I0655722

SHERLOCK HOLMES AND THE BODY SNATCHERS
(WHITECHAPEL VAMPIRE II)

By Dean P. Turnbloom

Copyright 2014

First edition published in 2014

© Copyright 2014

Dean Turnbloom

The right of Dean Turnbloom to be identified as the author of this work has been asserted by him in accordance with the Copyright, Designs and Patents Act 1998.

All rights reserved. No reproduction, copy or transmission of this publication may be made without express prior written permission. No paragraph of this publication may be reproduced, copied or transmitted except with express prior written permission or in accordance with the provisions of the Copyright Act 1956 (as amended). Any person who commits any unauthorised act in relation to this publication may be liable to criminal prosecution and civil claims for damage.

All characters appearing in this work are fictitious. Any resemblance to real persons, living or dead, is purely coincidental. The opinions expressed herein are those of the authors and not of MX Publishing.

Paperback ISBN 9781780921235
ePub ISBN 9781780921242
PDF ISBN 9781780921259
Published in the UK by MX Publishing
335 Princess Park Manor, Royal Drive,
London, N11 3GX
www.mxpublishing.com
Cover design by www.staunch.com

Grateful acknowledgment to Conan Doyle Estate Ltd. for the use of the Sherlock Holmes characters created by Sir Arthur Conan Doyle.

For Nanette...

Prologue

The canvas topping of the longboat provides little protection from the frigid night air; her hair, dampened by the spray of icy water, stiffens in the wind. Abigail Drake drifts into and out of consciousness, the cold stealing away her life. The storm tosses her from crest to trough to crest. During her more lucid moments she strains to see the silhouette of the *Animus Lacuna* as it tops a wave. Each time it does her spirit sinks as the lighting flashes show the ship more distant than before.

Cold, disheartened, and exhausted, she fights against the relentless onslaught of sleep, knowing it's a sleep from which she might never awaken. Only his promise gives her hope—a promise that now seems as remote as her Antonio.

"Can you forgive me?" he'd said as he cradled her in his arms. "I should never have brought you on this journey."

"Tonietto, don't. I wanted to come, to be with you."

"But the ship is lost, the hull breached. I'm not sure how long she'll hold together. Even with all my strength I can't protect you, can't shield you from the storm…from the cold."

"What will become of us, Tonietto?" tears streaming from her eyes.

"Abigail, you know what I am…you know I will survive…" the plaintive tone in his voice is more chilling than the night air.

"Yes, yes, I know, Tonietto," she answers. Frightened by his eyes as much as by the ominous sounds of twisting timber and water rushing into the ship, decks below, she draws his arms around her even more tightly.

"But there is a way we can still be together." His voice takes on a tentative tone, one she has never heard from his lips.

"How? What is it?"

"You must trust me. It won't be easy for you and you may find it too horrifying to contemplate but it's the only way."

"I don't want to die, Antonio."

Gently he caresses her face, smiling into her uncomprehending eyes, "I can't prevent that, but if you trust me, you can survive. We can survive together."

"But how?" Her eyes plead for an answer.

"Do you trust me?"

Introduction

Once again I set pen to paper in order to chronicle the exploits of my good friend and colleague, Mr. Sherlock Holmes. However, this particular tale is in need of a bit of explanation as it appears to start in the middle of the story. And for good reason, for it is the middle of the story that begins this account. Let me explain.

This tale concerns the vile murderer Baron Antonio Barlucci. With regret, I am unable to relate the entire story of how he became known to us owing to a promise I've given both to Mr. Holmes and to the Home Secretary, Mr. Henry Matthews. The reasons for this are varied but it suffices to say that the portion of the story that occurred in England must, of necessity, be omitted.

Anyone who has followed these chronicles must recognize it has been some little while since I've found the time to do any writing at all. Scarce as my articles have been since Holmes has retired, they've been all but non-existent in recent years. That isn't to say the material is lacking. I've piles upon piles of cases that faithful readers would undoubtedly find entertaining, but for quite some time I'm afraid I've been occupied with a number of personal misfortunes that have stayed my pen. Not the least of these was the too recent passing of my adored third wife.

Her sudden illness and subsequent passing caught me so much

by surprise that I fell into a fit of despondency. So deep was my depression that I thought it likely I might never climb out of it. There were times, I'm ashamed to say, that I contemplated crossing the Acheron on my own sixpence, so to speak.

I fear my dark mood must have found its way into my correspondence for in less than a week after posting a letter to Sussex, who should show up on my door step but Sherlock Holmes himself. He claimed some pretense about attending a gathering of apiarists in London and hoped I might put him up for a few days. The look on his face when first he saw me made me realize I must be further gone than I imagined.

Just seeing him once again, full of his characteristic vigor, was like a tonic for me. After a few days, during which we reminisced about our adventures together at Baker Street, he admitted to me he suspected I was a bit down and decided to come see for himself. Once satisfied it was nothing irreversible, he recommended my getting back to work again, perhaps writing about one of our former cases. On his suggestion I agreed to take a trip. He told me oftentimes he had noted a change of scenery is just the medicine needed to shake out the doldrums and get a body back in the pink. I suggested, of course, that he accompany me but he declined, saying this was something I needed to do alone.

With his visit concluded, Holmes returned to Sussex and I began to pack for my trip. I gathered my notes from some of the more grotesque cases that lay gathering dust while I was incapacitated with grief. I thought I might take a cruise on the Mediterranean and ready a few for publication. But while searching for a tweed jacket I intended to take upon the trip, I happened upon a leather-bound journal and a small bundle of papers tied up with brown twine. These were the notes I'd kept on the Barlucci case, which became the basis for this account.

I immediately pulled them out and examined them, thinking I might be able to organize them into yet another chronicle of Mr. Sherlock Holmes while on my cruise. As I explored their pages, it became evident to me why I'd not chronicled the story before. The case was, of course, one of the most unusually grotesque I've had the pleasure to accompany Holmes upon. But due to the myriad details and loose ends of which Holmes and I were not privy at the time it was quite unsuitable for recording.

I determined at once to change my plans and instead of relaxing on a cruise I should root out those missing details and travel instead to America. I would find the missing pieces and perhaps therein find some usefulness to my remaining life.

Now, having just completed that trip and having composed my notes with all relevant material that can be ascertained assembled, and after consulting once more with Mr. Holmes, I am ready to put the entire story, or rather, that part of the entire story that occurs in America, down on paper. I ask only the forbearance of my audience for certain departures of style, which are owing to the way in which this particular story came together. Where I've needed to resort to literary license to reconstruct what is most likely to have occurred based upon the result I've checked my reasoning with Mr. Holmes and have received his blessing that it is sound.

I hope I've pieced together this extraordinary tale in such a way that does not embarrass anyone who has assisted me in ascertaining the facts as they were, or exasperate any of my faithful readers.

Chapter 1

The end of the beginning…

It was a late November morning in the year 1888 and I was having a leisurely breakfast with Mr. Sherlock Holmes. Mary, my fiancée at that time, was still visiting in the country and Holmes and I were recovering from recent exertions on a case—a case I was under a strict promise not to chronicle, but which is inextricably connected to the case on which we were unknowingly about to embark.

The day was bright, though bitter cold out of doors. We were, however, warm and comfortable with a roaring fire and some of Mrs. Hudson's finest German sausages and potatoes. A recent trip to France had afforded us a chance to purchase some excellent coffee and while we consumed the breakfast Mrs. Hudson had served, we were both enjoying a steaming cup of espresso from the machine Mr. Holmes had constructed from a design he'd acquired while in Italy during the Moriondo forgery case. I recall with amusement Mrs. Hudson's reaction to the contraption when Holmes first set it up; she was apparently scandalised that he was "distilling spirits under her very roof".

Although our recent exploits did not turn out in an altogether satisfactory conclusion, our moods were light and carefree as we discussed that part of our endeavors that resulted in the exoneration of a young immigrant wrongly accused of the murder of a young woman on the high seas while they both made their transit from Italy to England.

It was as we were congratulating ourselves that there was a tentative knock on our door. "Come in," Holmes said in a voice loud enough and congenial enough to overcome the hesitancy of the would-be visitor. The door opened and standing there was a young lad of no more than 12 years, one of the dirty, bedraggled street Arabs that I'd so often seen in the employ of my friend, although I didn't recognize the face perched beneath this particular ragged haircut.

"G'day, Mr. 'Olmes. I got the information you wanted," he said, looking from Holmes to me in such a disapproving way that I immediately felt I was intruding on a confidential business meeting.

"That's all right, Wittmore, Dr. Watson here is an associate of mine."

Looking back to Holmes, the lad said, "I did what you asked. I stayed out at Potterman's until his ole lady left and followed her straight to Muggy's saloon."

"Excellent, Wittmore, you'll find the half-crown I promised you on the secretary by the door. I'll have Wiggins contact you if I need your services again." Holmes pointed toward the door with his fork and then turned back to attack his sausages.

The young lad hesitated at the secretary, and then turned and said, "Thank you, Mr. 'Olmes," before he scurried out the door and down the stairs.

"If I were you, Holmes, I'd check to see if anything else were missing from that secretary," said I as Holmes rose from the table and gazed out of the window in a contemplative pose.

"I don't have to. I already know he's made off with my

Fomby's pocket watch."

"You know? Why didn't you stop him?"

Holmes calmly walked over to the secretary and picked up the remainder of the coins he'd left there. "Well, aside from the half-crown, the pocket watch is all he's taken," he said after counting the coins and putting them in his pocket.

"I don't understand. You mean he left some spare change, but stole your watch? Why on earth…?"

"I think that's obvious enough. He must believe that if he's ever questioned about the watch he can deny it was there, reasoning that had he been a thief he'd have hardly left hard currency in favor of stealing a watch. What possible use could a watch be to a street urchin?"

"What use indeed. He could sell it."

A strange and if I'm not mistaken a pained look came across Holmes face, "A watch, Watson, is a symbol of constancy in what is surely an inconstant existence for such a boy. I think he may have taken it on impulse. When the time is right, he may think better of it. His character, still forming at his tender age, depends upon it."

"To hear you speak of it one might think you left it there as some sort of test."

"One might indeed."

At that moment Mrs. Hudson announced the coincidental arrival of Inspector Frederick Abberline of Scotland Yard. I say coincidental because it was he who involved us in a murder case that was integral to the solution of the homicide involving the aforementioned Italian immigrant. But this case had a decidedly less satisfactory conclusion. It was, in fact, the same murderer in both cases. But where we were able to extricate our young Italian client, the real culprit, one Baron Antonio Barlucci, managed to elude capture on his way to points unknown, though it was rumored he was heading to New York. To make the coincidence even more poignant, it was to bring us news of the murderous villain Barlucci that Inspector Abberline visited us on this day.

"Ah, Inspector," Holmes greeted Abberline as he entered our rooms. "Have you eaten breakfast?"

"No, no I haven't, Mr. Holmes, but I—"

"Then I insist you join us. I assure you, Mrs. Hudson's sausage and potatoes are the best in London. Watson and I were just sitting down."

"No, Mr. Holmes, that's quite all right. I'm here on official business."

As he said this, I could see the whole demeanor of my friend change, as if he could sense the tidings to come. "Official business, you say? Have you word from your young inspector? Andrews I think his name was."

"Yes, Inspector Walter Andrews. He was making inquiries about Barlucci's barque at the offices of the American Shipmasters' Association. It so happened while he was there a wire came in from one of their agents in Newfoundland." The inspector consulted his notebook, "One Edward Burford. He reported a longboat bearing the name *Animus Lacuna* has been recovered by a fishing boat. He also reported a lot of debris being carried down from the north by the currents."

"Ah, yes, the Labrador current, I expect, a portion of the Viking Gyre," Holmes said.

"Yes, at any rate, we believe the ship has been wrecked somewhere to the north, possibly striking an iceberg."

"You say a longboat from the ship was found?" asked Holmes. "Was there any evidence of possible survivors? Barlucci, perhaps?"

"No, no survivors were found. From the condition of the longboat it's suspected there wasn't time to launch it as a proper lifeboat. Most of the protective canvas topping was still fixed in place as it would have been when stowed. The only thing found aboard was the body of a young woman."

"Good heavens," said I. "You don't think…"

"That it might be the body of Miss Abigail Drake, Watson?" Holmes said in answer. "I think it could hardly be anyone else."

"Yes, that is exactly what we believe. We've sent a wire for Inspector Andrews to travel to Newfoundland just as soon as he can to make an identification of the remains."

"Is he acquainted with the young lady?" I asked.

"No, no, he's not."

"But he does have with him a recent photograph of Miss Drake," Holmes said. "I suggested to Sir Charles that he part with the photo in order to better inform the New York City constabulary that they might intercept the wayward Miss Drake." He paused as he turned over a bit of sausage on his plate. "I'm sorely aggrieved it will find use in such a somber cause as the identification of her remains."

"As will Sir Charles be, I'm sure," Inspector Abberline said. "He was quite shaken when he discovered his niece had taken up with such a man as Barlucci."

"As I understand it," said I, "it was Sir Charles' friendship with the baron that made their tryst possible."

"Which would make the wound all the more grievous and difficult to close," Holmes said. "We can only hope the recovery of her remains will ease his mind."

"Yes, we hope that's the case. He was a great man, despite his shortcomings," Abberline said.

"All great men have their shortcomings, Inspector, it's what makes us human."

Chapter 2
Morbid discovery...

While Inspector Abberline visited our apartments at 221B Baker Street, across the Atlantic the story rapidly unfolded. Much of what is written below was taken from the personal journal of Inspector Walter Andrews. The remaining events are the results of the first interviews I conducted of all the surviving principles in Canada and I believe the account to be as accurate as can be ascertained.

It begins in Newfoundland in the fishing village of St. John's, where the *Intrepid Mariner* is appearing out of the fog.

Jeremiah Callahan tossed the half-eaten apple core at a raven sitting on the bollard at the end of the pier. He spat a brown spew of tobacco juice as he brought his chair forward from its customary position tilted back against the Caumaghaun Fishery and pointed toward the inlet. "Look a'there." A fishing boat was just appearing from out of the fog. "The *Mariner's* on'er way into port. She must'a had some awful good luck to be comin' back this early in the day," he said, tilting back into his former position.

"Naught...too high in the water to have a full catch, Cal. I'll wager there's somethin' else goin' on," said Colonel Morris J. Fawcett, Inspector and Chief Superintendent of the Newfoundland Constabulary. Sensing something was amiss, he stayed put on the dock as the *Intrepid Mariner* tied up. Fawcett was tall and lean with reddish hair and mustache that contrasted amiably with his blue uniform. Handsome and well liked, as Chief Superintendent he was in charge of the approximately 100 members of the Newfoundland Constabulary. With such a wide area of responsibility and so few officers, most of the men were on continual patrol, with only small contingents in each town and village deemed large enough to warrant a constant presence.

When Captain Richard Halfyard stepped off the boat, Colonel Fawcett hailed him, "We didn't expect you back today, Dick. Is there trouble about?"

"Aye, Major, there is and of the foulest nature too," Halfyard strode up the dock with quick steps as he spoke. "We were out near Ballister's Bar when we ran up on a deserted longboat adrift in the fog. But it wasn't near as deserted as we'd thought." As he said this, the cook and a seaman appeared on deck carrying the body of a woman on a litter.

Fawcett watched as they carried their burden with great solemnity. "Who's that?"

"That's the young woman we found in the longboat."

"She was dead when you found her?"

"Aye, for days, we expect..." Then he added in a low voice, obviously not wishing to be overheard, "...though she looks better dead than half the women around here look alive."

"Do you know who she is...er, was?"

"No, she had no papers on or with her." Halfyard reached into the pocket of his foul weather jacket. "The only thing we found on her, aside from her clothes, was this." He held up a chain with a signet dangling from it. "She was wearing it round her neck."

Taking the chain and bauble from the captain, Colonel Fawcett turned it over in his hand several times, "It appears to be a crest of some sort. Maybe it'll help in identifying her." He put the chain and signet in the breast pocket of his jacket.

"The boat had the name '*Animus Lacuna*' on the gunwale," Halfyard said.

"That's something, at least. I'll have the Shipmaster's agent wire London and New York right away to see where she's registered and if they've a record of her sailing. We might get a manifest, if we're lucky." With this, the colonel took his leave of the captain.

"Good luck, Colonel," called the captain, then added, almost to himself, "...more's the pity."

Colonel Fawcett caught up with the litter carrying the woman's body as he came up to the head of the pier. It was a bit more than mere professional curiosity that had him halt her progress to the town's only mortuary. He pulled down the sheet covering her face to see for himself if the captain's description was accurate. He gazed down upon her delicate features and thought to himself, I see what the captain means. Her face looked as though she were only sleeping, but a touch of the cheek revealed skin as cold as hoarfrost.

Fawcett walked the short distance to the branch office of the American Shipmasters' Association. "Ed, we've got a line on all that debris that's been reported lately."

"Oh? What've ya got, Colonel?" Ed Burford was the local agent and surveyor for the American Shipmasters' Association, an organization with offices in nearly every port large enough to have a commercial shipping presence. The Association not only certifies the qualifications of mariners, but also keeps tabs on ships entering and leaving port making it a valuable source of information.

"The *Mariner* ran across a longboat in the fog this morning. There was a name on the gunwale, the *Animus Lacuna.*"

"*Animus Lacuna*, you say?" Burford asked as he pulled down a ledger from the shelf above his desk. He thumbed through the pages. "A-N-I-M-U-S…no, she's not been through here before." He closed the book. "I'll wire our New York office. They maintain records for all the ships on the eastern seaboard. We'll find out where she's registered and what her last port was."

"Ed, when you do, tell them there was a body onboard, a young woman."

"Dead?"

"I'm afraid so. See if you can get a manifest of passengers."

"Sure thing, Colonel." The shipping agent sent the following:

FROM AMERICAN SHIPMASTERS ASSOCIATION OUTPOST ST JOHNS NEWFOUNDLAND

TO PORT AMERICAN SHIPMASTERS ASSOCIATION HEADQUARTERS NEW YORK UNITED STATES

REQUEST INFORMATION ON REGISTRY OF SHIP ANIMUS LACUNA STOP LONGBOAT FOUND WITH BODY OF WOMAN ABOARD STOP POSSIBLE SHIPWRECK VICTIM STOP

ED BURFORD ST JOHNS ASSOCIATION SENDS

As Inspector Abberline informed Holmes and myself, it so happened Inspector Andrews was paying a visit to the New York offices of the Association making an inquiry concerning the *Animus Lacuna* at the time that wire was being sent. As soon as the wire was received, Andrews notified Scotland Yard and Inspector Abberline. Abberline quite properly paid a personal visit to Sir Charles Warren, former Metropolitan Police Commissioner, to inform him of the possibility that his niece may be a victim of a ship wreck. Within an hour of the wire's receipt, Inspector Abberline sent this reply:

FROM SCOTLAND YARD LONDON

TO AMERICAN SHIPMASTERS ASSOCIATION

ANIMUS LACUNA OBJECT OF MURDER INVESTIGATION SCOTLAND YARD STOP WOMAN FOUND POSSIBLE NIECE SIR CHARLES WARREN STOP DIRECT INSPECTOR WALTER ANDREWS SCOTLAND YARD TRAVEL ST JOHNS STOP HOLD BODY OF WOMAN FOR IDENTIFICATION STOP

INSPECTOR FREDERICK ABBERLINE SCOTLAND YARD SENDS

Chapter 3
Requiem

The ferry from New York's Whitehall Street terminal took an unremarkable four days to travel to St. John's, Newfoundland. During the trip, Inspector Andrews had plenty of time to contemplate his bad luck at being assigned this mission. At first he had been excited to be sent to New York. Even more so to be on the trail of the man Inspector Abberline and the redoubtable Mr. Sherlock Holmes himself believed to be "Jack the Ripper". He figured if he were able to capture Barlucci, it would go a long way toward making his career. But the wire from the Shipmasters' Association indicated the ship on which the supposed "Ripper" made his escape from England had apparently been lost at sea and the subsequent wire from Inspector Abberline directing him to make his way immediately to the city of St. John's in Newfoundland, Canada changed everything for the young inspector. Once he arrived in St. John's, he was to contact Colonel Fawcett of the Newfoundland Constabulary. His new mission there was to identify whether or not the remains of a young woman found adrift in a longboat was Miss Abigail Drake, the niece of former Metropolitan Police Commissioner, Sir Charles Warren.

The mission on which he was originally dispatched from Scotland Yard, to warn the New York City Police of a possible

17

murderer on their shores and to alert them that Sir Charles Warren's niece might be in his company, had transformed from an opportunity to become a hero by capturing the "Ripper" into the morbid duty of identifying a dead body and possibly transporting the remains back to England.

The ferry arrived on the afternoon of the fourth of December and the town of St. John's was engulfed in a thick, wet fog that only served to dampen Andrews' already dismal mood. Before the boat had been made fast to the landing, Inspector Andrews had already identified Colonel Fawcett. He stood on the pier in the distinctive blue uniform and white helmet of the Newfoundland Constabulary. Andrews watched from the deck of the ferry as the Colonel approached a distinguished looking gentleman with iron gray eyes and dark hair, peppered with gray, beneath a black billycock. Andrews guessed from the colonel's swagger that he had mistaken the gentleman for the inspector from Scotland Yard. Once the colonel spoke, there was no longer any doubt.

"Inspector Andrews, it's a great honor to make your acquaintance, sir." Standing ramrod straight the Colonel extended his hand.

"I beg your pardon?" The look of confusion on the face of a banker, who'd come to St. John's on holiday served to lighten Andrews' mood.

A puzzled Colonel Fawcett stammered, "Aren't...aren't you Inspector Andrews of Scotland Yard?"

"Pardon, Colonel." With an amused look on his very young features, Andrews said, "I'm Inspector Andrews."

Looking past the banker, Colonel Fawcett smiled broadly, "Please forgive me, Inspector; I was expecting a much older man."

The banker, straightening his Prince Albert coat front, said under his breath, "Older man indeed!" as he stormed off the ferry landing, wounded ego in tow.

"Perfectly all right, Colonel…happens all the time. I see you got my wire that I'd be arriving today." Inspector Andrews offered his hand, "I'm Inspector Walter Andrews, Scotland Yard, at your service."

"Colonel Morris J. Fawcett, Newfoundland Constabulary, sir, equally at your service." The Colonel displayed that stiff formality Andrews felt he probably reserved for those he wished to impress. As they shook hands, Andrews took stock of the Colonel, who in truth was only a few years Andrews' senior. He found his grip to be firm and his gaze steady, though somewhat vacant. "I'm very pleased to make your acquaintance, Inspector. Scotland Yard's reputation is not unknown to us here in Canada."

"Thank you, Colonel. And I must say I've heard only good things about the Constabulary Police." In truth, he didn't know much about the NCP, or Canada for that matter. On those few occasions when he'd taken the time to think about Canada, it was only about how primitive and backward it must be. Nothing he'd seen thus far altered that impression. So far as Colonel Fawcett was concerned, he impressed Andrews as a bit dull-witted, provincial, and prone to making up his mind without sufficient data. He wondered if perhaps a prolonged period spent in such a desolate post might not dull the senses of even the most alert detective.

"I've taken the liberty of booking you a room at the St. John's Inn, just down the street. It's clean, it's reasonably priced and it has the best dining room in town," Colonel Fawcett said proudly. "If you like, I can take you there now, so you can freshen up."

"Thank you very much, but I'm sure you can appreciate your wire has caused quite a stir in London. There is a great deal of interest in discovering whether or not the young lady you've found is or is not the niece of Sir Charles Warren. I'm afraid he didn't suffer the news well, particularly considering the circumstances, and the sooner I can substantiate or refute the matter of his niece's death, the better."

"The circumstances?" the Colonel asked, confusion once again stealing across his face. "Ah, yes, the circumstances...I understand perfectly," which of course told Andrews that Fawcett didn't understand at all. "I've a carriage awaiting us and we can go to the mortuary at once."

Instructing the driver to go directly to Witherspoon Mortuary, Colonel Fawcett and Inspector Andrews climbed inside a brougham fixed with snow runners for the short trip to the outskirts of St. John's. The carriage was pulled by a single Belgian draft horse and the runners slid easily over the hard packed snow in the streets. It was obvious to Inspector Andrews that although St. John's was backward by London standards it was a growing, thriving town. There were several new buildings going up despite the harsh winter weather. By the time they reached the mortuary, Colonel Fawcett had given Andrews the complete history of the Constabulary. As they pulled up in front of the clapboard building with the coffin-shaped sign that read, 'Witherspoon's Mortuary', Andrews practically bounded down from the carriage, anxious to get away from what had become a tedious and one-way conversation. A sign in the window bade him to enter. Inside and just above the door a bell dangled at the end of thin, curved ribbon of metal in such a way as to ring as he opened the door to enter. They were met immediately by a small figure hurrying in from the back room to greet them. Andrews thought this must be Mr.

20

Witherspoon.

The mortician was a small, stooped man with long scraggly hair circumnavigating his bald pate. Wire-rimmed bifocals occupied the tip of his extraordinarily long, thin nose. "Come in, gentlemen, come in. Welcome to the Witherspoon Mortuary. Amos Witherspoon, at your service," he said with a flourish in a reedy nasal voice that whistled its s's. As he stood looking them over, he took a large bite from the apple he held in his right hand. After swallowing he said, "Please excuse me, I've missed my lunch this afternoon and I'm famished." He wore a black suit, single-breasted, over a starched and immaculate white shirt, the collar of which was adorned with a flowing string tie. "You are here to view the young woman, perhaps?" he asked with the practiced, caring smile and sympathetically furrowed brow of someone whose occupation was the comforting of the bereaved. "Won't you kindly sign the viewing book?" He extended a book and a pen in Colonel Fawcett's direction.

"This is Inspector Walter Andrews of Scotland Yard," Colonel Fawcett said with a tone meant to convey the importance of his visitor. "He is here in an official capacity," his voice ascending at the word, 'official'.

"I'm sorry, sir, but it's my 'official' capacity to ask each visitor of the deceased to enter their name in the viewing book, if you would be so kind."

"But—" Colonel Fawcett began, stopping short as Inspector Andrews pushed past him and took the pen from the wispy fingers of the mortician, entering his name on the ledger.

"Thank you, sir," the smiling mortician said, taking back his pen. He then turned to Colonel Fawcett. Tilting the pen in his direction he raised his eyebrows with patient expectation.

21

"Oh!" Colonel Fawcett took the pen. "If it will serve to quicken the process," he muttered as he too signed the book.

"Excellent. Now, gentlemen, right this way, if you please," sang the diminutive curator of the mortuary as he took another large bite from the apple. He deposited the remaining core in the central fireplace as he exited the reception room, leading them through the viewing room on the way to the 'chill' room.

The viewing room was richly paneled in dark mahogany and the floors were covered with thick, luxurious carpeting. The room was illuminated by gas jets near each door that did little to lighten the mood. Its high, arched ceiling gave it the feel of a cathedral, albeit on a much smaller scale. Muted light leaked into the space from above through three beautifully detailed stained glass windows depicting scenes, not from the bible, but from fairy tales. Regardless the subject matter, they lent a solemn mood, which was made all the more so by the article in the center of the room, an ornate copper-colored coffin adorned with gleaming brass handles. At the far end of the room was a set of double doors leading to the chill room.

As they passed through the doors into the 'chill' room it was quite evident that for obvious reasons the room was insulated from the rest of the building and was unheated. "I'm afraid my last shipment of arsenic was lost at sea. I'm expecting a new one to arrive today, probably on the same ferry that brought you to our little community, Inspector," Witherspoon explained as he lighted the candles that flanked the sides of the room. "Unfortunately, I've been unable to properly embalm our most recent guest. But I think you will find her in a remarkable state of preservation all the same."

Inspector Andrews took the photo of Abigail Drake from the inner pocket of his frock coat where it had been ever since he left

London. He then approached the table on which lie the young woman, her body covered with a sheet and a smaller, satin cloth covering her face.

He gazed down at the innocent face of Abigail Drake in the photo and then removed the cloth from that of the young woman lying on the table. It was evident in an instant there could be no mistake. Nevertheless, he stood there for a full minute looking down at her. It didn't seem possible that this young woman was dead. She looked so peaceful, as if she were only sleeping. Inspector Andrews had seen plenty of dead bodies in his time at Scotland Yard, but none whose coloring looked as natural as the young beauty that lay before him. Her lips were deep red. They even appear moist, he thought, as if she's only just this minute moistened them with her tongue and there is a pinkish glow to her cheeks. "It's her." His words left a grim trail of gray in the air as he spoke like smoke from a funeral pyre. "It's Abigail Drake." He turned back toward Colonel Fawcett, who stood a respectable distance away. "I fear Sir Charles will be quite broken by the news. I must wire London at once."

Witherspoon stood beside the body, absent-mindedly stroking Abigail's hair, "What a pity," he said, as much to himself as to Andrews and Fawcett. "She was quite beautiful. As you can see, she's remarkably preserved, even without the proper treatment."

Andrews noticed with some discomfort the unusual attention showed the deceased Miss Drake by the mortician, "I shall be claiming the body in the name of Sir Charles. Please make the necessary arrangements to have the body ready for transit back to England. I shall want to leave on the first ferry tomorrow morning."

"You'll be leaving so soon?" asked Colonel Fawcett in a somewhat disappointed tone.

Looking first to the form beneath the sheets, then to the mortician, who was nodding approvingly, Inspector Andrews commented, "I think it best not to tarry too long, don't you?"

As he caught on to what was so obvious to the other two, he wanted to be sure they understood that he now understood the Inspector's concern for haste, "Oh yes, yes indeed…of course. At least the weather is working in your favor."

"I shall make certain all is attended to properly, sir," Witherspoon said, wearing the same caring smile and the same sympathetically furrowed brow as when they'd first arrived.

"Thank you," Andrews said, then turning to Colonel Fawcett. "I'd like to send that wire immediately, if it's convenient, and then I should like to get some rest. It's been a rather long journey."

#

Amos Witherspoon entered the "preparation" room at 4:00pm. He'd received his shipment of arsenic, just as he'd predicted, and after tending to some of the more mundane duties to which a mortician must attend, he made ready to prepare the body of Miss Drake for her return to England.

The sun had already disappeared behind the trees but it would be another fifteen minutes or so before it would set in the southwestern sky of Newfoundland. Amos was used to working after dark, as the sun set quite early in the winter months. In fact, he preferred the dark afternoons of the winter months, especially when he was to prepare a woman for burial.

The preparation room was a small room built into but insulated from the chill room. It communicated with the viewing room through a hidden double door in the wall. This allowed Amos to permit some heat into the room, for his comfort, while preparing the bodies for viewing and subsequent burial. It also had a large skylight. An amateur astronomer, Amos had it installed telling his wife that it would make it easier for him to star gaze on cold Canadian nights.

Amos worked unconcerned about being interrupted. The doors to the mortuary were always closed at 3:30pm sharp and he knew Mrs. Witherspoon, by this time in the afternoon, would be blissfully under the influence of several glasses of merlot, of which he kept her well stocked, leaving Amos quite sure he would be undisturbed. On evenings such as this, when he was graced with the company of a woman in the preparation room, Amos took an early dinner. The ritual consisted of his setting two places, one for himself and one for his 'guest', as he liked to term them. Most times he used the side table on which he would later place his instruments. The preparation room was brightly lit by gas jets at regular intervals on the walls. Amos also had candles both on and around the tables. Making himself more comfortable, Amos removed his jacket and placed it over the back of a chair in the corner of the room.

An excellent and thoughtful host, Amos always made polite conversation with his guests, often asking them why they were so quiet, or why they weren't eating. It was a little game he played and he never ceased to be amused by it. Then, after having satisfied his gastronomic appetite, he made the necessary preparations to satisfy his carnal appetite. After cleaning up the remnants of his meal and removing the fine china to the kitchen, Amos flitted about the room turning down the gas jets and extinguishing candles as he removed his tie, all the while conversing with his guest, entreating her suggestively to prepare herself for what was to come. He had never been rebuffed in this request yet, and his present visitor was by far the loveliest guest to whom he'd yet appealed.

"A new moon makes the stars look all the brighter, don't you think?" he whispered to his guest as he drew down the sheets, exposing her lovely body to the dim light of the single candle he'd allowed to remain shining. He was fascinated with how fresh the body appeared, surprisingly so considering the length of time since death. But he supposed it was not in small part due to his knowledge and skill as a mortician, not to mention the ameliorative influence of the light from the single candle.

With a genuine affection his thin fingers squeezed her right foot, feeling the cool but pliable flesh. Slowly, he ran them up the back of her smooth leg, wrapping them around her calf up to and behind her knee. He gently pulled it away from the other knee, caressing her inner thigh while his left hand unbuckled his belt, allowing his trousers to fall to his ankles. Leaving them in a bunch on the floor, he climbed up onto the table as he prepared to mount his conquest.

Suddenly he found it impossible to breathe. His first thought was that he was having a heart attack, his second how horrified his wife would be to find his dead, naked body on top of the deceased Miss Drake. The mind is a mysterious thing, for in the split second before he died he thought about these things and still had time to see the pair of white fangs framed within blood-red lips coming toward him, and then he felt the sting of their bite. As his life was sucked from him he experienced an ecstasy unlike anything he had ever known. He thought to himself, *a final reward for my work ethic.*

Chapter 4

The body snatcher...

Andrews approached the brown clapboard building thinking it strange not to see a hearse out front awaiting his arrival. He wanted to be onboard the first ferry out of St. John's and was certain he'd made it quite clear to the mortician he'd be by early this morning to collect Miss Drake's remains. Instead, all was quiet. Walking up to the door, he knocked. At first there was no answer, but then from within he heard the high-pitched voice of Hillary Witherspoon, wife of the odd little mortician, "Amos! Amos, there's someone at the door. Where on earth are you and why haven't you opened the door by now?" By this time, she'd reached the door herself and changing her expression from one of scorn for her husband to one of practiced sympathy, she greeted the inspector, "Won't you come in?" She said, opening the door and stepping back, "How may we help you?"

Andrews tipped his hat, "Mr. Witherspoon is expecting me," he said.

"I see. Well, I'm sure Amos isn't far. Please, have a seat; I'll fetch my husband directly." Having shown the inspector into the greeting room, she excused herself to look for her husband only to return minutes later alone. "I don't understand where he could be. I'm terribly sorry, Mister..."

"Inspector Walter Andrews, Mrs. Witherspoon, Scotland Yard. I've come for the remains of Miss Drake." He stood and said, "I arranged to do so with your husband yesterday. Is there anything amiss?"

"I'm sure there is not, sir," she said with a bit of ire at the suggestion. "My husband is singularly diligent in his work. He was up very late last night making sure everything is ready. The casket is in the viewing room still." As if to excuse his absence and with a look of confused concern on her face she said, "Amos must have stepped out for a minute..." Turning, she continued, "...it's not like him to disappear like this." And then, regaining her composure she said, "No matter, please, come this way," and led the inspector into the viewing room.

The bright light streaming through the stained glass high above them contrasted greatly with the previous day, giving the room a lighter mood. There, in the middle of the floor was a much different coffin than had occupied that space just the day before. This one was much less ornate, of unpolished plain wood with iron handles instead of bronze. It was, in fact, a plain burial coffin. "This, of course, is the coffin in which Miss Drake is meant to be transported. We don't have much call for 'transport caskets' here, so my husband thought this simple coffin would do instead." With bewilderment that expressed itself in her voice as well as on her face she said, "But I would have thought Amos would already have had it loaded into the hearse."

"That was the understanding," Andrews said, making no attempt to hide his growing annoyance. "The ferry departs in little over an hour."

He could see the coffin was unlatched and as he approached he noticed a slip of cloth protruding from under the lid. Andrews looked from the coffin to Mrs. Witherspoon. "Are you quite sure your husband has finished his work?"

"Oh, yes, quite sure, sir. I've never known him to need more than a full evening to prepare even the worst cases." She practically beamed with pride.

"Then what is this?" He pointed to the cloth.

At first Mrs. Witherspoon glanced dismissively at the bit of material, but there was something about it that seemed familiar. Then it hit her, it was Amos's shirt-tail. Her mouth gaped open and a gasp leaped from her.

"What is it, Mrs. Witherspoon?"

"My…my husband's shirt," she said as she accusingly pointed to the strip of material as if it had committed some ungodly act.

"What? Are you sure?"

Looking now at the inspector, she displayed her own annoyance, "Of course I'm sure. I know my own husband's shirts don't I? He was wearing it yesterday. I laid it out for him myself."

They stood staring at what Mrs. Witherspoon identified as the tail of her husband's shirt and suddenly the cloth moved ever so slightly. The two of them looked at each other in stark surprise. Then, Inspector Andrews took a step forward. The cloth moved again, this time it seemed to jerk, then jerk again. Grasping the lid with both hands, Andrews opened the casket.

Before it was fully opened, a fat rat wriggled out from beneath the lid. Mrs. Witherspoon fainted dead away. Andrews jumped back, allowing the lid to slam shut, as the well-fed rodent skittered across the stone floor and into the chill room.

Andrews helped Mrs. Witherspoon into the parlor. He then grabbed a poker from the fireplace and went back to the casket.

Prepared this time, he opened the lid once more. Three more rats were feeding upon the remains of Amos Witherspoon. Andrews stabbed the first one, its squeal alerting the other two. The larger one turned its blood-smudged muzzle toward Andrews, baring its teeth. The other one sought refuge under Amos Witherspoon's arm. Andrews brought the poker down on the aggressive rodent, smashing its skull with the first blow. He then went after the third rat, jabbing beneath Witherspoon's arm again and again until finally he heard the squeal as the poker made deadly contact.

Looking around, Andrews spied a brass cuspidor in the corner of the room. Stumbling over to it, he vomited violently into its void. When he recovered enough to investigate the horrible scene, he saw the body of Amos Witherspoon, naked from the waist down with a look of abject terror frozen on his blood-splotched, rodent gnawed face. In addition to his conspicuously missing male appendage, there were numerous wounds on his bare lower extremities where the rats did the most damage. His nose was also partially missing and there were two ragged, irregular gashes cut deep into his throat. Most remarkably, a thing that Andrews at first didn't realize amid the horror of the scene, was that within the casket there was an almost total absence of blood.

#

By the time Colonel Fawcett arrived, Mrs. Witherspoon had been revived and was resting comfortably on a settee in the greeting room. A neighbor and good friend, Mrs. Agnes Walcot, had arrived to comfort her, as well as to discover what she could about the goings on in her neighbor's house. Inspector Andrews was in the viewing room scribbling in a small, leather-bound notebook. When the Colonel entered, Andrews moved to put his body between Fawcett and what he

30

was penning in the book. To his chagrin, the Colonel peered over his shoulder, a bewildered look on his face.

"What's that, Inspector?"

"Nothing at all, just some notes and impressions," Andrews said. "Where have you been? I sent for you over an hour ago. I'm afraid there's been foul play here."

"I got here as quickly as I could, Inspector. I was out on Waterford Bridge Road; there was a fire last night."

"A fire?"

"Yes, the Fenster house burned to the ground. Fenster, his wife, and their two youngest were visiting his sick mother. They left their oldest son, Tommy, home but he's turned up missing. And, well, they say misfortune occurs in sets of three, you know, so when I got your message—"

"Missing, you say…interesting."

"Yes, I went out to their place, they live about a mile out of town; I wanted to look through the ruins to see if young Tommy might be…well, you know…" The Colonel hung his head and fiddled with his hat band. After a moment, he asked, "So, what's happened here?" He edged his way toward the coffin in the middle of the room. "I wasn't given any details, just got word to get here quick," he said as he approached the still open casket. "Dear God!" he exclaimed as he saw Witherspoon. Closing the lid he crossed himself three times.

"Yes, quite," Andrews responded to the Colonel's reaction. "I'm afraid all I know for certain is that Amos Witherspoon's been murdered and the remains of Abigail Drake appear to have been stolen. I've not yet made a thorough exploration of the property."

"My men will handle that," offered the Colonel.

"Your men? I was under the impression you were your men,"

Andrews said, raising his eyebrows.

"Actually, I have a good many men assigned to me, one hundred sixteen. Most of them are on patrol or at other outposts, but we've a few on hand in St. John's. As Her Majesty's legal representative in this province, I also have the authority to commandeer and deputize as needed."

"I see. Very well, Colonel, but under the circumstances and if you've no objection, I'd very much like to assist in this investigation."

"Glad to have your expertise, Inspector. Scotland Yard's reputation is quite well known and respected around here, of course."

"Incidentally, how old is the Fenster boy?"

"Nineteen, I'd say. Why?" asked the Colonel suspiciously.

"Colonel, we have a murder here, the remains of a young woman are missing, and now you give me the news there is a young man also missing? I'm not one who easily believes in coincidence."

"Now, don't go jumping to conclusions, Inspector. I've known the Fensters since before Tommy was born. He's a good lad. I'm sure he's not mixed up with this business."

"I'm not jumping to conclusions, Colonel. But just the same, I'd like to speak with the Fensters once we've concluded our business here."

"If you think it necessary," agreed the Colonel, reluctantly. "They are a bit distraught as you could imagine."

"For now, I think we should question Mrs. Witherspoon, if she's up to it," offered Andrews.

"Yes, quite right. She's in the receiving room. Mrs. Walcot is tending to her," the Colonel said as he turned and headed in that direction.

Mrs. Walcot was cooling the brow of Mrs. Witherspoon with

a damp cloth as Colonel Fawcett and Inspector Andrews entered. In truth, she was fussing over her like a mother hen, clucking and flapping about, alternately applying the cold compress to her forehead and then patting her hand, all the while repeating, "There, there, Hillary…it'll be all right. I'm here to help."

"Mrs. Witherspoon," began the Colonel, "are you up to answering a few questions?"

"Danny, why don't you let the poor thing alone. She's had a terrible shock."

"Please, Mrs. Walcot, I wouldn't bother Mrs. Witherspoon were it not absolutely necessary, I assure you. Now, Hillary…Mrs. Witherspoon, may we ask you just a few questions?"

"Hmmm?" Mrs. Witherspoon opened her eyes and held up her head, "Um…oh dear, I…I suppose so," she uttered in a despondent tone.

"When did you last see your husband, Mrs. Witherspoon?"

"Why, last night, just before I retired…I went to bed early, as I haven't been feeling at all well of late."

Colonel Fawcett rolled his eyes toward Inspector Andrews and when he was sure she wouldn't see, made a gesture indicating Mrs. Witherspoon's illness might be due to her predilection for drink. Mrs. Walcot gave them both a disapproving look.

"Amos was tending to some paperwork in his office."

"What time did your husband come to bed?" asked Inspector Andrews, ignoring the Colonel's pantomime.

"Why, he didn't go to bed at all," Mrs. Walcot said. "Anyways, his bed hasn't been slept in from what I can tell."

"Thank you, Mrs…?" questioned the inspector.

"Walcot, Mrs. Agnes Walcot. I live next to the Witherspoons.

Have for twenty years. Hillary is my best friend in all the world. I went in to check their rooms as soon as I heard the news." She gave him a smug smile, "It wouldn't do having things out of place with an investigation going on, so I was going to tidy up for Hillary, but there was nothing amiss at all."

"Mrs. Walcot," began Inspector Andrews, his tone calm, his manner quiet but authoritative, "while I can appreciate your concern, by tidying, as you put it, you've contaminated the scene of a murder. Though I'm unsure what we might have learned from the state of Mr. Witherspoon's room, I'm quite certain now we must disregard anything we discover there."

Mrs. Walcot's mouth stood open as the inspector spoke to her. Then she sputtered, "Well, I…I…hmph!"

"Also, I'm afraid I must insist you refrain from answering any questions directed toward Mrs. Witherspoon. I know it may seem unnecessary when you are aware of the answers, but we have procedures and protocols we must follow, which to you may seem arcane, but which I assure you are most necessary. We need Mrs. Witherspoon to answer, as best she can, any questions we ask at this time. You do understand, don't you, Mrs. Walcott?"

"I should say I do, sir," was her curt reply as she fell silent from the perceived insult.

"Now, Mrs. Witherspoon," continued Colonel Fawcett, "is what Mrs. Walcot said, here, true?"

"Yes, yes, I suppose it is true if his bed wasn't disturbed. I often don't know when Amos goes to bed. He works late many nights. He's so…" she paused with a sniff, and then sobbed before continuing, "…was so…" and began crying on Mrs. Walcot's shoulder.

"There, there, dear, it's all right…that's it," she consoled.

"I'm exceedingly sorry to have to put you through this, particularly under the circumstances, Mrs. Witherspoon," said the inspector, "but I can attest it's of the utmost importance." He looked about the room, not quite sure how to ask his next question, "Please forgive the indelicacy of this line of inquiry, Mrs. Witherspoon, but is there any good reason you can think why your husband would be in the viewing room without his trousers?"

"INSPECTOR!" objected Mrs. Walcot, who evidently had gotten over the previous insult, "Just what are you suggesting?" Pulling Mrs. Witherspoon's head down to her shoulder, she said to her, "Pay him no mind, Hillary, Amos was a good and decent man. Those rumors were put away long ago."

"What rumors would those be?" asked the inspector, but Hillary Witherspoon was sobbing too loudly for either her or Mrs. Walcot to hear.

Colonel Fawcett pulled the inspector aside. In a quiet voice he said, "I believe the proper term is necromancy, Inspector. Nevertheless, it was rumored from time to time that Amos may have dallied with some of his lady guests. I never believed it myself, but it cropped up now and again."

"I believe you mean necrophilia, Colonel."

Fawcett cleared his throat as his face flushed at his mistake, "Yes, of course, you're right."

Andrews smiled in spite of the situation, and then said, "In view of the circumstances of his death, and the apparent theft of the young woman's remains, I don't believe we need to add credence to that abhorrent rumor. Order your men to keep the casket closed. We'll keep his embarrassment between us, agreed?"

35

"Agreed. I'm sure Mrs. Witherspoon will appreciate our discretion in this matter."

"Colonel! Colonel!" a young man called from outside, "they've stolen Witherspoon's horse and buggy."

Stepping out onto the porch, Inspector Andrews close behind, he asked, "Are you sure?"

"Aye, Colonel, as sure as a beaver's got buck teeth."

Colonel Fawcett and Inspector Andrews followed the young man around the side of the building to the livery at the back of the house. The door stood open and the stable was empty, except for some spare tack hanging on the wall inside.

"Stolen, all right," he said as he inspected the empty building. "I'll wire the neighboring towns to be on the lookout." Turning to Inspector Andrews, the colonel said, "At least it shouldn't be difficult to find."

"Oh? Why is that?"

Striking a match on the livery door to light his cigar, he said, "Witherspoon only has one buggy—his hearse."

#

"Mistress? Mistress, I've done what you asked, kept a watch all day. No one's been by, not a soul." Tommy Fenster crushed the snow beneath his feet as he paced back and forth in front of the concealed opening in the rocks.

Abigail had been watching the boy even before she emerged from the small cave. She was quite torn over Tommy. He was so very young. As she watched him twitch and squirm like the poor rummies she used to see while riding through Whitechapel in the back of her comfortable landau, she knew his fate was set. But Tommy wasn't a rummy. He was simply a young boy who happened to be walking

36

down a lonely country road on a cold December night and now would never see his parents, or even the daylight, again.

Stepping into the cold starless night, Abigail gave a sad smile as she said to Tommy, "Yes, you've been a good boy, Tommy...a very good boy."

"You promised, Mistress, you said if I was good and kept a good watch you'd...you'd..." Tommy stammered, looking sheepishly. She could smell the need oozing from his pores, the craving he could not control, nor understand. She wondered if her Antonio would be disappointed at her taking such an innocent victim. But she knew there was no going back now.

"Yes, Tommy, and I always keep my word. But first I must ask you, are you very sure this road will take me to Petty Harbour?"

"Yes, ma'am," he said as he shifted from his left foot to his right, holding and rubbing his arms against the cold.

"And does the ferry to New York stop there?"

"Yes, ma'am. It stops there and straight on to New York. There's local ferries too, but the New Yorker from St. John's always stops at Petty Harbour." Tommy stopped talking and just stood there, bouncing and fidgeting, as if he needed to relieve himself. In point of fact, it was relief he sought, relief only Abigail could give him this evening—relief from the addiction to which she had introduced him on their first meeting.

Fortunately for Abigail, she'd run across young Tommy on the road out of St. John's not long after disposing of Witherspoon and stealing his hearse. Having just taken her first victim, there was still fire in her veins when she came upon him. The blood on which she gorged herself had had an intoxicating effect on her. Its warmth flowed through her like fine brandy. Had she not been so drunk with her first blood-meal she was certain she would have let Tommy go unmolested. But the orgy of blood left her wildly stimulated and she happened upon Tommy at just the wrong time, for him.

Tommy had been walking down Waterford Bridge Road, making his way back from his friend's house in town to his parent's farmhouse, some two miles outside of St. John's. Tommy heard the hearse coming down the road. It was obvious that it was being driven hard. He looked back over his shoulder to see Abigail standing in the forefront of the hearse driving the horses hard and fast along the darkened road. Frightened, he started to run as she approached, whipping the horses mercilessly in her attempt to put distance between herself and St. John's. At the same time, his young eyes could not resist trying to get a better look. Not having access to a proper wardrobe, Abigail had taken the mortician's pants and jacket. To a rural nineteen year-old boy in Newfoundland, she was a frightful, yet exciting sight, standing there with the wind whipping her hair, tugging open her jacket, her naked upper body seeming to gleam in the moonless night.

Coming up behind, she pulled back on the reins and leapt down onto the road, seizing Tommy by the collar of his woolen coat halting his flight. Turning him to her, she looked into his eyes with a malignant and animalistic violence. His scream fell dead in the cold air. There was no one to hear his cry. She silenced his scream with a bite to his neck.

Their fluids mixed, his blood and her spittle, and Abigail could feel the boy relax in her grip, no longer fighting against her, no longer trying to scream. Instead, he seemed to relish her 'kiss'. It was just as the baron had told her, when she asked about his victims. She knew Tommy must be feeling a warm, euphoric sensation spreading

38

from his neck throughout his body leaving him only wanting more, unable to think of anything but the pleasure he felt.

She drank and as she did, she suddenly felt compassion for this young victim. Unlike Witherspoon, he had done nothing to wrong her. Again she thought about the baron, in those wonderful days they were together onboard his ship. During the long, passionate nights they spent together aboard the *Animus Lacuna* before they encountered the storm, he told her what his life had been like during the centuries since he'd been a vampire and how he yearned for a cure. She had asked about his victims and he told her that he was acutely conscious of their humanity and that he always took great pains to select victims from among the most wretched of society. He hoped that in limiting himself in this way he would preserve some semblance of his conscience and thereby perhaps save his soul, if indeed he still had one.

Careful not to imbibe too deeply, Abigail disengaged from the youth. When she did, she could see he immediately felt weak and became feverish with the desire to have her continue sucking his blood. She suddenly felt a surprising feeling of shame at what she had done. At the same time the power she felt over her victim was nearly as intoxicating as her first taste of blood, a contradiction she didn't understand. It made her marvel at the way this young boy cowered, imploring her to continue. She resisted. She knew she could now take from him as much as she wished, without resistance. She also knew that she would need a guide if she hoped to get on her way to New York, where she and Antonio would once again be together. Young Tommy could be that guide. She would put him to good use in her escape from wherever she was now to New York. She ordered him into the hearse, in the seat next to her, and together they continued down the road.

Now, as her second night as a vampire began, she watched Tommy fidget. She knew his discomfort was more from want than from the cold. He had stood vigil throughout the day, his wide eyes red from lack of sleep. With yearning, pleading eyes, Tommy once again looked at Abigail, "Y-you said…" he repeated.

Abigail again felt pity for Tommy. The emotion seemed foreign to her and was mixed with a loathing for him at the same time. Tonight she had a difficult time even thinking of him as a person, for he had stopped being that for her when she had drunk the first drop of his blood. It was a strange mixture of feelings she had, almost as if she were of two minds, each pulling her in different directions.

But with Petty Harbour close at hand, she knew Tommy's usefulness to her was at an end and that she would soon need to dispose of him. Yes, there was pity, but the power she felt overwhelmed and subjugated that pity and she smiled, beckoning him to her, "Come here, Tommy," she cooed, "you have been a very good boy."

As she spoke, Tommy moved to stand in front of her, his hopeful, pathetic eyes looking into hers. She kissed his lips, gently, holding his head in her hands. He moved his body closer to hers. Her left hand caressed his cheek, then slid down to expose his neck that bore the marks from her first bite. He turned his head away, to give her better access. She kissed him again, then gently moved to his neck.

Tommy closed his eyes, shaking in anticipation of her bite. When it finally came, he exhaled a sigh of relief as the euphoria swept over him again. This time the euphoria did not end, not for Tommy. Finally, Abigail let his lifeless body fall limp to the ground. Young

Tommy Fenster lay dead at her feet as she callously wiped his blood from her lips. Looking down at him, she was once again moved to pity. Kneeling beside him, she made a cushion of loose pine needles for his head and then leaned over and kissed his cheek.

When she finished, she got to her feet and, stepping over his inert body, climbed up into the hearse in her new outfit, modest but stylish—from the closet of Tommy's mother. As the snow once again began to fall she snapped the whip over the head of the pale roan, leaving Tommy in a pool of his own urine.

Chapter 5

Realization and pursuit...

I had not long returned from attending my practice on a Thursday, the first week of December when Inspector Abberline once again came calling. The look on his face told us instantly all was not well. His face had such an ashen gray cast to it I at first believed he might be coming to seek medical advice. There was an epidemic of measles in Staffordshire and influenza was on the rise throughout London. But my professional fears were unfounded as his first words signaled a dilemma of another kind entirely.

"She's missing," he said to Holmes.

"Missing? Who is missing, Inspector," I asked as Holmes used his thumb to tamp the rough shag he'd just pulled from the slipper into his black Peterson billiard pipe.

"He means Miss Drake, of course," Holmes said from around the now clenched pipe stem in his teeth. His manner was unperturbed as he paused to retrieve a match from the cast iron match holder on the mantle, struck it on the side, and lighted the pipe.

"No," said I.

"I'm sorry to say Mr. Holmes is quite right."

"How could you have possibly known, Holmes?" I asked, amazed once more at Holmes' uncanny ability to grasp in an instant what most of us would fail to do so in an hour.

"Quite elementary, I'm afraid," Holmes said in that wry way of his. "On Inspector Abberline's previous visit, just last week, he carried the grave news that Miss Abigail Drake's body was possibly found in a longboat, apparent victim of a shipwreck. Who else would he be coming here to tell us is missing?"

Knowing Holmes methods as well as anyone I was quite surprised at this specious reasoning. "Well, I must say that's a fantastic leap of faith, Holmes. I would have thought your supposition would be on firmer ground than that."

"Supposition? I'm surprised at you, Watson. You know my methods, I never suppose. But then again, there is also this." Smiling in that offhanded and arrogant manner he has when he's just made a jest, he held out a hand-written message from Home Secretary Henry Matthews. "It arrived in the afternoon post." The note requested that Holmes personally look into the matter of the missing body of Sir Charles' niece as a special favor to the secretary.

"Well, you might have said something."

"There, there, Watson. You only just arrived minutes before Inspector Abberline here."

"Yes, I suppose that's true," said I. "Anyway, it's a terrible business."

Smoke poured from Holmes' lips as he withdrew the pipe to speak. "Yes, quite. I fear there may be something going on even more sinister than a misplaced corpse."

"What do you mean?" Abberline said.

"Consider. A madman is on the loose, one clever enough to elude a city-wide manhunt and escape with the niece of the then Metropolitan Police Commissioner. His ship apparently meets with what may be considered a natural calamity and goes down with all hands, save the body of the aforementioned niece, which now turns up missing."

"Do you think it might be coincidence?" I said.

"As you've heard me say many times, Watson, coincidence is the residue of design. I believe it's entirely possible we've not seen the last of Baron Barlucci."

Abberline started. "Barlucci? You think Barlucci may have somehow survived the shipwreck?"

"Of course, I suspected all along the ship wreck might be a ruse." Holmes paced across the floor in front of the fireplace. "The baron knew we would be hot on his trail and that his escape by ship would be temporary at best. A man as clever and ruthless—and as mad—as he might have conceived a plan to scuttle the ship, thereby putting the authorities off his scent."

"If indeed that was his plan, how did he expect to survive?" Abberline said.

"That, my dear inspector, is the puzzle. Perhaps he had arranged another ship to meet him on the high seas on which to transfer."

"That would take quite a bit of luck even for the most experienced seaman, don't you think?" Abberline said.

"Yes, but it's possible. The trouble with that solution is that there would be others alive that might give him away. Another possibility might be he planned to escape on that longboat with Miss Drake after scuttling the ship. That would take care of any telltale witnesses, as I'm sure he would see to it that any other conveyance that might be used to escape would be scuttled as well."

"I'm sure the crew might have had something to say about

scuttling the ship, eh?" said I.

"I'm sure they would, Watson. Evidently something went wrong. Perhaps it was just that. If his plans were to scuttle the ship with all hands while he and Miss Drake escaped, he would need to scuttle the crew as well. He might have planned to murder them in their sleep. Perhaps he was discovered. At any rate, somehow Miss Drake was set adrift in the lifeboat. The wreckage found in the vicinity implies the scheme to scuttle the *Animus Lacuna* was at least partially successful."

"Mr. Holmes," Abberline said, "This all appears to me to be the most tenuous supposition imaginable."

"Not supposition, Inspector, deduction. That Miss Drake's body was recovered is a fact, a fact that hints something went wrong. The initial conclusion was that a storm, or an iceberg, or other catastrophe caused the ship to founder and Miss Drake, by luck or design, was set adrift in the longboat in which she was found. Had that been the end of it and her remains returned to England, then the storm or iceberg or some combination might be the logical conclusion. But, that was not the end of it. The succeeding fact that Miss Drake's body was stolen and is now missing portends something much more malevolent than nature. Logic and reason draw me to the conclusion that Baron Barlucci is at the heart of this, that it is he who is the body-snatcher."

"Do you mean to go, then?" I asked.

"I'm not currently engaged in anything pressing, and I could hardly turn down a personal request from old Henry. Besides, the baron escaped me once. I don't intend to allow him to do so again. There may yet be a chance to bring him to justice. Yes, I shall leave immediately. Watson, are you up for a trip to America?"

"Well, I don't know. I've my practice...and then there's Mary..."

"Come, now, Watson. You told me yourself Mary's not due back in London for another month at best, and I'm certain you could get your neighbor Jackson to take on your patients in your absence. On those occasions when I've visited you, his waiting room has always appeared conspicuously empty, while your own overflows. You'd be doing him a favor."

"Well, yes, I suppose you're quite right. But it might take me a day or so to get ready. Oh, dash it all, yes, yes, it would be my great honor to once again accompany you on an adventure."

Inspector Abberline, who'd been silently watching as Holmes convinced me to accompany him, said, "Andrews is still in Canada, but I expect he will make it to New York before you. I'm sure he will be only too happy to assist you in any way he may."

"Splendid. Then the only thing remaining is to decide on transport." Holmes thumbed his way through the pages of *The Times*. "I see that the *RMS Etruria* is departing from Liverpool for New York in three days. That would be ideal, eh Watson?"

"Why, yes...yes, it would. That should give me ample time to make any arrangement required to secure my patients well being while I'm away."

"You'll make good time if you can get passage," Abberline said, "if you don't run into any American tramp steamers, that is." The inspector was referring, of course, to the collision and subsequent sinking of the *SS Iberia* by the *RMS Umbria*, *Etruria's* sister ship, just off Sandy Hook, New Jersey, the previous month.

"Yes," Holmes said, "she is a fast ship, one of the fastest of the Cunard line. We'll be in New York in a week's time."

"Gad, Holmes, what times we live in. Think of it, an ocean crossing in a week."

"Yes, we're most fortunate to live in a time and in a country where even the fantastic is a possibility."

Thus it seemed, Holmes and I were off together on yet another adventure, this one to the unknown dangers that awaited us in the wilderness of America.

#

The snow that fell on the evening Witherspoon met his end was still much undisturbed by either wind or new snow making it a fairly simple task for Andrews and Colonel Fawcett to follow the trail of the hearse on the morning after discovering it was missing. About three miles before reaching Petty Harbour, the trail veered off the road and into the woods. It stopped close to a small cave near an outcropping of rocks and a fallen tree.

"Poor Tommy," Colonel Fawcett said, choking back his emotion. Young Tommy was lying beside the fallen tree, his cheek and hair frozen to the pile of pine needles beneath his head. Two rough gashes were opened in his neck but like Witherspoon, no blood was found around the corpse.

"Where's the blood?" Andrews said, more to himself than to Fawcett. He looked around the body for signs.

"What's that? Blood? Oh, yes, well, there doesn't appear to be any, does there? Perhaps some animal came along and lapped it up?"

Bloody hell, thought Andrews, surely he can't be that dense. "Do you really believe an animal would come and lap up his blood but leave the body undisturbed?"

"Well, when you put it like that…no. That does make it queer, doesn't it?" He waited for Andrews to respond. When he didn't,

Fawcett said, "At least this clears young Tommy of being the body-snatcher. The Fensters will be glad of that...that is, they will once they've recovered from their loss," he said looking back at Tommy.

"But now we have a new mystery. What was Tommy's part in this?"

"Why, no part at all as far as I can see. He's a victim."

"Yes, a victim with what looks to be a fatal wound delivered to his throat but no blood, a victim who must have traveled with the murderer and body-snatcher from St. John's almost to Petty Harbour."

"Perhaps the murderer used Tommy as a guide. The ferry to New York makes its last stop at Petty Harbour; perhaps that is where your murderer is heading after all. Did you not say that is where the ship was rumored bound?"

"Yes, that's true. I suppose if he was reasonably sure he could make it the rest of the way on his own, he'd have no reason to take Tommy with him."

"Poor Tommy. The Fensters will be grief-stricken. To first lose their home and now their son. Horrible."

"Let's get on to Petty Harbour. There's nothing we can do for Tommy here." It wasn't that Andrews was bereft of compassion, but rather he was far more interested in catching the perpetrator of this travesty than in commiserating with Colonel Fawcett. "We'll wrap him in a blanket and tie him to your horse. We can get a wagon to take him home when we arrive in Petty Harbour."

With Tommy securely fastened behind Colonel Fawcett, they continued on their way toward Petty Harbour. Before they'd gone a mile further, they ran across Witherspoon's hearse. The horse was grazing on some pine needles that had fallen by the side of the road.

Fawcett climbed down from his horse and took an apple from

his saddle bag. With it, he coaxed the hungry animal to allow him to take the reins. "There, boy, take it easy. We won't hurt you. We just want to get you into town where you can be properly fed, that's all."

Once he'd eased the spooked horse's nerves, he set the brake and tied his horse to the back of the hearse. He laid Tommy's body in the back and climbed up into the seat. "There now, let's get on to Petty Harbour," he said and snapped the reins, pulling up alongside Andrews. "Might be more difficult now with no wheel tracks to follow."

"It looks like he went on by foot. The wind has partially concealed his tracks but it looks like he's still headed to Petty Harbour."

"If he's headed there to catch the New Yorker, then I'd say we've already missed him. Wonder why he decided to go on foot?"

"Perhaps he thought the authorities in Petty Harbour might be on the lookout for a hearse."

Colonel Fawcett looked sheepish, "I suppose they would have been, had I wired ahead."

After they'd gone another mile or two, Andrews broke the silence saying, "He must be a powerful man to carry the body all this way."

"The body? Oh, yes, the body...I'd nearly forgotten. Why, yes, he must be powerful indeed. Or perhaps he's gotten rid of the body. Too conspicuous."

"That's a possibility. But he's killed two people since stealing it, it's apparently pretty important to him for some reason." He was thinking about the baron and how Holmes had said he was mad. He must be mad to go to so much trouble for a corpse, no matter how much he may have been in love with Miss Drake.

"What's that?" the colonel said.

This broke Andrews out of his thoughts. "Where?"

"Up ahead, in the road, a couple of dogs."

Andrews spurred the sides of his mount and galloped forward fifty yards. Before he reached the scene he could see these weren't dogs. "Wolves," he cried. Reaching inside his coat, he found his Webley "Bull Dog" and fired three shots at the two wolves. The first shot hit its mark, felling the larger of the two wolves before they knew he was on them. The smaller wolf ran into the woods, howling as if in pain, though Andrews was unsure he'd actually hit the beast. By this time Colonel Fawcett had caught up with him.

They advanced slowly on the site where the wolves had been. What they saw in the middle of the road was a nasty scene of blood and gore, the body of a man, or what was left of it. It looked as though it had been pulled apart by wolves. "What's that?" Andrews said pointing to a clump of clothing, partially covered by snow, about fifteen yards back the way they'd come, off the side of the road. Andrews climbed out of the saddle, handed the reins to Colonel Fawcett and walked over to investigate. "It's another one, but the wolves didn't get to this one. He's got the same wounds on his neck as young Tommy."

"Are you sure, Inspector?"

"Of course I'm sure." Before he'd finished, Colonel Fawcett was leaning over his shoulder, examining the wound.

"Could be a wound from one of those wolves."

"Look around, Colonel. There's no blood here. That's why the wolves let this one alone."

"Still, we can't be sure."

"Have it your way, Colonel, but it appears to me that one, or both, of these men were the victims of the same murderer as Witherspoon and young Tommy, and if he's gone on to New York, I aim to follow him."

Chapter 6

Transit to America...

The voyage from Liverpool to New York was breathtaking. Two days out we navigated through a small field of icebergs. Holmes slept like a baby that night but I must admit I did not. I spent much of the night on the bridge of the ship making a perfect nuisance of myself to the Captain and First Mate. I did manage to sleep away the majority of the following day and upon waking was told it appeared we'd cleared the cluster of bergs and none had been sighted since mid-day.

That evening at dinner we had a delightful time. We were seated at a table with none other than Sir Henry Irving and his personal assistant, Abraham Stoker. Just the previous month I had the pleasure of attending Sir Henry's performance of *Macbeth* at the Lyceum, the premier theater in London that I discovered Sir Henry not only performs in, but also manages.

It was quite an evening. I have long been an admirer of Sir Henry, but Holmes, much to my surprise, took more of an interest in Sir Henry's assistant. In fact, while Sir Henry and I were enjoying coffee and cigars at our table, Holmes and Stoker went out on deck to smoke, an act quite odd considering the coldness of the evening.

Later, when I questioned Holmes as to what he'd found so interesting in Sir Henry's personal assistant, he merely said he had discovered they had a mutual acquaintance. Oddly, from that point on during our voyage Holmes seemed to spend a good deal more time than usual patrolling the decks smoking his pipe, deep in thought.

On the pages that follow, I've taken the liberty of recording from various sources bits of the story of this affair that were occurring as Holmes and I were traversing the ocean from London to New York. I feel it better serves the story to give just a bit of background on the various characters we will encounter in this adventure and what was occurring while we were steaming to meet them, rather than recount here any further impressions of the crossing.

At this juncture, I should like to describe one of the members of the police force in New York with whom Holmes and I would soon become acquainted on our mission to find the missing remains of Miss Abigail Drake. A most unusual character and one of whom we were unsure, when first we met him, how he might figure in this adventure once all was said and done. That which follows is an example of what from all reports was a commonplace occurrence in the life of one Mylo Strumm, Detective Sergeant in the municipal police force of New York. I relay it here not to denigrate him so much as to let the reader become acquainted with the man as we first knew him.

Mylo Strumm trudged through the storm. The driving sleet stung his cheeks and made his feet wet and numb with cold inside his worn shoes. He had to get to the hospital before it was too late, before his wife breathed her last. Just as he saw the hospital lights, a hearse, pulled by six black-plumed horses, rounded the corner and rushed by him throwing a torrent of slushy water up from the gulley all over his white suit.

"The great Mylo Strumm," the lead horse whinnied,

"detective, extraordinaire."

Strumm rubbed the sleep from his eyes, realizing it was the dream again. Opening only one, he saw Bernie O'Toole staring down at him, a look of amused disgust on his equine face.

Bernie O'Toole stood nearly six feet tall with a generous portion of mean within his wiry frame. Strumm had known O'Toole for just about two years, ever since Strumm had landed in the First Precinct, unceremoniously bounced from midtown after going on a two-month bender. "Get up, Strumm," O'Toole said as he kicked the bottoms of Strumm's feet. "For the life of me I can't figure why you haven't been sacked long before now."

"Because, Bernie," he said, still looking at O'Toole with just his left eye, "most of the detectives in this God-forsaken precinct, yourself being a prime example, could not find their arses with both hands and a proctologist's chart."

"That's rich coming from a barrel-fevered sot such as yourself."

"Even drunk I can see what hen you've been trimming, Bernie, and I don't believe Mrs. O'Toole would approve."

"What's that you're saying?" Bernie said, blubbering and blustering, his eyes narrowing their gaze at Strumm. "And mind yourself, I've heard about your tricks."

"You're one to be talkin' about tricks, Bernie. But I don't need tricks to see you've been dallying at a local bawd's palace. It's as plain as that malmsey nose on your ugly puss."

"Pyeh! That's a lot of gas," Bernie said, giving a furtive glance around the cell to see who might be within earshot.

"Okay, if you say so, but I'd shake that moll's powder from your lap before you go home." Even lying flat on his back Mylo could

54

see the cream-colored powder, a favorite hue of the midnight mollies on 4th Street, smudged on O'Toole's inner thigh.

"Ha, show's you for a fool, that's flour from a loaf of bread I bought not half an hour ago," O'Toole said, glancing around to make sure he was heard by the right ears.

"My mistake, I'm sure, but it appears your baker is a whole lot friendlier than mine."

"Eh?" A quizzical look came over O'Toole's face as he straightened up and scratched his head.

"Your wife has dark hair, doesn't she, Bernie?"

"What of it?" O'Toole said, pushing out his chin in defiance.

Raising himself up on one elbow, Strumm reached for O'Toole's crotch.

"Here, now," objected O'Toole.

"Take it easy," Strumm said as he snatched something from the air. "I see your baker is blonde," pulling a long platinum hair from O'Toole's fly. "And if it's with that flour he does his baking, it's little wonder he makes your loaf rise. Circus croissant?" he said, making a reference to the services offered by the prostitutes he knew O'Toole favored in what were commonly called French Circuses.

O'Toole's eyes widened and his face reddened. He moved over Strumm and was about to grab him by his throat when Detective Murray came to Strumm's rescue. "Let it go, Bernie." His low voice resonated with menace in the dank cell. Michael Murray stood only five feet five inches tall but was nearly as wide as two men with arms the size of O'Toole's legs. Every cop in the precinct knew of his prowess as a wrestler and they all took great pains to remain on Murray's good side. O'Toole backed away.

Murray didn't approve of Strumm's drinking, but he knew the

reason for it and made allowances because of it. He reached out his hand to help Strumm to his feet. "Another night in the tank eh, Mylo?" His voice registered his disapproval.

"I didn't start out there, Murray."

"No, but ya sure as piss wound up there, didn't ya? Again." He took the detective's arm as the two of them walked toward the desk sergeant to collect Strumm's personal effects, a beat up pocket watch, a near empty wallet, a key, a detective's badge and a police gun.

"True," Strumm replied, "but none the worse for the wear." He pocketed his meager belongings and then clapped his partner on the shoulder, "Now, Murray old boy, let's go to work."

"That'll have to wait. Captain wants to see you, Mylo." A look of concern showed on his face. "I think you're arse is in real trouble this time, if you catch my meanin'."

Captain Moses Cortright ran one of the poorest precincts in lower Manhattan. It was also one of the least graft-ridden in all of New York, and for Manhattan in 1888, that was definitely not the norm. While other precinct captains used their positions and the ever present crime in their districts to line their pockets with gold, Cortright turned his attention toward fighting crime, a novel endeavor in much of the New York City Police Department.

"Come on, Murray, how long we been doin' this, how long've you been my partner now? You think Cortright's gonna sack me? He knows I'm one of his best."

"Yeah, one of his best when you're sober, that is, and as far as how long we been doin' this, I'd say it's been two, two and a half years since I had the misfortune o'bein' partnered up wi' the likes o'you."

56

Strumm laughed,."Don't be that way, Murray old boy," he said as he reached up and mussed Murray's hair. "You know you've learned more about bein' a detective in the last two years with me than in the previous six you been here."

Murray laughed, but they both knew it was true. Despite his drinking, Strumm was a first-rate detective. Murray was glad when they were first teamed up, but at that time he didn't know Strumm was a broken man, a man whose world had come suddenly crashing down around him, a man who now sought his solace in distilled spirits, a man haunted by the guilt of a dead young wife—a death he could have prevented. Once Murray learned the whole story, he remained loyal to Strumm, despite disapproving his drinking.

The nearly two years in the First Precinct had been more or less a blur to Strumm. It was Murray who'd helped Strumm through the hardest of times and still keep his job. There would be stretches, up to a month or more, when he'd throw himself wholly into his work, foregoing the bottle, but then he'd backslide for as long a period or longer, nose once again pink with drink, as Murray put it. He'd never miss work, at least not entirely, Murray saw to that. Some days during his bouts he'd check into the precinct late or leave early, or both, but he maintained just enough of a presence not to be dismissed.

It was during those periods between cases that Detective Murray had his hands full trying to keep Strumm out of hot water. Strumm was an intolerable drunk who seemingly went out of his way to get into trouble. Case in point, and the reason Captain Cortright sent for him this morning, Strumm spent the previous evening in the drunk tank after escorting three ladies of easy virtue to the home of Thomas Sheehey, Commissioner of Charities and Corrections, telling them the commissioner's wife was out of town and he needed some company.

It wasn't that Commissioner Sheehey was unacquainted with the ladies in question and undoubtedly under other circumstances would have been delighted to entertain the trio of trollops. Unfortunately, last evening was the third Thursday of the month and the night when Mrs. Sheehey's bridge club met. When Strumm and the ladies barged in on the bridge party, accusations and fine china flew about the place until the police arrived, arresting Strumm and his strumpets. Commissioner Sheehey was left to clean up what was left of his china and his marriage. No doubt the commissioner had given Captain Cortright a personal call.

#

Also of paramount importance in this case is a young doctor of whom we had heard about before we departed England, a supposed principal player in the related matter of which I am sworn not to write. As it happened, he was newly married to a most delightful young woman of genteel manner and excellent breeding. We catch up with them as they learn, somewhat later than we had learned, of the probable sinking of the *Animus Lacuna*.

In a fashionable home in Upper Manhattan, Julia Cabot Tremaine and her husband, Dr. Alan Tremaine discussed the news of a ship wreck from the pages of the *New York World*. "I hope this means you'll give up your insistence on any public announcement of your latest experimentation," Julia said as her husband read to her a small article in the newspaper describing the suspected loss of the ship crossing from London to New York.

"They laughed at me, Julia, don't you see?"

"Yes, I know, but father and Uncle Ralph were only trying to keep you from being humiliated and ruined professionally just as you are beginning to make a name for yourself."

"But Julia, this was the most important medical and scientific find of the century. Not only had I discovered a true vampire, but I was well on my way to being able to cure his vampirism. Now it's all for nothing." He glanced across the room at the walking stick Baron Barlucci had given him as a parting gift when he left London.

Julia approached the chair where her husband was sipping his coffee, the newspaper now collapsed in a heap upon his lap. "Oh, darling, it doesn't matter now. Anyway, there's nothing to be done about it. Your baron is at the bottom of the Atlantic, and with him the secret of this vampirism." She brushed his hair away from his forehead as she sank down onto his lap. "Isn't there anything I can do to make you forget that awful man?" She leaned over and brushed his lips with her own.

Tremaine pulled her closer. Wrapping his arms around her waist he kissed her deeply. "I'm such a lucky man to have you, Julia," he murmured between kisses.

She only laughed and then nibbled on his ear lobe.

Taking her arms in his hands, he pushed her upright on his lap, "Now see here, Mrs. Tremaine," he said in a mock serious manner, "This kind of behavior is totally improper in the parlor." Upon saying this he slipped an arm beneath her knees and stood up with her cradled in his caress.

Julia tittered, "Oh my, Dr. Tremaine, and just what do you mean to do with me?" She locked her arms around his neck, laying her head on his shoulder.

"I'm going to take you to my bedroom, Mrs. Tremaine, and make mad, passionate love to you."

"Oh, dear," Julia said, giggling with delight.

As they were mounting the stairs, there came a knock on the

door, just behind them.

"Goodness, I almost forgot," Julia said as she wriggled to get out of her husband's arms, "Papa is coming over with some news. I wasn't supposed to say anything."

Tremaine remained standing on the third step as his precocious wife floated down the stairs to answer the door. Julia was the only daughter of Charles Edward Cabot, President of St. Vincent's Hospital, a stout, bald man with a large handlebar mustache that managed to retain much of its youthful reddish color, though his remaining hair was snow white.

A gregarious man, his broad smile revealed a gap between his front teeth that appeared nearly wide enough to slip a copper between them. Julia adored her father who doted on her and had always, he freely admitted, spoiled her shamelessly. He greeted his daughter affectionately, wrapping his arms around her and lifting her off her feet as he hugged her. "Ah, Julia, you're wasting away," he teased. It was evident his only daughter was the light of his life.

"Oh, Daddy," Julia said, "how is Momma?"

"The same, dear, I'm afraid she still isn't herself. She misses Charles so. I'm hoping that having you and Alan home for Christmas will bring her out of her doldrums."

"Dr. Cabot," Tremaine said as he descended the few steps down the staircase to the front door. "It's an unexpected pleasure to see you in the middle of the day like this." As he said this he gave his wife a look of disappointment and then continued, "We were just about to have s...um, some coffee. Would you care to join us? For coffee, that is."

"Yes, that would be excellent. I take it, then, Julia didn't tell you I was coming this morning?" Looking over at Julia he said,

"Good girl."

"I didn't want to spoil your surprise, Daddy." Taking her father's hand she led him and Alan into the parlor.

"Surprise? What surprise? What's this about, Dr. Cabot?"

"Charles, you must call me Charles, dear boy, especially since you will soon be working for me."

"Working for you, sir?" They sat down in front of the fireplace. "How? What does this mean?"

"There is an opening for head of the blood contagions department at St. Vincent's, and I put your name before the board."

"I see, sir, but isn't it a bit unusual, what with my marrying your daughter, for you to proffer me for such a position? Aren't you afraid it will smack of nepotism to the members?"

"Yes, yes, there is that, but when I mentioned you might be interested, they practically begged me to put you up for it. You're gaining quite a reputation, you know."

"Isn't it wonderful, darling?" Julia sat on the arm of Alan's chair, draping her arm around his shoulders.

"I don't know what to say. Yes, it is quite an honor, sir."

"I must say that I thought for a moment I might have made a mistake when you mentioned that vampire business to me, but Julia assured me you were just pulling my leg a bit." The elder man studied Tremaine's face as he shot a look of reproach to his wife, "It was just a jest, wasn't it?"

"Of course it was, Daddy." She gave her husband a stern look as she turned away from her father, "Don't tell me you were taken in by my husband's droll sense of humor. A vampire indeed. That's as likely as...as...as a sunken ship rising from the ocean." Though her father didn't get the connection, her husband did.

"I'm terribly sorry to have used you so poorly, Charles," Alan said with a laugh. "I'm afraid I sometimes let my imagination run away with me."

"No harm done, my boy," Dr. Cabot said, "so long as we hear no more about this vampire business."

"No, sir, I assure you," Tremaine said, "that is a dead topic." There was sudden silence, then all three burst out laughing.

"Excellent. Very good. Now, where's that coffee you promised me."

#

This brings us to introduce Miss Emily Drake, sister and twin to the late Miss Abigail Drake. Upon hearing of her sister's demise, Emily Drake returned to New York from Chicago to attend her sister's funeral. She'd gone to Chicago a little over two years ago ostensibly to prepare for her final vows to become a nun. What she'd discovered was that her vocation was more a reaction to loss than a calling to God.

"Dear me, Sister, we should be in New York soon now," Emily's best friend from Chicago, Sister Elizabeth said. Stout of body and quick to smile, Sister Elizabeth was traveling to Boston. A trained nurse, she was being assigned to the Carney Hospital as her first appointment since taking her final vows, so when she discovered Emily was traveling east, they decided to make the trip together as far as New York, as it was the last major stop on the way to Boston. Emily was happy for the company.

"You should get used to calling me Emily, Sister. I won't be using the title of 'Sister' any longer, I'm afraid," Emily said, surprised by the emotion she felt in saying out loud what she'd been thinking since the train left Chicago.

"That's true enough, Emily, but it sure makes me sad to think we won't be sistering together, after all."

"I know, me too, but I told you about my Aunt Lucie. Since Uncle Cedric passed, her letters have been more and more, how shall I say it, scattered. I simply must return to New York and take care of the poor dear."

"Well, yes, I suppose you must, but it's a loss to the order, that's for sure. You'll need to get some secular clothes once you get to New York or I won't be the only person calling you sister."

"True." Emily looked down at the rosary beads that lay across her lap, silent for a moment, and then said, "I think maybe this was coming anyway. For quite some time I've been considering whether this was the path I should take, after all. You know I entered the convent for mixed reasons of loss and obligation."

"Yes, yes…I remember you said you and your sister were separated after your parents died…"

"Yes…"

"She went off to England to live, didn't she?"

"Yes, I was supposed to go with her, but I got a nasty case of influenza just before we were to travel. She went on alone. I remember my heart was broken when she left."

"I'm sure hers was too."

"Well, if it was it was difficult to tell." Emily sat fiddling with the beads, then looked up at Elizabeth with just her eyes, "Abigail was always the strong one in so many ways." Emily looked out the window, remembering how when her parents died, victims of a tragic accident, their mother's sister and her husband, Mr. and Mrs. Cedric Belmont, took them in. But Cedric Belmont was not a well man and it was soon evident being responsible for two girls, who'd only just completed school, would prove to be too much of a strain for the Belmonts to bear. They contacted Sir Charles Warren, half-brother of the girls' father, who immediately and without hesitation insisted the girls come to live with him and his wife in London.

Childless, the Warrens were only too happy to open their homes to two vibrant young ladies. Unfortunately, Emily, who was always a sickly child, came down with influenza shortly before they were to make the trip and came very close to dying. Although it broke both the girls' hearts, it was decided that Emily was too weak to make the voyage and Abigail was to travel to London alone.

Shortly after her sister departed for London, Emily entered the convent of the Sacred Heart to begin her studies to become a nun. She was still despondent over the death of her parents and with the loss of her sister too, she thought perhaps she could find happiness in serving God. And though they never made her feel uncomfortable about staying with them, there was also her desire to move away from her aunt and uncle to allow Cedric to retire and recover his health.

"Would you like me to leave you alone with your thoughts, Sister...I mean, Emily?" Sister Elizabeth said, breaking in on her troubled reflections.

"Oh, no, Elizabeth, and you may call me Sister," she said looking down at her frock, "at least until I purchase some suitable clothing. Besides, it helps to have someone to talk to. I hope you don't mind."

"Gracious me, no. I have five brothers, it's refreshing to hear what life for two sisters was like. I was ten before I was even aware a family might not have to have brothers who put frogs in your bed or mud in your shoes."

"Oh my, brothers must be quite trying."

"Oh, they're dears, really, but just a bit on the rough-edged side."

"Did I ever tell you about the time when we were little girls and Abigail became lost?"

"Dear me, no. What happened?"

"Well, when were little, my sister and I were so close our mother used to say 'if Abigail gets a cut, it's Emily who bleeds'. Of course that was a bit broad, but I will say that I could always tell when my sister was in trouble. On this particular afternoon Abigail had been playing in a field behind our grandparents' house and had fallen into an abandoned well. Had this been a normal day, I would have been playing with Abigail, and had that been the case, we might both have fallen in the well and never been heard from again, but I was in bed with a terrible cold. I was napping when I sat bolt upright and screamed for my mother, 'Mummy! Mummy, Abby's fallen into a hole and can't get out.'"

"Goodness, what did your mother do?"

"At first she tried to calm me, insisting I'd only had a bad dream. I suspect she was afraid perhaps I was a bit delirious with a sudden fever. But after she checked my forehead and discovered it was cool and upon my insistence, she went to look for Abby, who, of course, she believed was playing just outside in the back yard. In short order she returned in a panic to my room, scooped me up in her arms and together we went to search for Abby. In my dream I had seen clearly where Abigail was and following my directions we found her fifteen feet down in an abandoned and partially filled in well."

"Oh my, that is quite a story."

"Yes, I only tell it because it was barely two weeks ago when I was once again awakened from a dead sleep with a premonition. It was the most powerful feeling I'd ever felt in connection with my sister. As I sat shivering in the cold darkness, I could actually feel my sister's life slowly draining from her body. There could be no mistake. Abigail was dead."

There was a long silence. Elizabeth took Emily's hand.

That was how she came to be on this train, headed to New York. When she first telegraphed her aunt, she received a response saying Abigail was expected soon, by ship, and that her guardian, Sir Charles Warren, in England, was much distressed at her leaving and bade she contact him at once upon Abigail's arrival, but without informing Abigail. It all sounded most mysterious, but her aunt told her she was sure it wasn't serious. Abigail had always been headstrong. It was three days later when Emily received another telegram informing her of the shipwreck and the recovery of Abigail's body.

Emily felt immense sadness for the loss of her only sister. She remembered how they grew up together, twin peaches of their parents' eye. She remembered how they'd played together, laughed together, and cried together. They were totally devoted to one another.

But now Abigail was dead. Emily felt a cold emptiness inside her, like an empty tomb. But despite the feeling, her tears would not come.

Once again lost in her own thoughts, she sat silently watching the passing landscape. She passed off the sense of urgency she felt as a combination of grief and homesickness. It had been two years since she left New York, three since she'd last seen Abigail.

Interrupting her introspection, thankfully, Sister Elizabeth patted her hand and said, "Well, Sister, last leg of the journey." The train was pulling out after a brief meal stop in Schenectady. "I'm sure you'll be glad to be rid of me." Elizabeth laughed in that jolly way she had that was so contagious.

"Don't be silly," answered Emily. "I don't know what I'd have done with myself if you hadn't been here, you've been most indulgent."

"Not at all, dear…not at all. It sounds as though you and your sister were very close."

"We were. I'd do anything for her, and she for me. If it weren't for her I'd have been expelled from Our Lady of Hope?"

"Goodness, what on earth for?"

"Well, I'm afraid when I was a young girl I was a bit on the rebellious side. I didn't like to study, was very lax in obeying the rules, etc."

"Oh dearie, weren't we all," Elizabeth said with a bemused titter.

"Yes, well once, not too long before we were to graduate, I sneaked a boy into our rooms at the school."

"Oh my, you *were* a naughty one," Elizabeth laughed.

"It was all quite innocent, but Mother Superior was incensed. I can hear her ranting to our parents, 'rules are rules, and young Mistress Emily has crossed the line once too often'."

"Oh dear, she was going to expel you?"

"Yes, and with only six weeks to graduation."

"How terrible. How did you get out of that pickle?"

"My sister, my dear darling sister Abigail came to my rescue. You see, Abigail was the model student in every way. She excelled in academics and was a favorite of all her teachers. Abigail was a natural leader, very popular with the other girls as well as the sisters. In truth, I believe at least some of my rebelliousness was to compensate for

67

feeling less self-assured than my sister."

"That's a very mature observation."

"Yes, well, anyway Abigail told Mother Superior that it was she and not I who'd smuggled the boy in through an open window in the dormitory basement."

"Did they believe her? Oh, well they must have."

"Yes. They really had no choice. Our parents were summoned to the school and we were all in Mother Superior's office, Mama and Papa, Mother Superior, Abigail, Sisters Anna and Carmella, and me. The sisters couldn't tell us apart, so Abigail explained that she was so frightened when first she was caught that she told them she was me. Then she broke down into tears, begging my forgiveness. Mother Superior was quite embarrassed. Our parents consoled Abigail who was crying frightfully, pleading not to be expelled and promising never to misbehave again."

"What happened then?"

"Well, what could poor Mother Superior do? She couldn't very well expel me with Abigail protesting my innocence in such a forceful and dramatic way, although I don't believe Mother Superior was completely convinced, and she couldn't expel Abigail, who for four years, up until this incident, had been the very model of a fine student. We were both allowed to stay and graduate, though Abigail was not allowed to graduate with the honors she deserved. I felt terrible about that," she said.

"Oh dear."

But then she laughed, saying, "She was so convincing that I nearly believed her myself."

"What a devoted sister."

"Yes, we've always been so. There was never anything she

wouldn't do for me, nor I for her."

"Excuse me, Sisters," the conductor said as he tipped his hat in reverence, "we'll be arriving at Grand Central in New York in about fifteen minutes."

"Thank you," she said to the conductor, and then turned back to Elizabeth. "I'd better gather my things. Aunt Lucie will be waiting at the station. You must meet her."

As Emily stepped down from the train she saw her Aunt Lucie almost immediately. In truth, although slight of form, Aunt Lucie was difficult to miss. Barely over five feet tall, she was attired in a lemon-yellow dress beneath a bright red, belted greatcoat of velveteen with white ermine cuffs and collar. Atop her flaming red hair was perched a grand wide-brimmed hat with an immense yellow ostrich feather that matched her dress. The feather reached a height of seven feet, making it possible to follow her progress through the throngs of travelers even when she could not be seen directly. It was fair to say Aunt Lucie stood out from the crowd.

"Oh my," Sister Elizabeth said in a conspiratorially quiet voice, "your description of your aunt was certainly not exaggerated. She appears quite outgoing."

"Yes, she's such a dear, really, but has always enjoyed being the center of attention. It does my heart good to see her so, for her letters of late have been a bit confused, particularly since the death of Uncle Cedric. I'm glad to see she looks her old self," Emily said as she waved to her aunt.

"Emily!" Aunt Lucie called from across the platform. "Emily, it's so good to see you," she said as she closed the distance and wrapped her arms around her in a rather embarrassing attempt to lift her into the air. Settling back down, she turned to Elizabeth, "Oh dear,

you and your sister have grown so much since last I saw you."
Confused, Elizabeth looked at Emily.

"When Emily mentioned she was traveling with her sister, I was so happy to know that Abigail had been found again, but I must say I was a bit confused."

Emily asked, "Confused, Auntie?"

"Why yes," she said turning to Emily, "How ever did she get all the way to Chicago from Newfoundland?" Turning back to Elizabeth, "How did you manage, dear?"

"Oh my…" Elizabeth said, not quite knowing how to answer.

Emily rescued her, "Why Auntie, that's a perfectly wonderful hat you have on, wherever did you get it?"

"Why I bought it just yesterday, at B. Altman's," she said. "Isn't it a tart?"

"Just so, Auntie, just so. Oh dear, I'm afraid I haven't introduced you to Sister Elizabeth. She was traveling to Boston and was kind enough to accompany me as far as New York."

Turning back to Elizabeth, as if for the first time seeing her, Lucie said, "It's so nice to meet you. Are you staying in New York?"

"No, I'm afraid I'm continuing on to Boston, Mrs. Belmont," she said looking at Emily with the obvious question written across her brow.

"Auntie, wait right here and I'll get my bag," she said and pulled Elizabeth away. "I'm afraid she isn't quite herself. I've a feeling this is going to be a bit more difficult than I'd thought."

"Would you like me to stay a day or two."

"Oh, you're such a dear, that's very nice, but I'm sure we'll be all right. Aunt Lucie is just a bit confused about time and events, and people…she's been somewhat this way for many years, though as I said, Uncle Cedric's death must have pushed her a bit further than I knew.

Emily retrieved her bag from the train and hugged Elizabeth good-bye, "If I get the chance, I'll visit you in Boston."

"You promise? Oh, that would be wonderful. Please take care of yourself, and your Aunt, and again, I'm so sorry to hear about your sister."

"Thank you," she said, making her way across the platform to her aunt. She hired a cab and as they climbed in, Lucie had a queer look on her face. Emily asked, "Auntie, what's wrong?"

"Emily, I'm afraid I have some distressing news. I was so happy to see you I'd quite forgotten to tell you."

Emily braced for what was to come.

"Emily, I'm afraid there isn't going to be a funeral…at least not as we'd planned."

"I don't understand, Auntie. What do you mean?" she asked, feeling a flutter of hope, thinking but not thinking, 'Could she be alive?'

Lucie handed her a telegram, from Sir Charles Warren. It read:

> FROM SIR CHARLES WARREN, SCOTLAND YARD, RETIRED
>
> TO LUCIE BALDWIN, NEW YORK
>
> BODY IN NEWFOUNDLAND IDENTIFIED POSITIVELY AS ABIGAIL STOP INSPECTOR ANDREWS INVESTIGATING STOP BODY STOLEN STOP GOD REST HER SOUL STOP
>
> SIR CHARLES SENDS

"Her body was stolen?" Emily asked.

"Whose, dear?"

Chapter 7
Dead end…

Upon arriving back in New York, having hitched a ride on one of the two Newfoundland Constabulary's police boats, Andrews went directly to the office of the Ferry Master at the Whitehall Street Ferry Terminal.

"Excuse me, where might I find the Ferry Master?" Andrews asked a round woman with an even rounder face who sat behind a desk stacked with piles of what looked to be ledgers and folders of correspondence. He wasn't quite sure she had heard him over the sound of her own labored breathing until after a few moments she looked up.

"If this is about yer luggage, we tole'ya before ya'boarded to keep an eye on it. It ain't our responsibility if it gets snitched in transit." After saying this in two or three labored breaths she went back to work on the file she had open before her as if that were the end of the conversation.

An annoyed Andrews then announced, "This is not about missing luggage, Miss…" he read from the name placard on her desk, "…Miss Wolniac, it is about a missing body." She stopped writing but did not look up. "I am Inspector Walter Andrews of Scotland Yard," he said as he laid out his badge and credentials on the desk in front of her, "and I'm here investigating the theft of a corpse, the corpse of a young woman by the name of Abigail Drake."

Miss Wolniac picked up the badge and identification in her hand, looked at it for a minute or so as if forming in her mind the response she quietly uttered, "Scotland Yard, y'say? Well, that don't hold no truck in this vicinity, Mister. But if this is truly a case of, as you say, the theft of a body, I'll see if the Ferry Master can see you. Please have a seat over there," indicating a gray, wooden bench on which slept a man who had the appearance of not having bathed in quite some time.

"Thank you," Andrews said, "but I think I'll just wait here."

"As you wish," she said with a grunt. She leaned forward in an effort to hoist herself out of her chair, pressing her knuckles onto the desktop. The position of her arms and the grimace on her face reminded him of a bull dog getting to its feet as she raised her great girth from the chair and slowly made her way to the office of the Ferry Master. A few minutes later, Miss Wolniac returned to her desk, where she closed her eyes and plopped down into her chair, her breathing more labored than ever. After a moment her eyes opened and scanned the room falling at last upon Andrews. With a motion of her hand that appeared calculated to use the least amount of energy possible, she waved him back over to her desk. When he arrived, she looked up at him and between gasping breaths said, "Mr. White, the Ferry Master, will see you." With a quick nod of her head, she indicated the door from which she had so recently emerged, "Just through there."

The Ferry Master's office was also cluttered with stacks of paper, in this case maps, manifests, etc., and at first Andrews thought he must have entered the wrong door, not seeing a soul inside. But as he stood in the doorway, he heard from behind one of the stacks of charts a coarse phlegmatic cough and a voice that said, "Come in, come in...don't stand there with the door open."

Andrews entered the room and approaching the desk he saw a very small and thin man who appeared even smaller as he was reaching down into a deep drawer in the bottom of his desk. "I'm Inspector Walter Andrews, of Scotland Yard and—"

"Yes, yes, Miss Wolniac has told me. You are here about a missing body."

"That's correct, sir."

"We don't have it. We don't make a practice of transporting corpses, but on those odd occasions when we do, we don't lose them," he said in a manner apparently intended to end the conversation before it started.

"No, I'm afraid you misunderstand me. I don't believe you lost the body. You see, the theft occurred in Newfoundland, St. Johns, and, well, I'm in pursuit of the thief. I believe he left Newfoundland bound for New York. In fact, I can only be a few hours behind the ferry on which the thief must have travelled."

"How can that be? We have only two ferries a week from Newfoundland. You must have come on the latter, making you days behind, not hours."

"I arrived by the Newfoundland Constabulary Police boat."

"Police boat? You don't say. May I see your identification?" He held out a thin hand with unusually long, thin fingers. He took Andrews credentials and examined them carefully. "So, if you don't think we lost your corpse, what is it we can do for you, Inspector? And have you spoken to the police?"

"I've not yet been to the authorities. I thought it would be best to not lose time so I came here first. As to what you can do for me, I'd very much like to speak to the captain in charge of the last ferry."

"I'm quite sure that can be arranged. What is it, exactly, you wish to know?"

"The luggage, I want to know if there were any trunks transported and if so, who claimed them," Andrews said.

"Don't tell me you think the body may be locked in a trunk?"

"I can think of no other way the body might have been transported aboard a ferry without drawing attention."

"Yes, I see. Well, sir, you may be in luck. The *Rainbow Smelt* had trouble tying up. There was a bit of wind and it took out a piece of the pier when it arrived. The winch was broken and only hand luggage has been offloaded thus far."

"Where is the ferry?"

"Pier twelve-bravo," White said as he cleared his throat and pointed to his window. "You can see it from here. It's the only ferry we have in port just now."

"When do you expect to have the winch fixed? May I go onboard and search for the trunk?"

"Well, first I believe we should wire the police and have them meet you. This is a bit out of your jurisdiction, don't you think?"

Two hours later Andrews was standing on the pier by the brow waiting to go onboard when a detective from the first precinct arrived. "You Anderson?" he said.

"Inspector Andrews, Scotland Yard," he said, holding out his hand and correcting the detective. "And you are?"

"Detective O'Toole, First Precinct, New York Police." He looked Andrews over, "We don't get many inspectors from Scotland."

"I'm from London, actually," Andrews said. "Scotland Yard is the name of our Municipal Police."

"Huh," grunted O'Toole, "I'd've thought you'd name it after London."

"Well, you see—" Andrews began to explain, but Detective O'Toole was already walking up the brow onto the ferry.

"Come on, Anderson, they tell me you got the notion there's a body in a trunk."

"Andrews," he corrected O'Toole once again and hurried up the brow to follow the detective. The Ferry Master had arranged the custodian to show them to the luggage storage area.

The winch, by this time, had been repaired. The Ferry Master had allowed smaller items to be winched off onto the pier but kept the three trunks onboard for inspection. The owners of two of the trunks were also onboard. O'Toole explained to them this was an official investigation and they were to open the trunks. Although they were none too happy to oblige, oblige they did. O'Toole rooted around inside the trunks and then looking up to Andrews said, "Would you like to take a look, Inspector?"

Looking at the disarray in which O'Toole had left the two trunks and the angry but restrained faces of the owners, he waved his hand, "It's obvious nobody is in these two trunks. What about the third?"

O'Toole turned to the cargo master, "Where's the owner of this 'un." He kicked the remaining steamer trunk.

"He's not about, sir. The Captain said he was a foreigner, but no one's seen 'im since we arrived."

Barlucci, Andrews thought. It had to be his trunk. But where was he? Andrews looked out onto the pier up and down the dockyard.

Perhaps Barlucci was watching them now, knowing what they would find hidden in the trunk, or perhaps, somehow, he'd learned Andrews was on his trail and was cowering in some dark corner of New York.

O'Toole said, "Well, then, if he ain't here, he can't object. Force the lock, let's have a look."

Andrews stood nervous with anticipation as the cargo master used his crow bar against the lock. When the hasp popped off, he pulled open the trunk. It was empty.

O'Toole laughed and said, "Looks like you've been chasin' an empty box, Inspector."

#

After his humiliation on the ferry, where he felt Barlucci had somehow eluded him and absconded with Miss Drake's body, a disappointed Andrews wired Inspector Abberline from the Western Union office in the terminal.

The trail of Abigail Drake's body snatcher was now cold, as cold as the sinking feeling of failure in the pit of Andrews' stomach. He'd failed to arrest Baron Barlucci when he first arrived in New York, failed in returning the remains of Abigail Drake to her uncle, Sir Charles, and now he'd failed to track down the villain and murderer who stole her body. He didn't even have a lead in the case.

With nothing left for him to do, he felt it his duty to visit the Police Board of Commissioners office. There was the matter of jurisdiction to consider, as both the Ferry Master and Detective O'Toole reminded him, and it was after all only his intuition that told him the murderer he'd followed from St. John's to Petty Harbor had actually left Newfoundland for New York in the first place.

He told the Commissioners the whole story of Baron Barlucci, his suspected guilt in the Ripper murders, his escape from London with Miss Abigail Drake in tow, the subsequent recovery and then loss of Miss Drake's remains, and of his own investigations in Newfoundland. He gave them detailed descriptions of both Barlucci and Abigail Drake, although he purposely withheld Miss Drake's photo—that he intended to return to Sir Charles when he was back in London.

He hoped the local police would ask him to assist, if not lead, the investigation in a collaborative effort. In that way he might salvage what remained of his pride. But he was sorely disappointed. Not only did they not request his collaboration, they insisted he cease any further investigative efforts in 'their' city under 'their' jurisdiction. Andrews felt he had no choice at this point but to return to London with his hat in his hand.

But matters were about to go from bad to worse. When he checked the Western Union Office for a response to his wire, he was surprised to find a message awaiting him telling him that Holmes and I would be arriving in New York in just a few days. Instantly he knew Holmes and I we were coming to take over the investigation of the missing Miss Drake. Andrews' emotions were quite mixed upon hearing this. He was a bit put out that Inspector Abberline evidently did not have enough faith in his judgment about the viability of this investigation, but not having any type of lead and not knowing what else he could do, he resigned himself to be of as able assistance as possible to the illustrious Sherlock Holmes.

The Gilsey House Hotel was an extravagance in which he would not normally indulge on a junior inspector's salary, but as Andrews was unsure when he might ever be in New York again, he decided to splurge on a well deserved vacation while he awaited our arrival. Afterward, he would determine whether to return immediately to London, or stay on and assist Mr. Holmes, if there was indeed anything to assist him with.

The Gilsey was situated in Manhattan's Tenderloin district, an area rapidly gaining a reputation as an up-and-coming entertainment venue with playhouses, concert saloons and halls for the relatively new sensation, vaudeville. The rooms were luxurious with walnut and rosewood doors and casements adorned with bronze inlay, marble fireplaces, rich tapestries arrayed upon the walls and large crystal chandeliers throughout. Without a doubt it was the grandest hotel to be had. It was also a venue where the local clientele congregated to enjoy the arts.

It was the Gilsey's proximity to the theater houses of mid-Manhattan that drew Andrews to it. Not only was it near the theaters, but it was also frequented by actors and actresses. Aside from those enticements, he had never before stayed in such a grand establishment. At dinner that evening he hadn't even been thinking of Abigail Drake when he first noticed the young woman seated at the table next to his. It was her voice that first caught his attention. It seemed out of place among all of the New York accents that had assaulted his ears since he'd arrived. Not British by any stretch, but refined. Initially he wasn't even conscious of why it gave him the feeling of comfort it did. But as he listened to the tone and melody of it, he thought certainly she must have spent at least some time in England. It was less an accent than a manner of speech. Although he was unable to follow the conversation between her and the older man with whom she was seated, he strained to hear snippets, enjoying the melodic tone of her voice.

"I hope it's not too much of an inconvenience for you to conduct business here at my hotel, and at this time of day," she said, her voice low, with a hypnotic, seductive quality to it.

"Not at all, Miss Drake. For our 'special' depositors there is no limit to our accommodation." With the practiced fluidity of a banker used to the eccentricities of the very wealthy, Thaddeus Martin tried his utmost to reassure Miss Drake of the sincere and professional courtesy she could expect from Drexel, Morgan & Company. "And, although strictly speaking you are not a depositor, the instructions we received regarding the depositor's wishes were quite explicit. Anyone approaching our offices with the proper identification was to be given unlimited access to the liquid assets transferred to us, the full faith and credit of no less than the Bank of England standing good for it."

She handed him the signet she'd received from Antonio. He reached for it with greedy fingers, examining it with a jeweler's glass under the light of the table lamp between them, comparing it to the one he carried in a small felt-lined brass box.

The dining room was crowded and they sat at a small table near the entrance, but to one side. With her back to the wall she commanded a view of the entrance as well as the majority of the interior of the dining room. She glanced about, scanning the other patrons. There were finely dressed ladies and gentlemen enjoying their meals, laughing, talking, drinking wine. Her blood raced. This evening, she had purposely dressed in a way that if not provocative was at least enticing. From where she sat, even in the dim light of the dining room, she could tell that many of the men supping on the overpriced fare had noticed her and were reacting to her in an interested if not downright lustful fashion. It was a new sensation for her. She was surprised to note, however, that her companion showed not the slightest sign of interest in her other than as a client.

"Nevertheless, I should explain that I would have come to

your offices, but I suffer from an unusual sensitivity to sunlight, an allergy of sorts, that prevents me from spending too much time out of doors during the day."

"Quite all right, Miss Drake, you needn't feel you have anything to explain." He looked up at her and handed her back the signet. "There. It matches perfectly…undoubtedly struck from the same mold." A satisfied, if formal, smile attached itself to his face, "Now, how may I be of service to you."

She took a breath. "Well, first of all, I'd like to establish myself in a more suitable residence, perhaps a small house. Nothing too big, but it must be in a respectable area of the city where a woman alone can walk to church unmolested," she said with a slight smile.

"Of course, we can't expect you to go on living in a hotel indefinitely, can we?" he said in a formal tone. "A woman situated such as yourself should be in a setting that befits her station. Did you have an area in mind?"

"I was hoping you might be able to help me. I would prefer to live close to the park."

"I know just the place. Have you heard of the Dakota? It's a marvelously appointed apartment building with rooms arranged in the French style, with separate service entrance to the rooms and dumb waiters for meals from the dining hall."

"It sounds very nice. My only reservation is my need for privacy. I'm afraid I'm a bit eccentric in that respect."

"Of course, Miss Drake. Many of the apartments have private entries, but if you find an apartment unsuitable, there are a number of private residences in the same general area, near the park. Would you like me to arrange for a showing?"

"Actually, Mr. Martin, I'm afraid I'm in a bit of a hurry to get situated." She smiled sweetly as she added, "I'm really very set on a house with its own grounds, set back from the road if that's possible."

"I see," he said writing in a small leather notebook he'd taken from his pocket. "House…not too large…set back from road. There. Leave everything to me. I'm sure you won't be disappointed. Would there be anything else?"

"Yes. My…my sister was recently involved in a shipwreck…"

"I'm terribly sorry to hear that. Is she all right."

Smiling gravely, she said, "Well, I have every hope she will be. But anyway, about the shipwreck. There were others aboard who, I fear, were not so fortunate. I was hoping, since your company deals with shipping and insurance and such, that if you were to receive any word about the ship…well, I was hoping you could notify me."

"Certainly, we'd be most happy to." He smiled and poised his pen once more. "The ship's name and port of departure?"

"The *Animus Lacuna.* Last departed London, England."

"Very well, Miss Drake, if we hear anything on the ship, so shall you."

"One last thing. I find that I'm a bit cash shy just now. I wonder if I might impose on you for a draft…to enable me to purchase a few personal items. I would be very grateful."

"Of course, Miss Drake, without a doubt," he said as he withdrew a pen and draft paper from the interior pocket into which he deposited the signet. "I should have offered it at the outset. Will one thousand dollars be enough for a start?"

"That would be most generous," she replied, surprised at both the amount and the relative calm with which he offered it.

"Not at all, Miss Drake. You'll find the liquid holdings from which you may draw are quite extensive. This is but a pinch in a pail."

Smiling her sweetest, she said, "That must be a very large pail."

"Indeed, Miss Drake, indeed," he replied without the least bit of mirth. After handing her the draft, he asked, "Will there be anything else?"

"No. No, I think that will be everything I need, presently."

Standing, he extended his hand, "Then I'll be leaving you, Miss Drake. I'm certain we can find you suitable lodgings without too much trouble, and I shall speak with the hotel manager so you won't be troubled about your bill here."

"I must say, that is very kind of you," she responded shaking his hand, which had all the life of a lump of clay.

"Good evening, then, Miss Drake," he said and pulled back his hand.

She held it, and then asked, "There is just one thing more," releasing her grip, noting his discomfort.

"Yes?"

"There is a certain doctor in New York with whom I would like to make contact, but I seem to have lost his address. Would you know how I might discover it?"

Examining his fingers as if he expected them to be damaged, he replied, "I'm sure if you speak to the hotel staff, they can find his address for you."

"Thank you, Mr. Martin, and again, you've been most kind."

"At your service, Miss Drake," he replied and he walked away toward the front entrance to the hotel. She watched him as he passed through the lobby as if looking for someone, and then she saw a second man approach and take his arm. Together they departed the hotel. She smiled to herself, at once understanding Mr. Martin's disinterest in her. As she sipped her wine, thinking about what she must do next, she looked slowly around the room at her fellow diners, watching as they enjoyed their meal and laughed together quietly. She envied them their simple pleasures and wondered when she might again enjoy those same pleasures. Leaving a generous gratuity on the table, she rose to leave.

"Pardon, Miss," Andrews said in a soft voice.

She turned toward him, "Yes?"

"I believe you dropped this." He handed her a glove that had fallen to the floor.

"Thank you…"

"Andrews."

"Beg your pardon?"

"Andrews, Walter Andrews," he repeated, "at your service."

"You're British?" she said, somewhat surprised.

"Yes, guilty as charged, I fear. And judging from the slight accent I detect in your speech, I'd say you've spent some time in my home country yourself," he said smiling. "I noticed it when you came in. I was hoping for a chance to speak to you. It's so nice to meet someone with whom I might have at least a bit in common."

"You are very perceptive, Mr. Andrews, but I'm afraid it's been quite some time since I've been to England. Besides, I was just leaving. I doubt we would have that much in common."

"That's a pity. I was hoping we might get to know each other a little better, that is if you don't mind," he said in his most charming manner. "Are you staying here at the Gilsey House?"

"Yes, but only temporarily."

He smiled his most engaging smile but despite his abundance

of charm he felt she was suddenly in a hurry to get away. "Splendid. Perhaps we could find an opportunity to chat before you leave."

"Yes, perhaps, but just now I find I'm a bit late for an appointment. If you'll excuse me," she said, turning to leave.

"Of course, Miss…, Miss…?"

"Dr…umm…Drury."

"Then, Miss Drury, I shall look for you tomorrow," he said, giving a shallow bow.

With a hurried curtsy, she said, "Mr. Andrews," and glided out of the dining room.

Once he was sure she was gone, Inspector Andrews pulled his wallet from his breast pocket and removed the slightly blurry picture he carried there and studied it thoroughly. The face in the picture was very much like the face of the beautiful woman to whom he'd just spoken. There were differences, of course. The woman to whom he'd just exchanged pleasantries seemed older, more worldly, than either the woman in the photograph or the one lying in Witherspoon's Mortuary. Perhaps Abigail Drake had a sister or cousin. As he looked again at the photograph, a chill ran through his body. He had an uneasy feeling, as if he'd just met and was looking at the photograph of a ghost.

He knew, of course, that was ridiculous. Abigail Drake was dead. He'd seen her lying in Witherspoon's mortuary, cold as a stone. Her body was missing, to be sure, but there really could be no mistake that she was dead.

The longer he looked at the somewhat faded photograph, the more convinced he became that the young woman he'd just met had to be somehow connected to this case. What that connection was, wasn't clear to him, but he felt in his gut that there was one. The uncanny resemblance of Miss Drury to Miss Drake gave Andrews something to ponder and he thought perhaps there might be some investigations he could engage in before Mr. Holmes arrived.

Satisfied at last, he tucked the photo back into his wallet and resumed his meal. After settling the bill, which he thought quite dear, he exited the dining room and went directly to the front desk. There by the bell was a pad of paper and a pen with which he inked a short note to Miss Drury telling her he had two tickets, a lie he would need to rectify, to a play for the following Saturday night and if she would be so kind as to accompany a subject of the Queen, he would be quite delighted. He signed it, Walter Andrews, Room 419.

"Bellman," he said addressing the desk clerk, "I wonder if you would be so kind as to place this message in Miss Drury's box and give it to her next time she passes through the lobby?"

"I beg your pardon, sir," the clerk said as he perused the register, "did you say Miss Drury?"

"Yes, Drury."

"I'm sorry, sir, there ain't no one by the name of Drury staying at this hotel, man or woman."

"Are you certain, she's about 5'2", very beautiful, dark hair and striking green eyes…"

"Oh, you must mean Miss Drake," the clerk interrupted.

"Pardon? Did you say…Drake?"

"Yes, sir, that's right, sir, Miss Emily Drake."

On a whim, he wadded up the note he had already written and decided to leave quite a different note for Miss Drake. "I wonder if you might do me a favor," he said as he took another piece of desk stationery and began to write, "I want you to give this note to Miss Drake, personally."

"Very well, sir. She's just left, but I'll see to it to she gets it immediately upon her return."

"No, actually, I prefer you wait until I give you a signal."

"Signal, sir?"

"Yes, I want to gauge her reaction when she reads it."

"Very well, sir, I'll wait 'til you give the signal."

Chapter 8
Macabre murder in Manhattan...

Mid-December was cold and wet in lower Manhattan. Detective Strumm was just returning from a three day suspension for that little party he'd thrown at Commissioner Sheehey's residence and Detective Murray had been given the impossible task of ensuring Strumm didn't get into any more trouble. On his first day back on duty, they were assigned to investigate a murder in the docks area. Murray hoped it would prove to be a case that engaged Strumm's interest, and curb his drinking for a while.

Violence in the lower east side of Manhattan was anything but unusual and Detectives Strumm and Murray had seen their share of it, but they'd never seen anything like this. The victim's body was discovered naked, hanging by his heels from the otherwise empty clothesline in an alley just off Old Slip, one of many streets leading to the docks. An overturned garbage can spewed its contents, consisting chiefly of apple cores, egg shells and coffee grinds, beneath the suspended wretch. His throat bore two large wounds, but not a drop of blood was on the street below. Some of the local newspapers would report that a wolf was loose in the city, while other, more sensational tabloids would attribute the murder to Jack the Ripper, with the theory that London had become too on the alert, so Saucy Jack had come across the sea to strike at the heart of America's London.

At five feet, nine inches tall, dressed in a low derby hat and frocked coat, Detective Strumm did not look at all imposing. In fact, he had the appearance more of a cabman than a policeman. He attempted to hide his boyish face with a large mustache and at a distance he succeeded somewhat, but at close range he appeared all the younger for it. Also up close it was easier to see the bags under his eyes, the result of his hard-drinking lifestyle.

"What do you make of it, Murray?" Strumm asked as they walked around the suspended body, observing it from all angles.

"He's hanging there like a side of beef, he is. I'd say it was a big dog made them gashes, Mylo," he answered. "I would say it was a wolf, but we haven't had a wolf in lower Manhattan in over a decade."

"Maybe one's escaped from the zoo." Strumm posed the question as a statement, following Murray's line of thought.

"Nah...we'd a'heard somethin' by now," Murray answered, while he thumbed through a sheaf of dispatches and alerts he'd taken as they left the station.

"And how do you explain the oddball position of the body, hanging from the line there like Monday's washin'?"

"I've given that a great deal of thought, Mylo, and best I can figure, this poor fellow must have been trying to escape."

"Well that makes sense. 'Specially if somethin' or someone chasin' him could do that."

"Yeah. Here's how I see it," Murray said, rubbing his hands together as he always did when he had a fully realized theory about a case. "This poor fella was engaged in enjoyin' the attentions of some not so happily married woman when her husband comes home unexpected-like, if you catch my meanin'."

"That would explain the skimpy dress for this time of year."

"Yeah, I'd say he probly left in a hurry, maybe out a bedroom window. Then the husband, findin' his clothes strewn about the bedroom, sets his dog on this guy's trail using his own clothes to give him the scent...probably a big dog, a shepherd or a mastiff."

"I see, and the dog tracks the scent, finally catching up to him in this alley, if I follow your train of thought."

"Sure, he must have climbed up them trash cans there, grabbed hold of the laundry line, flung his feet up over so's the dog couldn't get at 'em. That's when he loses his grip. He was hanging there upside down and the dog tears his throat out." As he concluded his theory, Murray puffed out his chest in a gesture showing his pride in his deductive powers.

"You don't find anything missing in that story?" asked Strumm.

"Well, no, I...I don't think so. Seems to cover the facts of the case as we know 'em, Mylo," Murray said scratching his head. "Is there somethin' you see I don't?"

"It's not what I see, Murray, it's what I don't see that puzzles me," Strumm said as he walked around the body, still hanging from the clothesline.

"I don't follow, Mylo."

"Look at the alley underneath the victim, Murray," Strumm directed.

"I don't see nothing."

"Exactly my point. I would a'thought with wounds like this and hangin' upside down like he is, we'd be standing ankle deep in this poor bastard's gore."

"Well," Murray stammered out an explanation, "I suppose the

91

dog could've just lapped up all the blood, don't you think?" not wishing to give up his pet theory.

"Yeah, I suppose that might explain it. Still, for there to be not even a drip or a drab..." Strumm stood silently contemplating, "...very odd, queer even." Pacing around the hanging corpse, Detective Strumm theorized, "Maybe the victim wasn't murdered by a dog at all; maybe he was murdered by a man, or men. Killed somewhere else and then hung here, out to dry so to speak, as a warning of some kind." Looking at Murray he asked, "Has there been any trouble recently on the docks? Labor unions perhaps?"

"When aren't there troubles you may well ask," Murray said. "But there's been rumors of late about some organizing, I suppose that could be behind this," he reluctantly agreed.

"I think that scenario fits the case a bit better, but I can't completely discount your theory, Murray," he said in a manner calculated not to offend the subordinate officer. "To be truthful, I think both theories are a bit short of the mark and don't account for so complete an absence of blood...I find that very queer. It's the blood, I think, or more the total lack of it, that's the telling clue here. We'll know more after the Medical Examiner gets a look at those wounds."

#

It was while the late supper crowd was beginning to thin that she descended the stairs on her way out to visit Dr. Tremaine. The desk clerk met her as she crossed the lobby, "Miss Drake, your luggage has been sent on to the address you requested, and on behalf of the staff and management of the Gilsey Hotel, may I say it's been a pleasure to have served you during your stay with us."

"Thank you, Ernie, you've all been very kind. Is my cab outside?"

92

"Yes, Miss Drake," he said as he reached to open the door. Then he stopped saying, "Oh gosh, I almost forgot," as he fished into his jacket pocket. "This message was left in your box."

"A message?" she asked as she took the folded slip of paper from his fingers and opened it deliberately. Her pleasant smile faded as she read the note. She crumpled it, her eyes scanning the lobby.

"Is there anything wrong, Miss Drake?"

She smiled once more, but not pleasantly. "No, not at all...tell me, the gentleman who left this note, have you seen him this evening?"

"Uhm, no...no, Miss Drake, not this evening," he lied.

She looked at him with eyes he would later tell me seemed to penetrate his very soul. Ernie shuddered despite himself.

"Thanks again, Ernie," she said as she walked out the door. She climbed into the waiting cab and it drove away.

Andrews rushed past Ernie and into the street, depositing a silver dollar in Ernie's hand as he passed. "Thanks, Ernie." He jumped into a trap that had been waiting at the curb and hurried after Miss Drake.

Chapter 9

The Trap…

Andrews, in a light trap, followed at a discrete distance behind Miss Drake as she traversed the lower docks area of Manhattan. Her coach finally turned into a dark alley of an area so seamy he wondered what business she could have there. Perhaps she was meeting Barlucci. As he rounded the corner he could see little. The light from the quarter moon reached only sparingly into the alley but through the shadows he caught a glimpse of a woman's dress and stylish shoe disappearing into an open door. Just a glimpse, yet he was sure it was Miss Drake.

Perhaps the baron had somehow convinced Emily that Abigail was either not dead, or that she could somehow be brought back to life. With Emily Drake now in possession of a private residence it appeared the time may have come for her to reunite with her accomplice and claim her prize.

He resolved to bring in the local authorities in the morning as well as telegraph his still immature theory to Inspector Abberline. His heart beat faster, the hunter closing in on his prey. He stopped the carriage and walked the remaining fifty yards to the door, watching for any movement. Hesitating at the door, he strained his ears to catch the sound of the slightest movement within. Hearing nothing, he opened the door only wide enough to allow his entry, and then quickly and quietly closed it behind him.

If it had been dark in the alley it was pitch inside the warehouse. The air was still and quiet. He stood motionless, waiting in futility for his eyes to adjust to the blackness. He was aware of the sound of his wool suit rubbing against itself as he breathed. With conscious effort he slowed his breathing, trying to make no sound at all, while his ears were tuned to hear even the smallest sound. A full minute passed, and then another before he could make out even the faintest edge of a shadow. He inched forward. Suddenly to his left, at a distance he judged to be in excess of twenty feet, he heard a scuffing sound. Slowly, he moved in the direction of the sound, a thin film of sweat forming on his brow despite the cold. Again he heard the sound as of something being dragged over a wooden floor. This time he judged the sound to be closer, but behind what were probably crates stacked in front of him. He reached out his hand and touched the rough side of a large wooden crate. His fingers followed the edge while with the stealth of a cat cornering a mouse he made his way around the crate to the other side. The sound, this time just inches from him, caused his head to snap up and to the left. Atop the stack of crates he saw the faint silhouette of a woman.

"Miss Drake?"

There was no answer, just the same sound once again. He realized it was the sound of the heel of her shoe scraping the side of the crate on which she sat, almost as if...she were luring him. He called again, in a firmer voice, no longer a question, "Miss Drake."

A low laugh came in response, feminine, but somehow beast-like. Inexplicably, he was filled with dread. Suddenly he wondered who was the cat and who the mouse.

"Miss Drake, I only wish to help you."

"Do you, Inspector Andrews? Do you really?" The low laugh came once again. There was no levity in it. "Why?" She drew out the word like the purr of a jungle cat.

"Yes, I do. I know about your sister. And I know what you've done. Please come with me to the police. I'm certain you never meant to hurt anyone. Come down so we can sort this out."

"A bit off your beat aren't you, Inspector? This is New York, not London. And what is it we should sort out?" Now the voice was directly behind him. He'd seen her shadow shift, but heard nothing. The darkness was intense.

"I know about the body."

"The body, Inspector? What body would that be?"

"Why, Abigail's body, of course. Your sister, Abigail Drake."

Her laughter echoed inside the near empty warehouse, seeming to come from all directions at once. When it subsided she asked, "Indeed, Inspector, and what do you presume to know about the body of Abigail Drake?"

"I know it was found in a longboat off the coast of Newfoundland; I know that the longboat came from the ship, *Animus Lacuna;* and I also know that your sister was on her way to New York when the ship she was on, which was owned by Baron Antonio Barlucci, was struck by an iceberg and sank."

"How do you know these things, Inspector?"

Andrews felt encouraged by the evident interest in her voice. "I know because I saw her lying in the mortuary in St. John's."

There was a lengthy pause before she said, "Did you meet the mortician, Inspector?"

The question startled him. "Yes, yes I did."

Her voice took on a harsh edge as she asked, "How did Mr. Witherspoon look the last time you saw him?"

The image of Amos Witherspoon's horrified face flashed before him. He didn't know how to answer her. His mind raced. Did she know the circumstances of the little man's death? If she did know, how, and why would she bring it up?

Matter-of-factly she tossed off, "He was a pathetic little pervert, you know."

Her dismissive tone, a tone not unlike scores of murderers he'd heard seeking to justify their heinous crimes, triggered the policeman in him. Almost instinctively he asked, "Is that why you killed him, Emily?" hoping to trap her in a denial.

What she said next and the way she said it froze him in his place, "Emily didn't kill him, Inspector. Abigail did."

Again her laughter echoed through the warehouse and Inspector Andrews knew beyond doubt that Miss Drake was mad. He was glad he'd taken the precaution of bringing along his Webley special. It was safely tucked in a holster fastened to his belt at the small of his back. "But Abigail is dead, Miss Drake, we both know that," he said.

"Do we, Inspector?"

"Of course."

"Yet when first we met you thought I might be she."

He remembered having that very thought, but how could she have known…

"Do you deny the thought crossed your mind, Inspector? What if I were to tell you that Abigail Drake still walks the earth?"

"I'd say you were delusional, Miss Drake." He was unnerved by the easy confidence her voice portrayed. There was no desperation, no fear in her.

"Oh, I'm not delusional, Inspector, though were I in your shoes I'd think much the same thing, I suppose."

In the darkness he felt the air move as she came around him noiselessly.

"Don't misunderstand me, Inspector. I'm not denying that Abigail died in that longboat, the cold slowly stealing her life from her, a bit at a time, slowly and with each breath. It's true. It happened just that way. But…"

He had to stop her mad rambling, "But, Miss Drake? There is no but. Abigail Drake is dead. And for reasons I've yet to fathom, you either stole her remains or, much more likely, you are involved with someone else who stole and deposited those remains here, in this warehouse."

"Is that so, Inspector? And for what purpose?" she asked, unfazed.

"Madness is its own purpose. You were obviously very close to your sister. I believe you were so driven by grief and an inability to accept your sister's death that you had her body stolen. But you should know your accomplice is a particularly ruthless man. Did he tell you he murdered four men on his way to New York? One just a boy, barely 18 years old?"

"Poor Tommy," she said with a wistful tone, "he begged for my kiss. What could I do, Inspector? I simply obliged him."

"What? What do you mean? What are you saying, Miss Drake?"

"Yes, Inspector, you are closer to the truth than you know, but alas, you cannot wrap your feeble mind around the real truth. That is my greatest advantage and your greatest failing, a failing that tonight will cost you your life."

Using the darkness to hide his movements, Inspector Andrews had slowly reached behind himself until the handle of his Webley was now solidly in the palm of his hand. Turning his body slightly away from where he judged Miss Drake was standing, he pulled the gun from its holster. "Not tonight, Miss Drake."

Her laughter was even louder this time as he struck a match to show her the game was up.

She glared at him, her emerald eyes glowing in the match light, "Do you foolishly believe I didn't see the bulge at the small of your back when you entered the warehouse, or smell the gun oil with which you recently cleaned it? And, if I'd been so unobservant as to miss those obvious bits of information, do you think I could have missed seeing you reach behind your back or hearing the sound of metal sliding over leather as you withdrew it? It's time you knew with whom you are dealing, Inspector Andrews." As she finished speaking, she blew out the match. Inspector Andrews pulled the trigger on his Webley before the glow from the match died. But when the muzzle flashed, Abigail was nowhere to be seen. He fumbled for another match in his waistcoat. As he was about to strike it, he felt a deathly cold kiss on his throat below his left ear. Before he could turn, Abigail grasped both his forearms from behind, preventing him from moving. She purred into his ear, "You should always trust your first instincts, Inspector. I am Abigail Drake. Too bad you won't live to tell anyone."

He fought in vain against her grip. He continued to fight when he felt her cold lips press against his neck. But as her teeth pierced his flesh and her saliva mixed with his blood, all thought of resistance left him and he understood why Tommy had begged for her kiss.

#

The study was well lit and Julia was knitting as Dr. Tremaine came into the room. He lighted a cigar as he prepared to read the evening edition of the *New York World* newspaper. He let out a great plume of smoke just as there was a knock on the door.

"Who on earth can that be at this hour?" Julia said.

"I'm sure I don't know, unless it's your father." He smiled at his bride, "He has a habit of showing up at the most inopportune moments."

"Don't be silly, dear, it's much too late for Father to be about. I'll see who it is," she rose and met Annie at the entryway. "That's okay, Annie, I'll get the door. Dr. Tremaine and I will have our coffee in the study."

"Yes, ma'am," said Annie. With a small curtsy, she turned and headed back to the kitchen.

When she opened the door the first thing Julia noticed were two beautiful green eyes looking at her. Behind those eyes was an equally beautiful woman. "May I help you?" Her tone was colder than she had intended. Over the young woman's shoulder Julia could see she had the cabman waiting for her.

"I would like to see Dr. Tremaine."

"Is he expecting you? He rarely sees patients in the evening."

"Who is it, darling?" Tremaine called from the next room.

"Just a moment, dear," she answered before turning back to the woman. "I'm sorry, what name shall I give my husband?"

"Drake, Emily Drake."

"She says her name is Emily Drake, dear," she said, turning back towards her husband's voice, steadfastly not allowing the very beautiful young woman past the threshold.

Dr. Tremaine approached, "Drake…Emily

100

Drake…hmmm…why is that name familiar?"

"Dr. Tremaine?" She peeked over Julia's shoulder. "Dr. Tremaine, I believe you knew my sister, Abigail. You met her in London, at a party in the Alexandra Hotel. She was with my uncle, Sir Charles Warren."

At the mention of Sir Charles, recognition flashed in the doctor's eyes, "Of course, I remember now. Your sister, you say? I would have sworn you were she. The resemblance is most remarkable."

"Yes, we're twins."

"Ah, I see…identical, no doubt…" Addressing his wife, he said, "Darling, Miss Drake is the niece of the Commissioner of Police for Scotland Yard. That's correct, is it not?"

"Yes, it is. My uncle would be pleased you remembered."

With the realization that the beautiful Miss Drake was not a threat to her 'territory', Julia's manner changed from protective wife to gracious hostess. "I'm so sorry, Miss Drake, please forgive my abruptness. I'm Julia Tremaine, Alan's wife, won't you come in." She opened the door ushering Emily inside, "It's just that my husband has been working so hard of late. We rarely have guests at this hour and, well I guess I'm a little over-protective. You will forgive me?"

"Of course, not at all. I'm very pleased to meet you and it's I who should apologize for calling at this hour. I hadn't intended to be so late, but I was unavoidably detained. I don't mean to intrude."

"Nonsense. My husband and I were just about to have some coffee. I insist you come in and join us. You can tell us what brings you out on such a dreary night." The three of them moved into the study. "If you'll excuse me, I'll let Annie know there'll be three for coffee. Please, make yourself comfortable." She showed Emily to a small settee while Dr. Tremaine sat in his overstuffed leather chair facing her.

Julia left the two of them alone. When she returned, she heard her husband say, "Very well, but I must tell my wife."

"Tell me what, dear?" Julia asked as she entered the parlor carrying a coffee service with three cups. She could see a startled look on her husband's face but Miss Drake appeared completely calm.

"Miss Drake, dear, has just..." he paused as he glanced toward Emily, "...informed me that her sister's been lost at sea."

"How dreadful!" Turning her attention from her husband, she continued, "I'm terribly sorry, Miss Drake, is there anything we can do?"

"Thank you for your sympathy. I was hoping your husband might be able to provide some information regarding my sister's life leading up to her voyage, how she spent her last few weeks."

"I'm not sure why you think my husband can help in that regard, but I'm sure Alan will be only too happy to assist you as much as he can, won't you, Alan?"

"Of course, but I'm afraid my wife is right. There isn't much I can tell you. I barely knew your sister. I believe I may have seen her in passing once or twice after the party where we met, but beyond that..."

"That's true, I know, but I thought perhaps you might be able to tell me a bit about how her fiancée spent his time before he departed London."

"Who was her fiancée, dear?" asked Julia.

"Why, it was Baron Antonio Barlucci."

Chapter 10

Perplexing circumstances…

When Holmes and I arrived at the Battery Park in New York City, we'd naturally expected to be met by Inspector Andrews, but he was nowhere to be found. From the dispatch office, we sent a telegram to Abberline at Scotland Yard to discover whether there'd been some unexpected developments in the case. We learned that Andrews had recently wired that he was taking a room at the Gilsey Hotel, but little else could be discovered. Holmes and I passed quickly through the office of the Collector of Customs for the state of New York and immediately hired a hansom cab to drive us directly to the Gilsey Hotel on Broadway.

"It's not like an inspector of Andrews' reputation to leave us without escort, Holmes."

"That's true. It leads me to believe he must be onto some new development after all and has not yet had time to report back to Scotland Yard."

"Well, that would be very good news, indeed. Perhaps he's all but solved the case. That being the circumstance, we might catch the next ship back to London and be done with America."

"Come, come, Watson, we've barely arrived. Don't tell me you've soured to the adventure already."

I looked out the window of the hansom at the rows of squalid buildings and the garbage in the streets. "Well, I must say that I'm certainly surprised at the grappling and squalor we're seeing in what is purported to be the 'London' of America and the 'land of opportunity'."

"I don't think you're being quite fair to our American cousins. After all, what we've seen thus far is certainly no worse than Whitechapel, and perhaps a bit better."

"No worse, you say? Well, perhaps, though I would certainly doubt it's better than even the worst of what Whitechapel has to offer."

"Be that as it may, there is no great nation that exists in which there are not a goodly number of its people trapped in poverty. The question is whether or not there are avenues of opportunity which, if taken, will allow the poor to better their circumstances. I believe that in America, even more so than in England, those avenues are plentiful and open for those who choose to take them."

We sat in silence for some time as the cab passed from the poverty stricken five points area in lower Manhattan into the more commercial area along Broadway. By the time we reached the Gilsey, my perception of New York was a bit more favorable. "There now, this certainly seems to be a well established building." The Gilsey was truly grand to look at. It was a large white structure built in the classic baroque style of the second empire. Standing seven stories high with the main entrance facing the corner of the street, a heavily bracketed cornice separated the seventh floor from the ones beneath. Above it was a mansard roof with a cast iron railing.

"There, Watson, I knew you'd come around. Now let's go and see what young Andrews is up to." Holmes was out of the cab and bounding up the steps to the hotel. I followed close behind.

The lobby was walled in marble with plaster pilasters giving a Romanesque feel and the floors were richly carpeted. The main desk stretched from one wall to the other with a hinged drawbridge at one end that allowed the desk clerk and bellmen to traverse from the lobby into the business office behind the desk.

Within seconds of Holmes tapping the bell, a clerk appeared. "Good evening, may I help you?"

"Yes, I've an acquaintance staying at your hotel. I wonder if you would ring his room?"

"Your friend's name?"

"Andrews, Walter Andrews."

The clerk scanned the registry. "Ah, yes, Mr. Andrews. He's in room 419. But I'm afraid it won't do any good to ring his room. His key is still in his box. As a matter of fact, he hasn't been back to his room for three days."

"Tell me, do you keep such close watch on all your guests?"

The clerk smiled a toothy, but amiable, grin, "Not on purpose, sir, but my cousin has the shift after mine and I worked a double yesterday. He told me Mr. Andrews went out and neither of us has seen him since. He's a most congenial guest and often passes the time with Ernie and me."

"I see. Well, my associate and I," Holmes said, indicating me, "will be staying a few days in your fair city and as we've no other plans, we may as well stay here as anywhere. Don't you agree, Watson?"

"What? Oh, well yes, that would be grand."

"Very good, sir, we have a few vacancies..." he said as he opened the ledger. "I could put you in room 309?"

"Would you be so kind as to place us in a room somewhat closer to Mr. Andrews? On the same floor, if that's possible."

"Certainly, sir. I can put you in the room right next door. Room 421."

"Splendid. Now, one more thing."

"Yes?"

"You mentioned your cousin, Ernie. What time does he come on duty?"

#

Murray picked up the pale of warm beer and slowly poured the contents down into Strumm's sleeping face. Sputtering, Strumm said, "What the..." as he rolled off his sofa and fell flat on his face against the green threadbare rug.

"Mylo," Murray said, his voice a mixture of concern and disgust. "What're ya doing? The Captain's been asking for you for two days now."

"Is that so?" Mylo didn't budge.

"Yeah, that's so. He wants to know where you are on the docks murder case."

"Eh? Docks murder?"

"Christ. Yeah, the docks murder. I been coverin' for you. Told the Captain you was running down some leads. Now, pick yourself up, man, I'll put on some coffee." Murray walked across the room Strumm called home and lighted a fire in the stove, measured out an extra strong portion of coffee and set the Manning pot on the stove top. When he turned back around, Strumm was sitting up on the floor, elbows resting on his knees drawn up close, his back against the sofa.

With his left palm he rubbed from his eyes to the back of his head and let out a long, tortured sigh before saying, "Now I

106

remember…the naked guy hangin' from the wash line. Ohh, my head."

"Yeah, that's right…crushed shoulder and not an ounce of blood in him," Murray said, ignoring Strumm's discomfort.

"What does the Captain expect me to discover about that?"

"Who did it for starters, I imagine," Murray said, rinsing the sludge out of two cups on Strumm's counter.

Strumm looked up at Murray, an incredulous look on his face, "Come on, Murray, we been over this." He yawned and then continued, "We get a murder on the docks every month or so. Some do-gooder tries to organize the steeves, then the shippers send out their muscle to wise 'em up. Now and then it gets out of hand and a body pops up as a warning. No big mystery."

"Yeah, well the *Globe* got wind of this one and they're kicking up a fuss, if you catch my meanin'."

"A fuss? Over a dock murder? I'd hardly think they'd notice—or care."

"Probly wouldn't normally, 'cept they're sayin' it looks like a lot like them Jack Ripper murders across the pond in England."

"What gas."

"Sure, you and me knows that, Captain too. But the commishes wants an arrest to shut down that talk. Ain't good for business, they don't want other papers to start pickin' up on it."

"Oh, sure, that's just what I need to do, arrest some boss for a two-bit dock murder."

"Nah, just the muscle, you don't need to go to the bosses."

"Well, then, we can take our pick, so long as we can make it stick. Most of the usual suspects got at least one murder under their belts."

"Gawd, Mylo, what's happened to you? There was a time you'd go without sleep 'til you locked up some petty thief. Now look at you…some poor bastard gets murdered, in a Gawd-awful savage way too, I might add, and you want to just pin it on some other poor sonofabitch."

Strumm stared up at Murray as if to say, '*You know what happened to me*'.

"I know, I know, you've had a rough patch—I got it. But you ain't doin' yourself no good this way. Besides, you've solved less heinous crimes than this since, and stayed sober to boot."

"Ah, well," Strumm smiled, "there've been a few that were just vexing enough to keep the ole' think-tank engaged." He tapped two fingers to his temple.

Murray poured two cups of steaming coffee and set them down on the small kitchen table. "Well then, maybe you'll have something to get up about. There's been another murder." He picked up a chair off the wooden floor and sat, his considerable frame testing the chair's strength. Strumm climbed up off the floor and joined him.

"At the docks?"

"In a warehouse near the docks. The warehousemen found the body this morning and Cap'n wants us to check it out pronto. Says it's a bit queer the way it's set up."

"And I suppose he wants it kept quiet too, eh?"

"'Spect he would, yeah," Murray said with a grunt. Then he brightened up and added, "Well, maybe we'll be lucky and this really is that Jack Ripper fellow," a smirk on his ruddy face.

"That'd be lovely, Murray," between sips of the steaming coffee. "But I don't think 'RIPPER' is his name."

#

Even with the warehouse doors open, there was a stench permeating the air. Murray munched on a Cortland apple as he walked around inspecting the exterior of the wooden crate. Strumm was high above with the loading dock foreman, Dolph Lonnigan, inspecting the interior of the crate stacked above.

"I found him just as he is, Detective. Not a thing's been moved," Lonnigan told Strumm. "I know how you gents are about things like that. My cousin Leo is a copper in Queens."

The two men were holding handkerchiefs over their noses, peering down into one of only a half dozen crates of various sizes in the nearly empty warehouse. This crate was stacked atop two other crates, which were beside the two on which they stood.

"Good work, Lonnigan. I expect the smell is what caused you to open this crate?" Strumm said to the foreman.

"Gawd-awful, ain't it? This warehouse has been empty for weeks, locked up tight. We wouldn't a'been opening her up today but the *Lodestar*'s a'comin' in from Bogatá. She's got a load of coffee, tea and spices, coca too, I believe, though that ain't my taste, you understand. Old man Morgan wouldn't a'heard of it in his day, but since Pierpont's taken over operations there's been a lot of changes, not all for the better if you was to ask my opinion."

"Tell me about this morning, will you?" Strumm said, ignoring most of the foreman's banter. They climbed down the ladder. Murray was speaking to some of the other workers but stopped to steady the ladder for his partner.

"Well, when we opened the doors this morning, the stench nearly did us in. Harry, there, lost his breakfast, he did," he said, pointing to a large dockworker with a nose that changed direction no less than three times as it ambled down his face. He stood in the open door of the warehouse. "You wouldn't think a Stevie that's been working the docks as long as Harry'd've lost his biscuits, but he surely did," laughed Lonnigan. "You should have seen him...Lordy."

Detective Strumm made notes and sketches of the position of the body, position of the crates, etc., as he continued to ignore the chatter of the foreman. "And you say no one else has been up here this morning?"

"No one, Detective."

Murray, knowing the morbid curiosity of inhabitants around the lower docks, regardless of their station, said "You ain't been allowing no peeps for the curious, have you, if you catch my meanin'?" Murray asked him,.

"Not a one, sir. You have my word."

"Then how do you explain this?" Strumm asked, waving in the air a bit of fine lace he'd removed from a splinter of wood on the crate top.

"How should I know? No one's been up here, I tell you. Maybe him that dumped the body in the crate left it."

"Perhaps," Strumm said lifting the lace to his nose beneath his handkerchief. Even through the stench in the air he detected the hint of a women's perfume on the lace. He tucked it into the pocket of his waistcoat and scribbled down some more notes. "All right," he said at last, "let's get the crate down and get the body out so I can examine it."

The foreman gave the order and a crew of men rigged the crate with ropes and a system of overhead belts and pulleys slowly moving the crate from its position on top of the two crates down to the floor of the warehouse. Once the lines were clear, and upon the order of Detective Strum, Murray pried loose one side of the crate and lowered it, drawbridge-like, allowing Strumm access to the body. It was obvious that moving the crate had disturbed what Strumm considered his 'crime scene', but it could not be helped.

As Strumm set to work examining the body in a swift and efficient manner, Murray continued to scour the area around the crates looking for anything that appeared out of place.

Although the gaping wound in the victim's neck appeared to be the obvious cause of death, Strumm minutely examined every inch of the victims body for signs of other trauma. After satisfying himself as to the cause of death, he checked the victim's pockets for anything that might tell him who he was. Carefully he turned out every pocket, laying out each item on the floor of the crate beside the victim: pocket watch, chain and fob; loose coin of both American and British mint; a pocket knife; and a small leather-bound notebook. The last item was a man's wallet with eleven dollars inside, along with a badge and the identification of the victim. "Murray," Strumm called. "Take a look at this."

Murray came over to where Strumm was kneeling on one knee. He took the identification card from Strumm. "Chooey...Inspector Walter Simpson Andrews, Metropolitan Police of London. Mylo, this stiff's from Scotland Yard."

"Yeah, Murray, what do you know about that? And his wounds are almost identical to that wash line steeve. This case is startin' to pique my interest."

"Glad to hear it," Murray said. "We'd better wrap this up and let the captain know about this inspector."

"You're right, I'm about done here anyway." Strumm inventoried the items, writing in his notebook, and placed each in turn inside a small cardboard box, except for the victim's notebook, which he tucked into the inside pocket of his jacket.

As he finished, he noted that one of the victim's hands was clenched tightly shut. He bent over to pry it open when one of the men who'd rigged the crates came running from across the warehouse, "Detective...Detective... A gun, I've found a gun." Strumm looked up and saw the man turning the gun over and over in his hands as he examined it."

"Where did you find that?" he asked in a harsh voice.

The worker's countenance changed from that of a proud father showing off his new baby boy to that of a child caught pinching penny candy. "Why, over yonder by them rags, there."

"Weren't you told not to disturb the crime scene?"

"But sir, I didn't touch the body. I just looked at it."

Strumm shot a glare at the foreman and continued, "This entire warehouse is a crime scene until I've cleared it, do you understand?" Realizing under the circumstances he might be coming down a bit too harshly, he added, "But good work finding this gun. It may or may not have anything to do with the crime or the victim, but good on you for finding what my men missed." Murray, kneeling beside the body, shot him a glance that seemed to say, 'we hadn't widened our search that far yet'.

The kindness changed the worker's disposition and he walked away happily after handing Strumm the weapon. Strumm turned back to where he'd left the body. Murray was walking toward him, examining something between his thumb and forefinger.

"Mylo, look at this."

"What do you have there?"

"It looks like a button, but it don't look like any of the other buttons on him."

112

"Oh? Where'd you get it?"

Murray handed the object to Strumm. "It was clutched in his hand."

Chapter 11
Andrews, and Emily Drake…

"Dear Lord, please show me the way," Emily said in whispered prayer sitting in the rearmost pew of the chapel at the Sacred Heart Convent.

She had always felt comfortable here, in this chapel, where she began her novitiate, which tonight seemed so very long ago. Prayer had always given her peace and she needed peace just now very much. It was here in this chapel, in fact, where she had made her decision to become a nun. And now she was here again, feeling not a little like she had let her Lord down by leaving the sisterhood, but it was a decision she had long prayed over and knew was the right one, despite the feeling.

"I needn't tell you, Lord, how very much I loved…love my sister. When she's needed me, I've always been there for her, as she has been there for me—and she needs me more now than ever she has."

Tears flowed down her cheeks. "Lord, I know certain things have occurred, that the man she loved…loves is suspected of having done horrid things but I cannot believe my sister would have anything to do with someone capable of those acts."

She felt somehow confused as her mind raced between her

sister, her sister's fiancée, and the doctor who was supposed to cure them both. "If he can help her, help them, I would do anything…will do anything in my power—anything in my power to bring my sister back to me, back to her family, back to her life."

Quietly, she blessed herself. Her mind made up and at peace, if peace was possible for her until she had her sister back, she rose and left the church.

#

On the second evening Holmes and I spent at the Gilsey, we took dinner in the hotel restaurant. The fare was moderately flavorful, but a bit overpriced for my purse. While we ate, Holmes discussed his disappointment in the dearth of information we'd thus far uncovered. We had, of course, Andrews journal, which we'd taken from his room, but it appeared to be woefully incomplete.

We'd waited all afternoon for the return of Inspector Andrews but to no avail. That evening we'd decided to take our meal in the hotel to wait for Mr. Abel Jenkins' cousin Ernie that we might question him as to the last time he saw Andrews. Had he been on duty the night before, we would certainly have been further along in our investigation. Unfortunately for us, Ernie had last night off. We had to content ourselves with picking the lock on Inspector Andrews' room and inventorying his personal effects.

As we were enjoying an after dinner cigar with our coffee, blowing great plumes of acrid smoke into the air, Ernie Jenkins came on duty. We were made aware of this when Mr. Abel Jenkins signaled his arrival by waving one hand in the air in a motion intended to compel us to leave our table and join them at the desk. When instead Holmes only waved back, pretending not to understand, both Mr. Jenkins made their way into the dining room to our corner table.

"Mr. Holmes, Dr. Watson, may I present my cousin, Ernie Jenkins." Mr. Ernie Jenkins bore a striking resemblance to his cousin, although the light in his eyes appeared to be a bit dimmer, but he had an even brighter smile and an affable disposition.

"Ah, yes, Mr. Jenkins, Dr. Watson and I are very pleased to make you acquaintance." He looked at the other Mr. Jenkins, "Abel, would you mind if we spoke privately with your cousin, Ernie? I believe your services may be needed at the register." Holmes motioned to front desk where a rather large man with a steamer trunk was looking about aimlessly.

"Yes, of course, excuse me." Turning to his cousin, he said, "Ernie, try not to be too long. I'd like to get home to Ophie before she starts squealing." With this admonition, Abel returned to the front desk.

"Please sit down, Mr. Jenkins," I said, pulling out a chair for our guest.

"Thank you," he said sitting down. "But please, call me Ernie."

"Of course, Ernie," Holmes said. "We understand you were the last person at the hotel to see a guest of yours, a Mr. Walter Andrews. Is that so?"

"Yes, sir, I was."

"What can you tell me about when you last saw him?"

"I don't quite know what you mean, sir?"

"Well, for instance, did he say anything to you at all about where he might be going or whom he might be seeing."

"No, sir, he didn't. After I gave her the note he just left."

"After you gave her a note?"

"Why, yes, sir."

"To whom did you give a note, Ernie, and it's very important that you remember the circumstances distinctly. Was the note from Mr. Andrews?"

"Yes, sir, I remember it perfekkly. Mr. Andrews gave me the signal and I gave Miss Drake the note."

"Holmes," said I.

"Yes, Watson. Drake is not such an unusual name. Still..." He had that look he so often gets when some bit of information has piqued his curiosity. "What was Miss Drake's Christian name?"

"Emily, sir, Emily Drake."

"Emily, well, that's a relief, eh Watson?" he said as he gave me a smile.

"I never said, I mean, I never thought..."

"Now, Ernie, do you know where Mr. Andrews went when he left? Did he leave with Miss Drake?"

"Well, I don't know where it is he went, sir, but I do know he didn't leave *with* Miss Drake."

"Do you think he followed her?"

"Yes, sir, I'm sure of it."

"What makes you so certain?"

"Well, sir, I'm sure of it because that's what he told me."

"Are you saying he told you he followed her?"

"Well, not exactly. He told me to give her the note, so he could follow her. He told me he was an inspector from Scotland Yard and that he was investigating a case and thought Miss Drake might have some information that would help him. He had me wait to give it to her until he gave me a signal."

"Do you know what was in the note?"

"Yes, sir." He suddenly appeared uncomfortable as Holmes

117

pelted him with questions.

"That's quite all right, Ernie, you can tell us. It's only natural that you read the note before giving it to Miss Drake."

"Oh, no, sir," he said with sudden force. "I'd never've read it at all, but Miss Drake had balled it up and tossed it toward the planter as she left, and, well, we can't have bits of waste paper in the lobby planters, sir. It ain't Gilsey manners. Besides, I didn't suppose Mr. Andrews might like someone else finding it. So, after he scooted out the door to follow Miss Drake, I went over to tidy up the planter, and, well, the note was crumpled but..."

"But you smoothed it out and read it. That's all right, Ernie. I suppose it doesn't recommend your discretion, but in this case, it could be quite important for you to tell us what it said. Can you remember precisely what was written in the note?"

"Not exactly, sir, no, but it was kinda' queer. I remember that." Ernie then reached into his jacket pocket and pulled out his wallet. "You can read it for yourself."

"Why, Mr. Jenkins, you never cease to amaze..." He took the note from Ernie and read it aloud, "'I know about you, Miss Drake, and about your friend.' Short and direct. And did Miss Drake have any particular reaction when she read it?"

"I'd say it worried her plenty, sir. She looked about the lobby and then dashed out the door. Mr. Andrews was quick to follow."

"I don't suppose Miss Drake is still at this hotel?"

"No, sir, she was leaving that same night. Checked out."

"Of course." Holmes paused as he dashed out the stub of his cigar. "One more thing, Ernie, do you know where Miss Drake went when she left the hotel?"

"Yes, sir. She had us send her bags to an address in upper

118

Manhattan. We have a record of it, I'm sure. We never throw records or guest correspondence away."

Holmes smiled, "Yes, so we discovered."

Ernie blanched and a bit of color rose above his collar. "It's not like that at all, Mr. Holmes. Inspector Andrews was very nice. He would spend time while I was on duty talking to me. As you can imagine, a bellman doesn't get to know many of the guests in a hotel. Most folks treat us like furniture. But he was different. I liked him." Then he asked, "You don't think anything's happened to him, do you?"

"That's what we intend to find out, Ernie, and you've been a great help to us. I hope we can count on you to keep this between us, for now. We may have cause to ask you further questions as the case develops."

"Of course, sir, if it'll help."

"Splendid. Now, you'd better relieve your cousin. I think his wife is waiting for him."

"His wife, sir?"

"Yes, Ophie."

Ernie laughed. "Ophie's not his wife, sir, she's his pig."

Chapter 12

Mauldin Manor...

"Pardon me," Emily said meekly to the woman sitting behind the typewriter in the outer office. "May I speak to Mr. Thaddeus Martin? My name is Emily Drake."

The offices of Drexel, Morgan & Company were richly appointed and located on the second floor at 27 Exchange Place, a six story gray building in lower Manhattan with four large columns spanning the first two floors in the front. "Of course, Miss Drake," answered the receptionist. Mr. Martin is expecting you. First door on your left."

Emily walked tentatively to the door of Thaddeus Martin's office and turned the knob. As she opened the door, she poked her head in, "Mr. Martin?"

"Yes?" came the distracted reply.

"I'm...your secretary said I should come in. I'm Emily Drake? I'm here to sign the papers for the house you secured in my name...?"

Looking up from a stack of papers on his desk, Mr. Martin gave her a smile of recognition, easing her discomfort somewhat, and said, "Ah, Miss Drake, of course, how good it is to see you again. I trust you are satisfactorily settled in your new home." Rising, he came out from behind his desk, meeting her just inside the door. "The papers are ready for your signature. Once you sign, Mauldin Manor—the house, the grounds, and all the furnishings—are all yours." He led her over to his desk and handed her a fountain pen. "Take your time. I'm sure you'll find everything in order."

The agreement was very simple and Emily glanced over it, only vaguely aware of the terms.

Taking the pen in her trembling fingers, she said, "Thank you so much for arranging this, Mr. Martin, and for getting the former owner to agree to my moving in before the final papers were complete." With an unsure hand she signed on the bottom of the three papers laid out before her.

"Please, think nothing of it, Miss Drake, it's what we do here," he said, a smile breaking out across his face. "Besides, the previous owners are in South America. They've left our offices in complete control of their transactions." Martin removed his glasses and after breathing on them to fog the lenses, he took a handkerchief from his jacket pocket and rubbed them as he said, "I'm glad to see your skin hasn't suffered from the day's bright sunlight."

"My skin?"

"Yes…your allergy," he said, looking with interest at her face. "You mentioned it on our first meeting."

"Oh, yes," Emily said, regaining her composure. "Thank you. I've been using a cream application on my skin. It's worked wonders. I nearly forgot I'd mentioned it."

"Excellent. I'm very glad to hear it." The smile faded from his face as he continued, "Now that the business is concluded, I'm afraid I have some additional news, news in which no doubt you'll be interested. But I fear it might also distress you somewhat."

"Oh? And what would that be, Mr. Martin?"

"Its…it's about the ship…the *Animus Lacuna*. It's been found."

"Found? What do you mean, 'found'? I thought…I was led to believe it had been sunk."

"Badly damaged, to be sure, but apparently not sunk. A sealing ship arrived in Boston four days ago with a strange tale of finding what remains of the *Animus Lacuna*."

"Then please, you must tell me. What strange tale did they tell?"

"I'm sorry, Miss Drake, but the tale they told is too fantastic. I should not have said anything at all. Sea-faring men are a superstitious lot and prone to exaggeration, I'm afraid, if not out and out fabrication. I wouldn't pay them any mind."

"You must tell me of any news, Mr. Martin, regardless how fantastic. My sister and her fiancée were passengers on that ship. My sister died when she abandoned it after it struck an iceberg in a horrendous storm…"

A quizzical look crossed his brow. "I thought there were no survivors, you speak as though you have some special knowledge…?" Mr. Martin's left eyebrow rose toward his scalp as he looked at her.

Emily's face flushed, "What I mean is…that is what the authorities have surmised. Beside, my sister and I were very close. Sometimes when twins are as close as we, they feel each other's experiences almost as if they were their own. I had just such a feeling. It was as if she was speaking to me…from the grave."

"Oh, dear, of course. How foolish of me, I have heard that twins have a special bond but I had no idea such a thing was truly possible. I'm terribly sorry, Miss Drake. I mean, I assumed you and your sister were close, but…well, I had no idea. How painful this must be for you."

"Then you'll tell me all you know?"

"I'm afraid I know very little of the real facts, Miss Drake. I can only tell you the tale as it was related to me." As he spoke, he retreated to his side of the desk. "Please sit down," he said to her indicating the chair to the side of his desk. Emily sat. "From what I was told, the _Blue Walrus_ was sailing the northern sea lanes looking for harp seal colonies when she was caught in a ferocious storm."

"I'm sorry, did you say _harp_ seals?"

"Yes, they're hunted for their fur, which is of the finest quality but the manner of hunting is really quite abominable, if you ask me. Let me see, where was I?" He adjusted his glasses on his nose.

"You were saying the _Walrus_ was hunting seals."

"Ah, yes…they were in the northern sea lanes and for three days the ship was tossed about in a storm without reprieve. They thought sure they'd be dashed to pieces by the passing icebergs, but somehow they survived the storm with only minor damage. When they were able to take a navigational fix, they discovered they were far to the north of where they should have been. As they again sailed south, they came upon the wreck of a ship, the _Animus Lacuna_, beached along the shore and practically encased in snow and ice…" he paused, appearing uncertain that he should go on.

"Yes, what is it, Mr. Martin?"

"I'm terribly sorry, Miss Drake, but to go any further with this lurid tale would be to give credence to a story which, by any measure of common sense, is too fantastic to believe."

"Mr. Martin, please don't concern yourself. I'm quite capable of separating fact from fiction."

"Yes, Miss Drake, I'm sure you are, but in some cases what may pass for fancy may signal a far worse reality."

"Come now, Mr. Martin. I've engaged your firm because of your reputation of unswerving loyalty and dedicated service. Surely you can see I'm not one who's taken to flights of fancy."

"Yes, of course, Madame, I'm sorry. I didn't mean to imply…but please understand that I felt it my duty to warn you first."

"And you have done that, Mr. Martin. Now, please go on."

"Very well, Madame. The captain had the ship anchor out and sent five stout hands in to the frozen shore by longboat. As they approached, they saw the ship was caught up on the rocks with a wide gash running down her side nearly from stem to stern. Within the gaping hole they could see all was snow and ice. They could also see the *Animus Lacuna*—it's name was emblazoned upon her stern sheet, visible despite the ice—would never sail again. Looking toward the beach, they could make out through the falling snow what appeared to be a camp up on the shore at the base of a sheer cliff.

"I'm afraid I don't know all the details, Miss Drake, but the meat of it is that by the time the crew of the *Blue Walrus* arrived there was but one survivor from the *Lacuna* and it was apparent he was quite mad."

"A survivor? Do you know his name? Is he in Boston too?"

"Please try not to get yourself too excited, Miss Drake. He's not in Boston and I don't know his name. In fact, we'll probably never know just who he was."

"What do you mean?"

"As I said, the man was quite mad, perhaps driven so by the experience of the shipwreck or…"

"Or what, Mr. Martin?"

"Or what he'd come to, Miss Drake, but let me continue. As I said, there were five stout men in this party, the ship's bo'sun, a coxswain, two lackeys and the harpooner. Most of what follows is supposition based on what sparse information they could get from the harpooner, the lone member of the party to survive."

"Oh, dear, what happened to the others?"

"It can't be said for certain, but it's believed the bo'sun had trudged ahead with the harpooner remaining back by the longboat. The others were somewhere between. The madman pounced from hiding and dealt the bo'sun a lethal blow of a most grisly kind. The remainder of the party was frozen by shock, but the harpooner, being farthest from the scene, had the presence of mind to grab a pistol and fire at the madman."

"Did he kill him?"

"Whether or not he hit the madman with the shot is really quite inconsequential as the shot itself apparently triggered some sort of avalanche, burying the madman, the bo'sun, and the remainder of the party, save the harpooner, who was found babbling, saying the madman was some kind of vampire. The additional members of the crew of the *Walrus* tried digging them out, but to no avail."

Emily sat stunned. "Whatever could have happened that would have driven a man to attack his rescuers?"

"I suspect we'll never know for sure, but the lone survivor of that expedition, the harpooner, was so shaken by what he saw he was unable to speak coherently for several hours. When he did speak, he spoke of vampires and refused to say more." Thaddeus Martin leaned over his desk and with a hand motion invited Emily to join him in a most confidential moment. When she failed to accept, or to comprehend his meaning, he went ahead as if she had, "If you ask me, since we all know very well there are no such things as vampires," and he leaned forward even more, "that poor man was probably driven mad by having succumbed to…" his eyes widened as his lips formed the word, "…cannibalism."

#

Holmes had already departed by the time I arose. Returning while I was completing my toilet, he burst into our room, "Come along, Watson, I promised Sir Charles I would pay his respects to his half-brother's sister-in-law."

"His sister-in-law you say?" I asked as I was wiping the blade of my razor and returning it to its case.

"Yes, and aunt to Miss Abigail Drake, Mrs. Lucie Belmont, wife of the now deceased Cedric Belmont. Also, I might add, and more to the point, aunt of Emily Drake."

"Ah, I see, then it's more than a social call."

"Watson, you know my methods. How could you possibly think anything else."

We hired a brougham and driver for the day and drove along Broadway to Sixth Avenue following it north. I found the elevated railway to be quite fascinating, an engineering marvel, although it has the tendency to make the street level a bit dark even at midday, especially with thick clouds hiding the sun. But for all its wonder it stands in poor comparison to our own underground system. Further on we saw a second astounding engineering fete, the Croton aboveground reservoir. The water in the reservoir is contained within walls fifty feet high, which gives the air of a grand Egyptian palace, but much larger than even the grandest of the pharaohs halls. It is said the surface is four acres and the walls are twenty-five feet thick and made of granite from the top of which one could observe a grand view of the city.

After about twenty minutes, we turned onto 54th Street and pulled up to 136 East, the address of Lucie Belmont. It was a fine, second empire style home with a small portico and veranda beneath a second story balcony. The cornice was decorated with dentils and the siding was clapboard painted a pale yellow with brown trim around arched windows and door. There was a turret at one corner of the house and both it and the main roof were of the mansard type with matching parapets. I noticed right away the paint was beginning to show signs of age and neglect, indicating that in recent times other priorities precluded prompt maintenance.

Holmes twisted the buzzer and was rewarded almost immediately when the door was answered by the most delightfully cheerful hello from a woman who, though obviously well into her golden years, had the verve of a woman twenty years her junior. She was dressed in a gay green dress that seemed to set off her brightly tinted red hair and green-gray eyes. "Good day, Madame, my name is Sherlock Holmes and this is my associate, Dr. John Watson, and you, I believe, are Mrs. Lucie Belmont are you not?"

"Why, yes, I am, Mr. Sherlock, is it? Just what kind of a name is that anyway?"

"Holmes, Madame."

"Of course I'm home, young man. Where else would I be?"

Holmes gave me a quizzical look and I interjected, "Mrs. Belmont, Mr. Holmes and I came to pay respects for your brother-in-law, Sir Charles Warren."

"You did, did you? And why didn't Charlie pay his own respects, might I ask?"

"Beg pardon, Madame, but Sir Charles is in London," Holmes said with a bemused smile.

"Oh my, and he sent you all the way from London to pay his respects? I hope he pays you well for that. It must have taken you quite a while to get here."

I'd never seen Holmes quite so uncertain as to what to say next, but it was obvious to us both that either Mrs. Belmont was not in complete touch with reality or she was having a bit of fun at our expense. But Holmes, ever the straightforward pragmatist, pushed on, "I wish it were as simple as that, Madame, for you see we've come to New York to discover what has become of the remains of your niece, Abigail Drake."

"Abigail? The poor dear, she was ship wrecked, you know. At least, that's the report I got at first, but then they said they lost her body. Next, she'll be coming to dinner." She gazed off into the distance, growing suddenly quiet, as if she were remembering something. After a moment or two she looked directly at me and asked, "Would you like to come in for some tea? I've just brewed a fresh pot." I'm sure the look on my face must have convinced her we would answer in the affirmative.

"A nice hot cup of tea would be just the thing to take a bit of the chill off. Thank you, Madame, we'd love to," Holmes said even before I could formulate an answer myself.

As we walked through the door, Mrs. Belmont rang a small bell that was hanging beside the door. When she saw the look on my face she said, "Oh dear, pay no attention to me, it's just a habit I picked up, whenever anyone new enters my home, I ring this bell."

"Apparently a fairly new habit," Holmes said.

Looking a bit nervous, Mrs. Belmont said, "No, no…I've

been doing it for quite some years, I assure you."

Holmes only smiled politely as she showed us into a quaint little parlor in the front of the house with a large window that offered a view of the street. The atmosphere inside the home was thick with the odor of garlic. It was evident Mrs. Belmont was a bit of a cook. I, myself, had never acquired a taste for Italian precisely because I find the smell and taste of garlic most noisome.

Holmes and I made ourselves comfortable in two overstuffed chairs on either side of the fireplace, each with a small side table. Mrs. Belmont disappeared for a few minutes, but when she returned she was carrying a tray with a tea service and small cakes. She poured us each a generous cup of tea and handed it, along with a small platter of cakes, to us as we sat admiring the quaint décor of the room.

"Now, Mr. Sherlock, perhaps you can tell me what you meant by discovering what's become of my Abigail's remains."

"Well, Mrs. Belmont, we believe the man with whom she traveled may have something to do with the disappearance of her body."

"Oh dear, I was unaware she was traveling with anyone but her aunt. I thought it quite queer I'd heard nothing of her being involved in the shipwreck. My telegram to Charlie went unanswered, I'm afraid."

"No, Mrs. Warren took suddenly ill the month before they were to travel. Sir Charles had been very close to a young Italian financier, Baron Antonio Barlucci, and much to his later regret asked him to accompany his niece to New York. By the time he came around to understanding the full depravity of Barlucci, it was too late. It is Barlucci we believe who may be at the bottom of the theft."

"Oh dear me, what on earth would he want with her body, Mr.

Holmes?" she asked as she raised her tea cup to her lips.

I said, "We think the baron may be mentally unstable. He claims himself to be a vampire."

Her eyes opened widely at the word and her hand appeared to grow a bit unsteady as she sat her cup back in the saucer. "But surely that's ridiculous, isn't it Doctor? I mean, vampires are the stuff of fiction, aren't they?"

"Well, I certainly believe so, Mrs. Belmont," said I, "and so too does Mr. Holmes, I think."

"Positively. That is where the unstableness comes into play."

"What unstableness is that, dear?"

A bit exasperated, Holmes said, "Well, that doesn't really matter. I actually wanted to ask you about your niece, Emily."

"I thought you were here about Abigail. Emily isn't missing too, is she? Heavens."

"No, at least I don't believe she's missing. When was the last time you saw Emily, Mrs. Belmont."

"Why, just this morning. She arose early saying something about some errands."

"Did she say where she was going? We would like to have a word with her, ask her some questions."

"Well, I'm sure she doesn't know anything about this Barlucci fellow. My Emily is a good girl. She's nearly a nun, you know."

"No, Mrs. Belmont, we didn't know. Now, can you tell me where we might find her?"

"She mentioned something about Drexel and Morgan. I'm not sure who they may be but you might start with them."

#

Unbeknownst to Holmes and myself, while we were having that most delightful chat with Mrs. Belmont, Emily Drake was meeting with Dr. Alan Tremaine and converting her library into a first-rate laboratory.

"Ah, Miss Drake, these instruments are truly wonderful. They are even better than the equipment I had in London," Dr. Tremaine said as he removed two microscopes from a wooden crate filled with excelsior. "But please, I can take care of this on my own. I know even the muted light of an overcast day such as this is difficult for you."

"Think nothing of it, Doctor, the drapery helps and truly I'm not in any distress. I'm very happy you're pleased with the equipment. I told you I would spare no expense in your endeavors." Coughing while waving her hands in front of her face and blinking rapidly, she said, "I do wish you wouldn't smoke here though, Doctor. It's such a nasty habit."

"I'm terribly sorry, Miss Drake," he said as he crushed out his cigar. "I know it's an awful habit, I picked it up while I was in London."

She watched as Dr. Tremaine, clipboard in hand, walked from crate to crate. She marveled at how much he reminded her of a small boy opening his presents on Christmas morning. As she crossed the room, she saw a carriage coming down the long drive to the house. "Oh dear, who can that be?"

"What's that, Miss Drake?" he said without looking up from the dual centrifuge he pulled out of another small crate.

"There's a brougham with a driver coming down the drive."

"Perhaps it's another delivery?" he asked, looking up and smiling.

She was standing beside the window, moving the curtain just enough to allow her a clear look at the interlopers without alerting them that they were being observed. "No, I think not. The carriage appears to be one of the lighter types used for hire." Looking around quickly, she closed the door to the library. "Doctor, where is your carriage?"

"Why, it's at the back of the house, in the stable. I didn't wish for it to be seen from the street."

"Good. Stay in here and please be quiet. I'll go out and greet our guests."

"Who could they be?"

"I don't know," she said moving through the double doors, closing them behind her. Just before she disappeared behind the doors she said, "Lock this door behind me. I'll get rid of them as quickly as I can, but I don't wish to raise any suspicions."

#

After leaving the home of Lucie Belmont, Holmes and I continued up Sixth Avenue toward the address given us by Ernie Jenkins of where Miss Drake's luggage was delivered. Holmes had been unusually silent since we departed so after a minute or two I said, "Why didn't you tell Mrs. Belmont we have the address of the house Miss Drake purchased from Drexel and Morgan?"

"I was curious as to whether she was aware of the house and apparently she is not. Don't you find it a bit unusual that a young woman, a woman who's spent the past two years in a convent preparing to become a nun, has the wherewithal to purchase an estate such as Mauldin Manor."

"Perhaps she was left well off by her parents."

"I think not, Watson, else there would have been no need for Abigail to go to England to live with Sir Charles. No, the money for Mauldin Manor came from somewhere else, or someone. Undoubtedly, Miss Drake wished to conceal its existence from her aunt. Speaking of whom," he said with that half-smile he sometimes wore when he wished to test my perceptions, "Did you notice anything of particular import concerning Mrs. Belmont?"

I was quite used to Holmes asking me for my observations, discounting them one by one and then offering his own and I thought for a moment of keeping what I'd noted to myself. But old habits die hard and I was certain some of what I'd observed, while perhaps not germane to the case, would still be indisputable. "Well, the first thing I noticed, as I'm sure did you, was the aroma of garlic so thick in the house as to make it difficult to take a breath."

"Quite so, and what do you make of that?"

Clearing my throat, I said, "The most obvious reason would be that Mrs. Belmont is fond of Italian cooking. I don't care for it myself, but it is becoming all the rage in some circles, I hear."

"Posh."

"Posh?"

"Posh. There was cooking quite beneath that acrid aroma, a healthy proportion of corned beef and cabbage. I'm surprised you didn't salivate for that in spite of the garlic. No. Mrs. Belmont isn't a connoisseur of fine Italian cuisine. Of this we can be quite certain. Now, what else did you see in the room."

Thinking back to our encounter with Mrs. Belmont, visualizing the room in which we sat my mind seized on something. "She's a bit of an untidy housekeeper, I would say, but that might be blamed as much on her servant as herself."

133

"How so?"

"Well, I noticed on the window sill a small pile of nuts or shells. I wondered to myself at the time how long might they have been there."

"Excellent, Watson. I suspect they've been there since the summer, and they were not just ordinary nuts, they were acorns."

"Ha. Not even edible. More evidence of sloppy housekeeping."

"Not at all, old boy. Did you notice the mirror in the foyer? It was recently moved and fixed in its present place so as to reflect the entry door to anyone approaching it. And there was also an upturned horse shoe above the entryway door, as well as that business of ringing the bell upon our entry. Mrs. Belmont is a very superstitious woman."

"You base that on an upturned horseshoe? Preposterous."

"Indeed, it would be preposterous if that were the only clue. It's well known that a horseshoe, upturned will hold onto the luck it portends, but if you turn it such that the opening is down, the luck is said to run out. What is not so common these days, though it was in times past, is the use of acorns on a window sill as a precaution to keep lightning from entering and ringing a bell to ward off evil spirits. And then, there is the mirror and the garlic. I would venture to say that Miss Lucie Belmont is afraid."

"But I don't understand you, Holmes. Yes, perhaps she indulges in a bit of superstition. I myself have seen you toss a bit of spilt salt over your shoulder. What on earth does the mirror or the garlic have to do with this?"

"You are forgetting what Baron Barlucci told me while I was his…guest." As he said this, he straightened his coat. The coach lurched around the corner as we turned down 71st Street.

"And what was that? That he is, or was, a vampire?"

"Yes, common folklore has it that the vampire casts no reflection and that the smell of garlic is baneful to him."

"Are you saying…?"

"What I'm saying is that it appears Mrs. Belmont is afraid of something or, more likely, someone she believes to be a vampire. The only one I know who proclaims to be such a creature is the baron, Barlucci." Holmes looked up. "Ah, here we are, this must be the drive leading to Miss Drake's house."

At first it appeared that the house and grounds were deserted but as we approached, Holmes directed my attention to the soft glow of firelight inside the front window, "And look, there's someone watching us from that window."

"Where? I don't see anyone?"

"Of course you don't. They don't wish to be seen. Look there, the curtain, it moved again."

"That? Possibly a breeze or draft causing it to move of its own accord, don't you think? I must say you are ever on the alert for anything untoward."

"The secret to my longevity in this line of work."

"Yes, quite right," I admitted. Sometimes I contradict my friend strictly to annoy him. A grievous fault, I'm sure, but one that brings me a modest amount of amusement from time to time.

Once again we had the driver wait as we alighted from the carriage and rang the front bell. In less time than it took for Holmes and I to exchange looks at the disrepair of the house, the door was answered by a young woman that we would soon confirm was Miss Emily Drake.

This was my first glimpse of Miss Drake, as I, unlike Holmes, had never seen the picture of her twin, Abigail, and I must say that such a vision of sweet innocence I have not seen since the day I laid eyes upon my own dear, sweet Mary.

"Good afternoon, Miss Drake, allow me to introduce myself," Holmes said. "I am Sherlock Holmes and this is my associate, Dr. John Watson."

"Mr. Holmes, Dr. Watson," she said with a voice that was pure and lovely even though her eyes revealed she was somewhat shocked at our appearance. "To what do I owe the pleasure of your visit, sirs."

"Miss Drake, we are here to discuss the disappearance of the remains of your late sister. Do you mind if we come in."

Looking around in obvious embarrassment she said with a grace that became her, "Certainly, Mr. Holmes. Please come in, but I'm afraid you'll have to excuse how the place looks."

Holmes instinctively stepped toward the double doors that appeared to open onto the room in which the window was where Holmes had observed our being observed.

"This way, if you please, Mr. Holmes, I'm afraid the library is in need of repairs and isn't suitable for guests just yet."

I noticed Holmes nostrils flaring as she dissuaded us from entering that room, signaling his disappointment. But with a most gracious manner and smile she showed us into a dark parlor off to the right of the foyer.

"I've only just bought the house and I haven't had a chance yet to set things right in it. In fact, it's a bit of a mess." As she said this, she laughed a sweet delicate laugh that had the sound of music with it and crossed the room lighting one lamp after another to give the gloomy room some light. Before sitting on the worn divan, she stirred the fire and brought the drowsy embers to life with weak flame to which she added another log as the room was quite cold.

Holmes stood and looked about, "No need to apologize, Miss Drake, your house looks very clean, if you were to ask me."

"Well, yes, I've managed to give it a good scrub, but it's in such disrepair. Please, sit down. Make yourself as comfortable as my poor furnishings will allow. Now, how can I help you?"

"These things take time, my dear," I said, wishing to soften her obvious embarrassment as I took a comfortable looking chair near the fire. It looked a good deal more comfortable than it felt.

"Dr. Watson is quite right, and if you don't mind, I'd prefer to stand. I must say, that is a lovely dress you have on. Italian silk?"

"No…I believe the silk is from China. Thank you."

"You are very welcome," Holmes said with a smile. "Now, as to the reason we are here. As you know, the body of your sister has been stolen."

"Yes, I'm aware of that."

"We've been asked, by friends of your uncle…"

"Uncle Charlie?"

"Yes, Sir Charles Warren. Friends of Sir Charles have asked Dr. Watson and myself to look into the disappearance."

"I don't understand? Are you from the police?"

Holmes shot me an amused glance, "In a manner of speaking. I'm what you might call a consulting detective and Dr. Watson is my associate. Scotland Yard calls me in from time to time to…"

"Did you say Scotland Yard? But I thought they were in England and you said you were from the police. I assumed you meant here, in New York. I must say, I'm a bit confused."

"Yes, I'm sure it's all a bit confusing, my dear, but it should suffice to say that the official police call on Mr. Holmes' unique talents whenever they are faced with a challenge too difficult or too unusual for them to solve."

"In this case, since your sister was the ward of Sir Charles and he is a personal friend of the Home Secretary, Henry Matthews, I have been asked to assist in the official investigation of one of Scotland Yard's finest officers, Inspector Walter Andrews."

"And where is Inspector Andrews?" Miss Drake said, with all the guileless innocence of a child.

Holmes looked at me as he said, "We were hoping you might be able to tell us, Miss Drake."

"I? But how could I tell you…"

"He was last seen following you as you left the Gilsey House Hotel."

"But I've never…"

"You've never what, Miss Drake," Holmes said, a bit too sternly for my taste.

Miss Drake sat quietly, twisting a glove she held in her hand before answering, "I've never been the sort of girl who takes up with strangers, Mr. Holmes." She met Holmes' glare dead on, showing an inner strength that was masked by her gentle demeanor.

"Then are you saying you never met Inspector Andrews?"

She looked down at her lap as she said in a calm, even tone, "I may have met him in passing, Mr. Holmes. One meets a good many

138

people while staying at a hotel, no matter how briefly." She looked up, apprehension now showing in those beautiful blue eyes, "Did he...did he say we'd met?"

"As a matter of fact, he did. But as you say, it was only briefly and it appears you made a larger impression on him than he did on you, Miss Drake. Nevertheless, he was last seen leaving the hotel shortly after you. The clerk thought perhaps he was pursuing you on some pretense or another and that you might have seen him."

"No, Mr. Holmes, I'm sorry to say I have not. Then is he missing too? Like my sister?"

"I'm afraid he is. He hasn't been seen since and he's not returned to his hotel room."

"Oh dear."

"Tell me, Miss Drake, you haven't seen any other strangers about, have you? Strangers who might have shown an interest in either you or your sister?"

"Why, no, Mr. Holmes, I haven't."

"I see. Well, if you should, please contact me immediately. Dr. Watson and I are staying at the Gilsey House, Room 421," he said, handing Miss Drake a small card with the address written on the back.

"Of course, Mr. Holmes."

"Thank you, Miss Drake, you've been most helpful and are indeed as charming as your aunt described you."

This sudden bit of news, that we'd spoken to her aunt, appeared to disturb Miss Drake. "My aunt? Aunt Lucie?"

"Yes, delightful woman," I said.

Recovering somewhat from the shock, she said, "Yes, she's a dear sweet woman, though I suppose you noticed she's somewhat confused at times." A touch of crimson crept up her neck and into her cheeks.

"Nonsense," Holmes said. "We found her to be most delightful and informative." Turning to me, "Come along, Watson, we've taken up too much of Miss Drake's time as it is."

"Good-bye, Miss Drake," I said. "I hope we'll have the pleasure to meet again under less distressing circumstances."

She took my hand into her own, delicate and warm, "I hope so too, Doctor."

Holmes bowed slightly as he lighted his pipe. "Good day, Miss Drake. You won't forget to contact me should anyone show an interest in your business, will you?"

"Of course not, Mr. Holmes," she said, showing us to the door.

Once inside the brougham with the doors shut, I saw the smug look of contentment on Holmes face. "What did I miss?"

"Nothing, old boy, nothing at all," he said as he drew on his pipe and blew rings of smoke in the air. "So, tell me, how did you find Miss Drake."

"Charming woman, just as you said. Such delicate features and a delightful laugh, almost musical, I'd say. I must say I was surprised that you didn't ask her about the note Andrews had the clerk, Jenkins, give her before he disappeared. I would have thought that would have been of paramount importance."

"Indeed it may turn out to be, but to reveal my knowledge of its existence too soon would be to tip our hand, I think."

"You speak as if you still harbor the idea she could be involved, or worse, culpable in the disappearance of young Andrews.

How could such a delicate, demure young woman be involved in anything of the sort?"

"Did you notice the scent of cigar smoke coming from the library?"

"Not particularly, but what of it. She's probably had several craftsmen about the place with the view of making repairs. It doesn't appear unlikely some might smoke a cigar."

"I doubt they would smoke this particular brand—a Cuban blend, very distinctive in aroma, from the factory of Don José LaMadrid Piedra. They are quite dear, not exactly what a tradesman would smoke."

"I still say Miss Drake is too genteel to be involved with murder."

"You look too superficially, Watson. Miss Drake is charming, yes, but undoubtedly a liar, or if not a liar by nature, for she certainly wasn't very good at it, she lied to us on at least two occasions during our short conversation."

"Really? I wasn't aware of any signs of deceit."

Clapping me on the shoulder Holmes laughed as he said, "Of course you weren't, old boy, you were too busy enjoying the music."

Chapter 13

Unwelcome news…

She knew her sister's mind as well as her own. In fact, she'd always thought in some peculiar way the two were a part of each other, like two sides of a single coin. But rather than being opposites, they were just different aspects of the same substance, as if one were an extension of the other. So when Abigail arose to find Emily awaiting her, she knew instantly Emily had bad news on her mind.

"Something's wrong. Emily, what is it? Was there something amiss with the paperwork for the house?"

"No, not at all. Everything was in order and I signed all the papers. The house and grounds are yours, or mine I should say, though I certainly don't want them." She looked at Abigail, as though she wanted to say something but couldn't form the words.

"Good. And I see the instruments for Dr. Tremaine have begun to arrive. I trust he was pleased with their quality?"

"Yes, very pleased. He was a bit like a boy with new toys." Emily sat down near the fire. "Abigail, while Dr. Tremaine was here, and I was pretending to be you, we had visitors, a doctor by the name of Watson and a Mr. Sherlock Holmes."

"Holmes?" Abigail said sitting down abruptly beside Emily. "Are you sure it was Holmes?"

"Yes, do you know him?"

"I know of him. What did he want?"

"He said he was investigating…" Emily paused, as if embarrassed to go on.

"Oh? And what was he investigating?"

"He said he was investigating the theft of your remains as a favor to the Home Secretary." Emily looked down, obviously uncomfortable with the suggestion.

"Oh, I see. Of course, dear Uncle Charles, I suppose this has all been very difficult for him and Aunt Maggie. Did Mr. Holmes appear satisfied by your answers?"

"Not entirely, no."

"I'd have been surprised if he had been." Abigail looked at her sister with sympathy, "I know this is all very difficult for you, sister, I mean pretending to be me one minute, hiding the fact the next, seeing me like this, living shut away in this mausoleum of a house." She moved closer to Emily and put her arm around her shoulder. "But I know you understand the importance of my little subterfuge. Dr. Tremaine must be the only one who knows I'm not dead, at least not entirely." She smiled. "Also, as a consequence of my surviving the ordeal on the *Animus Lacuna,* of my becoming a vampire, I must shun as much as possible the light of day. How I must repulse you, sister… " she said, knowing how to draw sympathy. Deceiving her sister came surprisingly easy to Abigail. She justified it by telling herself she was sparing dear Emily the pain and guilt she would feel if she knew the whole truth of her dark secret. But in fact she was concerned if Emily knew, she might withhold her support.

"No, Abigail, don't. You could never repulse me, dear sister. I can only imagine how it must be for you."

"It's quite all right, Em, I know it's difficult for you too, to see me this way, to know the humiliation I feel living in darkness along with the other indignities of my condition. I know you feel it too, my dear, sweet Emily," skillfully playing on her sister's emotions, drawing her closer within her web, increasing her sister's sympathy toward her by feigning shame at her condition. As she spoke, a convenient tear trailed down her cheek just before she turned her head away to look down at the floor.

Emily turned and hugged her sister, "I'm so sorry."

There it was. Abigail knew she'd carried it off. Her sister would now not question any request made upon her. She kissed her sister on the cheek and pulled gently away as she stood and moved to the fireplace stirring the embers back to life. After several seconds when neither spoke, she looked at her sister and said in a cool voice, "Thank you, Em, you don't know how much I appreciate your support. But let's not talk about that anymore. I sense it wasn't Mr. Holmes visit that had you so upset. Tell me, what is it?" She could tell from Emily's expression that in the emotion of the moment she had forgotten about the bad news she carried and that had been written across her face when Abigail entered.

"Oh dear me, yes, but I'm afraid it's distressing news."

"Please, Emily, there's nothing you can't tell me. We're sisters."

"It's about the *Animus Lacuna*."

The words shocked Abigail to her core. All the cool confidence she felt only moments before was gone. Now she was reduced to the vulnerable little girl she'd just been imitating. Her knees suddenly weak, she sought the security of a chair, gripping the arms as she sat down hard. "The *Animus*? What about the *Animus*?"

she asked anxiously.

Emily related the essential parts of the story she'd been told by Thaddeus Martin. Abigail sat intently listening to every word in silence, all the while she could feel herself getting more and more enraged. When Emily reached the part of the story about how the ice and snow was dislodged by the harpooner's gunshot and buried all but the harpooner himself, she shrieked "No," and ran from the room. Emily sat stunned at the sudden emotional outburst.

She'd expected her sister to react strongly to the news, but she'd also expected her to reach out for the comfort they'd always given each other. In the first days after they lost their parents, the only consolation either of them found was in the warmth of each other's arms. But this reaction took Emily completely by surprise. Instead of leaning on her sister for support, Abigail chose instead to separate herself, preferring to grieve alone. Emily could hear the muffled screams and breaking glass as Abigail worked through her pain.

After what seemed like hours, Abigail come back into the room, her eyes red and swollen, but with a smile of resignation on her face. "Emily," she said, "I should like to speak with the harpooner from that ship, the *Blue Walrus*."

"Abigail, why?"

"If my Antonio is truly gone, I should like to hear it from the lips of the only witness. Will you journey to Boston and bring him here to me?"

"But Abigail…"

"Please, Emily, do this for me," she said as she took Emily's hand in her own.

Relenting, Emily said, "Of course, if that is what you want." She patted Abigail's hand. Suddenly she asked, "But what about Aunt

145

Lucie? I can't leave her this close to Christmas, not even for a day or two, it would break her heart. She is so looking forward to the holidays. Mightn't I wait until after?"

"Ah, Aunt Lucie. I almost forgot. We don't want her to be upset, now do we? I suppose this can wait until after Christmas. And Emily, I think it best for you to tell her as little as possible about this."

"Well, I suppose I can tell Aunt Lucie I am visiting a friend."

"Splendid. You are sure you're comfortable deceiving her like that?"

"It will not actually be a lie. The harpooner is a patient at the Carney Hospital where my good friend, Elizabeth, is a nurse. I just won't tell Aunt Lucie the underlying reason for the visit. I'm quite good in conscience with that, sister."

"Emily, Aunt Lucie doesn't know," she paused, "about me?"

Emily looked at her sister. "Poor Auntie is a bit confused since Uncle Cedric passed. And she was very distressed about your being found adrift. She put up a good front in public, but her heart was broken over you. It really wasn't fair to let her mourn so. So, yes, I've confided in her about you. I tried to explain it to her as best I could, but just how much she understands about your…situation, I cannot say."

"It's probably just as well. But I think the fewer people who know the truth of my condition, the better."

"Absolutely, sister, until you are cured of course."

"Yes," Abigail said quietly, "of course, until I'm cured."

146

Chapter 14

The fate of Inspector Andrews...

As we descended the stairs to breakfast the following morning, Abel Jenkins was standing behind the desk reading the morning paper, looking as though he were waiting for something or someone. Glancing up in our direction, he got an agitated look on his face, folded the paper in thirds and came around the desk headed in our direction, "Mr. Holmes...Mr. Holmes," he called as he closed the distance between us. "Mr. Holmes, it's awful...just awful."

"Tell me, Mr. Jenkins, what it is that's so awful." Holmes said.

"Why, it's murder, Mr. Holmes. That nice Mr. Andrews you been asking about."

"What?" said I, grabbing the paper from the clerk's hand. There, in a small article Jenkins had circled with the pencil he kept tucked away behind his right ear, was the description of what had befallen Inspector Walter Andrews. The article, buried on page fourteen of the newspaper between an advertisement for mustache wax and a story about an accident involving a cat, a bicycle and a cart full of fresh fish, noted that Walters had been found at the bottom of a stacked crate in a warehouse along the docks.

147

After I read the short account aloud, Holmes took the newspaper from my hands, examined it and asked, "I see this edition of the paper is a couple of days old. How is it you are just reading about it this morning?"

"I went lookin' for it after those detective fellows came around yesterday."

"What detectives? You say they came around yesterday?"

"Yessir, Mr. Holmes. Didn't Ernie tell you?"

"No," I replied. Ernie was preoccupied when we arrived back at the hotel last night. We didn't speak to him at all."

"Then you don't know. There was two detectives here from the First Precinct, name of Scrum and Scurray, or something like that. I'm not sure of their names, but they searched your friend's room."

"I thought as much. The items appeared to have been rearranged this morning."

"You been in his room too, Mr. Holmes."

"Of course," Holmes replied, lighting his pipe. "Thank you for alerting us about this new development, Mr. Jenkins. I shall put in a word to the management of the hotel about your diligence."

"Thank you, Mr. Holmes."

"Come along, Watson, I'm famished," he said and led the way into the hotel dining room. I checked my purse as we entered.

After we were seated comfortably, I asked my companion, "You didn't seem shocked or terribly upset about young Andrews. Wasn't the news of his murder surprising to you?"

"On the contrary, I'd have been surprised if we'd found that he was alive and well and had merely neglected to meet us. Although, I had hoped he was merely kidnapped and perhaps held as 'a guest' of the baron's. There is precedent for that sort of thing," he said with a wry smile. "Ah, here's the waiter."

We ate our meal in near absolute silence. I was of course used to Holmes quiet while he was working out some problem, but this was quite out of the ordinary. I've chronicled his contemplation habits many times and most often they are accompanied by copious amounts of acrid smoke from his pipe, during which time he eschewed any other form of sustenance. But he attacked his breakfast this morning with alacrity bordering on savagery. Generally speaking, Holmes could be grand company in the social setting of a good meal, but this morning that side of him was sorely lacking. While we ate I was stricken once again, as I had been during our crossing, with the feeling that my friend was dealing with some inner turmoil or conflict that, although he didn't wish to discuss and was trying his best to conceal, was causing him great distress.

#

Our visit to the First Precinct was extremely informative. We found Captain Amos Cortright to be a man of high intelligence and honor. He told us that Andrews had been found inside a crate in a docks warehouse and that the board of commissioners, the same ones Anderson had appealed to about Barlucci and Miss Drake, wanted the murder covered up as a possible attack by an escaped zoo animal. They were apparently concerned any similarities with this murder and the Ripper murders in London might cause a general panic and interrupt the flow of money from their vice halls.

Captain Cortright also informed us that Detective Mylo Strumm and his partner Detective Murray, had been investigating the Andrews murder when another, higher profile, case was discovered in

Central Park. Cortright had been obliged to loan out the two detectives to the Nineteenth Precinct to find the culprit responsible.

When Holmes produced a letter of introduction from Henry Matthews any reticence on the part of the captain to our viewing the murder site and conducting our investigation disappeared. In fact, he provided us with a letter of introduction of his own that we might give to Strumm to gain his cooperation. We thanked Captain Cortright and made the short trip to the scene of Inspector Andrews' murder.

The row of warehouses along the wharf all looked very much the same. There were three sets of double doors on Number 33 that opened onto the dock. The backside of the warehouse had a similar set of two double doors opening onto an alley, with a single entry door between. The docks were bustling when we arrived and the warehouse was half full. From the description we'd received from Captain Cortright, who it turned out was a most amiable sort, Andrews had been found in the empty southern-most end of the warehouse. We'd been given the name of the foreman, Lonnigan, and found him tucked in a corner out of the cold eating his lunch on some packing from one of the crates.

"Pardon me, sir, we are looking for Dolph Lonnigan, foreman for the Belham Stevedoring Company."

He looked at us suspiciously over his sandwich wrapped in brown paper, "Who are you and what do you want with Lonnigan?"

"My name is Sherlock Holmes and this is Dr. Watson. We're investigating the murder of an inspector from Scotland Yard. He was found in this warehouse."

When he heard this he chewed faster and struggled to his feet. Wiping his hands on his pants he said, "I'm Dolph Lonnigan, Mr., uh, Mr…"

"Holmes, Sherlock Holmes."

"How can I help you, Mr. Holmes?"

"We'd like you to show us exactly where the body was found and to recall as best you can everything that occurred when the police investigated."

"Well, surely I can do that. Let's step inside and I'll show you where we found the body." We moved into the warehouse proper. "The crate he was in is still in there, shoved over in a corner. The wharfies are a bit hinky about using it, they say it's a bit like re-using a coffin."

"I see. That will be excellent, Mr. Lonnigan. I'd very much like to take a look at the crate. Let's start there."

"It was a horrible sight, Mr. Holmes. I ain't never seen nothin' like it." He turned his head to the side as he described what he'd seen, "He was a-lyin at the bottom of the crate, face pale and bloated. But the damnedest thing was the blood."

"The blood?" I asked.

"Yeah, the blood."

"What was so unusual about the blood?" Holmes said.

"That's just it, there warn't none." As he said that I could see the look in Holmes eyes and knew my friend was somehow pleased.

Mr. Lonnigan showed us to the southern end of the warehouse and described with animated delight how they'd come to discover the body, having opened the warehouse and noticing a most disagreeable odor. He also described Detective Strumm and Detective Murray in such detail that we were quite certain we could pick them out should we meet them on the street.

By the time we'd concluded our tour it was late afternoon and we were certain we'd wrung every memory possible from Mr. Dolph

Lonnigan. Holmes shook Lonnigan's hand as we departed and asked one last question, "Has there been any form of security to prevent people viewing the scene and most especially the crate?"

"Nah, Mr. Holmes, but n'airy a soul's been in that end of the warehouse since we found the feller. Wharfies and steeves are a superstitious lot. They don't mind eyeing over a dead man, but once the body's gone, they don't hold much with visitin' his coffin, especially when it's empty."

"Thank you. Come along, Watson, we've got work to do."

As we climbed back into our brougham, I said, "I say, why were you asking about others viewing the scene? Surely you're not thinking there could be still be evidence at the scene."

"It's probably nothing, but I did find this trapped in the splintered edge of the crate's lid." Between his thumb and forefinger he held out a single thread, looking at it against the light coming through the window of the coach.

"A thread? Dear me, what good do you think that might be. Could have come from one of the longshoremen or even one of the detectives for that matter."

"I think not, Watson, unless they are accustomed to wearing fine Chinese silk."

Chapter 15
Come together…

The mutilation murders in Central Park had caused quite a stir in upper Manhattan. Both victims were found with horrible lacerations to their throats. When it was discovered that one victim was a wealthy business man and the other a common street prostitute, the newspapers picked up the story, connecting it to the murder on the docks some weeks before, proclaiming 'Jack the Ripper' to be alive and well in New York. The headline in the *Evening World* read 'Saucy Jack Plunges Over Pond, Pounces on Park'; the *Sun* said, 'Ripper Moves Uptown'; and the *Tribune* declared, 'Whitechapel Ripper Rips Manhattan'.

Central Park was an idyllic place of natural splendor but it had long been known to have a dual personality. During the day it was a place where mothers strolled with their trams and toddlers, and older children played safely unsupervised, but at night, the park took on a completely different and somewhat sinister character. It became a meeting place and playground of another kind entirely—a playground of vice where drugs, gambling, and prostitution could be had for the taking.

Violence, though not unknown there, was usually restricted to disagreements occurring during the course of some illegal transaction, and was rarely fatal. As such it was even more rarely reported. But a double murder in which the victims were at the opposite end of the social spectrum as well as being mutilated in a ghastly fashion was irresistible fodder for the newspapers. This motivated the New York Metropolitan Police to want the case solved as quickly as possible, so they called on Detective Sergeant Strumm to investigate.

Captain Cortright was pressured by the Board of Commissioners to put current investigations on hold and loan Strumm and Murray to the Nineteenth, the same precinct where Strumm had once been a rising star. Even though it had been two years since he'd regularly worked this area, his uncanny nose for detective work and his tenacity when on a case were well known. His real talent was in connecting the dots, finding patterns and understanding their meanings. It came so natural to him that he was forever amazed that other people found it so difficult to see what was in front of their eyes, what was so obvious to him. It sometimes amused him and other times irritated him that his colleagues and superiors thought he had some sort of supernatural talent.

Had it not already been decided, Strumm would have requested Murray accompany him on this case. They'd worked together from the time Strumm was first assigned to the First Precinct and Strumm felt that although Murray lacked a certain finesse, he could be depended on in a tough situation. Besides, he genuinely liked Murray and felt that there was somehow a synergy in their working together that made him a better detective than when he worked alone.

"What's wrong, Strumm? You been actin' edgy ever since the Captain told you you was comin' up here to work the Park case."

"You know why, Murray. It always feels strange as hell comin' back to upper Manhattan," Strumm said as the landau pulled up to the front of Number 220, East 59th Street. Strumm looked up at the façade, "The precinct house hasn't changed much."

"What'd you expect? Nothin' changes much around here, you ought'a know that better'n most. Look there, there's Tommy Carlton comin' out…he's been here in the Nineteenth forever."

But Strumm couldn't hear what Murray was saying. The very air felt different to him whenever he came back here, always chaffing, always cloying, nearly choking him. He knew it was just the flood of emotions long suppressed rising to greet him. It was as if he could smell death and Danny Fitz in the very walls of the building.

Holmes and I were in the precinct house when Strumm and Murray arrived. Holmes had read about the murders at breakfast. There was a piece in the *Daily Mail* that morning in which the scene was detailed. A park ranger found the bodies in the back of a Clarence, or Growler, parked beside a structure locally known as Cop Cot, a favorite site of lovers as it has a nice view of The Pond. The assumption of the paper was that Mr. Francis Josephson, owner of the carriage, had let his driver go for the evening—a fact later verified according the *Mail* reporter—and drove himself through the area around 93rd Street, an area worked by the other victim of the crime, a young Jewish prostitute named Ruth Nussbaum. What caught my friend's attention was not only the description of the victims but also the appellation attributing the murders to 'England's Saucy Jack' who, the paper asserted, was now working the city of New York. Of particular interest was the description of the scene being devoid of blood.

As I said, we were in the station house ahead of the aforementioned detectives ostensibly to discover who was investigating this case that we might offer our assistance. They walked up the steps and through the double doors into the precinct house before the desk sergeant had answered our inquiry. Shouldering past us with barely a glance they asked the desk sergeant, "Where's the bodies?"

"What bodies?"

Murray held out his identification for the sergeant's inspection. "We're here on special assignment from the First Precinct to work the Park case."

"Oh, you must be Strumm."

"He's Strumm. I'm Murray."

"Ah, sorry…" he said as he read the identification. "The bodies are still down in the morgue," the desk sergeant said, pointing to the floor. "The stairs are—" he started to say, but Strumm cut him off.

"I know the way, thanks." Strumm didn't need directions, he'd been there many times before. He led the way, stepping around large stacks of newspapers. Just as they were about to enter the stair well Holmes called out, "Just a minute, Detective."

Murray, who'd been lagging behind, turned around first. "Excuse me?" he said. Strumm stopped, holding open the door to the stairs.

Holmes closed the distance between himself and Murray. "I couldn't help overhearing. You are Detective Murray, are you not? And the gentleman holding the door would be Detective Strumm?"

"Tha's right," Murray said as he squared his body in front of Holmes. I quickly came up from behind. "Do we know you?"

"No, I'm sure you do not. My name is Sherlock Holmes. Dr. Watson and I have just come from the scene of a murder you are investigating. The victim was an inspector from Scotland Yard."

"Did you know the victim?" asked Detective Strumm, who by this time had allowed the door to swing shut and was standing beside us.

"Yes, and if you don't mind, I'd like to examine the body."

"I'm sorry, Mr. Holmes, that investigation is officially closed. Your friend was attacked by a large jungle cat, which was later caught and disposed of, neat as you please. I don't know how you do things in England, but here in New York we don't just let anyone examine the evidence of an investigation, active or not. I'm afraid we have jurisdictional procedures that must be followed." His manner was cordial, but I could tell he had no intention of allowing Holmes to examine the body of Inspector Andrews.

"I'm quite aware of your jurisdictional procedures, Detective." He pulled out the paper Captain Cortright had given him and with an obvious coldness said, "Perhaps this will change your mind."

Strumm read the note. "How well did you know Inspector Andrews?" he said, his manner shifting from matter-of-fact professionalism to conciliatory.

"Not well, only professionally."

"Then you know why he was in New York?"

"Yes. He was investigating the disappearance of the remains of Miss Abigail Drake, niece to former Metropolitan London Police Commissioner Sir Charles Warren. Now, I wonder if you would answer a few questions for me."

"If I can, yes," Strumm said. "Why don't we go down into the morgue, we can talk there, while you examine Inspector Andrews' body."

Strumm descended the stairs and entered the morgue as we

followed behind. Inside, sitting on a stool with his back to the door, was a man in a lab coat. From our vantage point, the figure at first appeared to have no head. After a second, a disheveled thatch of gray hair rose above the lab coat's small shoulders. Strumm seemed to recognize him immediately.

"Rudy," Strumm called to him. We watched as the ancient head slowly straightened, and then turned as he dismounted the stool and faced the door.

"Mylo?" the raspy-voiced response came. Clearing his throat several times, a still quiet but clearer voice said with a vague European accent, "Mylo, it is you. My God, how long has it been? How have you been?" he asked as he progressed across the room, his hand extended. Murray, Holmes and I were standing in the entryway just inside the door, not wishing to intrude on the obvious reunion.

Strumm closed the distance between them and took the doctor's hand, "Two, maybe three years, Rudy, and I'm fine, just fine."

Sniffing the air between them, Dr. Rudalac said, "Fine, *phyatt*! You are still drinking too much. I can smell it oozing from your pores, Mylo." There was a gentleness in his eyes that belied the affectation of disgust in his voice.

"Rudy, I didn't come here for a lecture on my drinking, not even from an old friend. Besides," he said ruefully as he noticed the open storeroom door behind which he could see a slightly unkempt cot, "I see you still have some old habits too."

"Eh, what's that you say?"

"Still sleeping here rather than going home, Rudy?"

"Ah, touché, Detective, touché, and after so long a time since I've seen you, I don't wish to lecture you, my boy," he said patting

Strumm on the shoulder. "But humor an old man, won't you? I worry about you, Mylo. You can't go on drinking like that."

"I'll try, Rudy, I promise," he said trying to sound sincere. The blank look on Rudy's face made it difficult to tell how well he succeeded.

"Who're your friends?" Dr. Rudalac asked, finally taking note of the rest of us.

Strumm looked around, "Gentlemen, this is Dr. Dragomir Rudalac, the best ME in Manhattan...hell, in all of New York. Rudy here's been medical examiner in the morgue at the Nineteenth Precinct as long as most here can remember."

"Detective Strumm is prone to hyperbole, but I have been here a good many years. And you are?" he said to Holmes.

"Holmes, Sherlock Holmes, Doctor. Rudalac, that's Bulgarian, is it not?"

"No, it is Romanian," the doctor said with an odd look on his face.

"Oh, forgive me, Doctor," Strumm said interrupting. "Mr. Holmes, and his associate, Dr. Watson, are here to look into the manner of the death of a friend of theirs, Inspector Walter Andrews."

"I see," Dr. Rudalac said, surveying Holmes and I closely. "Doctor, Mr. Holmes, it's a pleasure to meet you."

"And this is Michael Murray, my partner and confidante."

Murray came forward haltingly, "Good to meet you, Doctor."

"What is it, Detective, you look as though you'd seen a ghost," observed Dr. Rudalac.

"I...it's...I don't..."

"Murray doesn't like morgues, Rudy."

Dr. Rudalac laughed out loud, "A New York City police

detective who's squeamish around dead bodies?" He maintained an amused look on his face, as if he didn't quite believe what he was being told.

"It ain't the dead that bothers me," Murray said.

"What, then?"

"Well, it's just that..." He hesitated and then with an air of frustrated frankness said, "Look, I seen plenty'a dead bodies in the street, victims of crimes and all assorted accidents... That's natural, that's life, I got no problem with that. But a morgue...it's just that...well, a morgue makes my flesh crawl...it's a warehouse...a warehouse for the dead, if you catch my meanin'."

"Aha, I see, you are right, of course. But the alternative is what, Detective? The dead must be processed, especially in the case of murder."

"Aaaah...yeah, I know...it's just so...revoltin'."

"And that brings us to the reason we are here, Doctor," Holmes said. "Would you be so kind as to direct us to where young Andrews is being kept?"

"Of course, Mr. Holmes, please come this way. He is in the reefer." He led Holmes and I into the refrigerated vault through the heavy steel door in the far wall. Gleaming metal encased the refrigerated room. The morgue at the Nineteenth Precinct was one of the largest in the city and the only one with a working refrigeration unit, a 'reefer' as Dr. Rudalac called it. Officially it was known as the 'cool room'.

There were three bodies in the room. In addition to young Andrews, who was in a rather advanced state of decomposition compared to the other two owing to the amount of time he spent hidden in the warehouse crate, there was a man and a woman. Holmes removed his glass from his coat pocket and went to work examining in minute detail the body of poor young Andrews. This was a venue with which Holmes was very familiar and often at his best, examining without emotion every mark and trace of possible evidence a corpse had to offer.

After completing his examination of Andrews he moved first to the man and then the woman victim lying on tables nearby. After about thirty-five minutes during which time he had said not a word, he walked out of the refrigerated room and asked Detective Strumm, "I should also like to examine the clothing in which Andrews was found—as well as the item you found in Inspector Andrews' right hand?"

"I beg your pardon?" Strumm said. "What makes you think we found something in his hand?"

"Come now, Detective, surely you didn't think you could keep a thing like that secret."

Strumm reached inside his coat pocket, then stopped. "I'll show you if you tell me how you knew he was holding something."

"Quite simple. While I was examining Andrews' hands, I noticed in the palm of his right hand three small half-moon shaped bruises. I then noticed his fingernails extended beyond the tips of his fingers, with the exception of one finger. From there it was a small matter to compare the marks to the nails. The match was perfect. Ergo, Inspector Andrews must have been clutching something in his hand. May I see it?"

"Remarkable," Strumm said and held out his hand to Holmes. "It was a button." He let a small wooden button fall from his hand into Holmes awaiting palm.

Holmes held up the button under the lamp on the table, using his glass to examine it. Detective Murray cleared his throat as if he wished to say something, but a sharp look from Strumm caused him to fall silent. "You found this button clutched in Andrews' hand?"

"Actually, Murray is the one who found it, but yes, he was holding it tightly in his fist."

"It appears to be a decorative button...perhaps from a woman's dress," Holmes said.

"Yes, that's exactly what we thought. My intent is to take it to a seamstress shop, several in fact, if need be, to see if perhaps we might be able to find a dress with the same type of button, perhaps with one missing."

"An admirable line of inquiry, though I shouldn't bother. You'll likely find dozens of ladies' dresses with the exact match of buttons. This is a Duckwold-fine, a common celluloid button with a wire ferrule most likely made by a certain company in Massachusetts, Nashawannuck Manufacturing Co., although undoubtedly it could be any one of a half-dozen manufacturers here and in England."

"You seem to have a good deal of knowledge about buttons, Mr. Holmes," Dr. Rudalac said.

"I did a study on the various types during a case I investigated a few years ago for Lady Thackeray. I wrote a small monograph on the topic."

I found myself being quite amused and a little proud at watching the small group being equally amazed by my friend's demonstration of that unique talent of deduction and observation to which I've become accustomed. I myself am quite used to these seemingly incongruous demonstrations and it was refreshing to observe their reaction to it.

Holmes, apparently oblivious to their astonishment, said,

"Now, I wonder if I might have a look at the inspector's clothing?"

"There," Dr. Rudalac said, indicating a side table near the door. "You will find his personal effects in the small box beside them."

"Thank you," Holmes said. He spent a few minutes examining each piece of clothing and then turned his attention to the box. "I don't see the inspector's pocket notebook here."

"Don't tell me you found a square indentation on his arse-cheek, Mr. Holmes," Murray said, only half in jest I estimate.

"Not at all, Detective. Your Captain Cortright told me that the contents of that notebook told you Andrews was investigating the disappearance of Miss Abigail Drake's body."

"That's a relief," Murray said.

"May I have the notebook?" repeated Holmes.

Detective Strumm reluctantly reached once again inside his coat and pulled out a leather notebook with the initials 'WA' engraved in the lower corner. He handed it slowly over to Holmes.

"Thank you. One more question, please. The other two victims you have in the refrigerator, where, precisely were they found? I'd like to have a look around at the scene."

"Why is that?"

Holmes looked at him as if he were surprised by the question, "Isn't it obvious? They were murdered by the same hand."

Chapter 16

Strumm comes clean...

Once out of the station house and after a period of strained silence, Holmes said with a touch of petulance, "If Detective Strumm was unaware these cases were connected, then I'd say Captain Cortright has an overly generous estimation of his investigative prowess."

"Yes, even from where I stood it was obvious the wounds in all three victims had the all too-similar characteristics of those lateral tears cleanly through both the sterno mastoid and the sterno hyoid and into the internal jugulars. Too similar by half to wounds we've seen before."

"Yes, quite so. Too similar, too precise to be coincidental," he said, growing quiet and contemplative.

I said, in order to draw him out a bit, "It appears Strumm's predilection to alcohol pre-dates his removal to the First Precinct, if that Rudalac fellow is any evidence."

"Yes, it astounds me that he's apparently got both Cortright and Dr. Rudalac making excuses for his addiction."

I tried to ignore the irony of his statement as I mumbled some agreement and then fell silent as we continued into the park area.

It was a short carriage ride from the station house on East 59th

Street to the scene of the Parks murders in the southeastern corner of Central Park known as The Pond. It was a well travelled area during the day, which meant the snow was cleared from the path, but at night, it was obviously isolated. The coach in which the bodies were found had been near a locked gate that led into the main road leading to a large pond used chiefly by children ice skating or playing on their sleds. There was an excellent small hill that led down to the pond for sledders to get a good run. After the unfortunate accidental deaths of a number of children the Parks Department prohibited entry to this area after dark.

We'd barely arrived when Holmes bounded out of the carriage to survey the area. After less than fifteen minutes he returned to the carriage. "I'm afraid there's little to discover here, Watson. The hordes of children tromping through here have obscured any useful footprints and what they haven't, their horses have." Somewhat dejected he climbed back into the coach.

"Perhaps we'll have better luck tomorrow," said I in hopes of consoling him. I looked down at his shoes and observed, "You might wish to clean your shoes before we return to the hotel. I see you've stepped in some slush."

"What's that?"

"Your shoes, they've collected some wet clay; it must have been slushy out there."

"Oh, yes, I see. It must be a combination of the bright sun and the constant equestrian traffic." He scraped the mud off his boots with his Sheffield pocket knife and instructed the driver to take us back to the Gilsey Hotel.

#

It wasn't until doing research for this book that I discovered, through interviews with Detective Strumm and Dr. Rudalac, what transpired in the morgue once Holmes and I departed. I record it here as it bears directly on this tale.

"Mylo, I hope I didn't embarrass you. I never would have mentioned your drinking had I noticed you had company with you."

"No harm done, Rudy. Murray here is well familiar with my sins and we only just made the acquaintance of Mr. Holmes and Dr. Watson. I doubt we will see them again. I expect they will collect the inspector and toddle back to England. But tell me, Rudy, you acted almost as if you expected me. What gives?"

"I know why you are here. I recommended you to the new precinct captain, Captain Pruitt."

"You recommended me?"

"Of course...wasn't it you who discovered the body on the docks, hanging like so much dirty laundry?"

"Yes..." Strumm began, "well, I didn't discover it...I..."

Dr. Rudalac interrupted, "...and the one from the warehouse?"

"The Scotland Yard inspector, yes."

"Well, then, who else should investigate what appears to be a series of very similar murders?"

It was Murray's turn to laugh now, "Don't tell me you buy into that Holmes fella's dribble. Or worse yet, all that Ripper business, do you, Doc?"

"I didn't say that," began Dr. Rudalac, but he was interrupted by Strumm.

"What do you mean, similar? A dock hand being used as a warning and a Limey policeman who probably stumbled onto some smuggling ring, tea I'd expect. What would they have in common with a merchant monarch and his pavement princess?"

"Mylo, this is Rudy you're talking to, I examined all four bodies."

"Ah, but I've only seen the two," Strumm said with a smile.

"We've only seen two," Murray corrected him.

The old man's eyes popped open wide and he exhaled a wheezing laugh, "You'll have to forgive an old fool, Mylo. Of course you haven't seen the latest two. Why didn't you examine them with the English fellow?"

"I thought the quicker he was in and out, the better, to tell the truth," Strumm said.

Dr. Rudalac motioned with a thin hand, "Come, they're in the reefer." Dr. Rudalac watched as Detectives Strumm and Murray approached the body. Strumm's meticulousness contrasted with Murray's cursory perusal. Strumm examined first the body of the young prostitute and then that of her wealthy client. When he'd finished, he gave Rudy a sly grin. "Rudy, you know that Holmes fellow is right, don't you. You know they are all connected."

"Yes, and you've been in exile in lower Manhattan for too long. It's time you came back home."

"Thanks, Rudy," he said trying to choke back unexpected emotion.

Dr. Rudalac asked, "So, Detectives, what do you conclude?" He watched the younger detective, excited to once again see him in action. He had always admired the way young Mylo would talk his way through his thoughts. But it was Murray who spoke first.

"Well, Doc, if ya' ask me I'd say there's some obvious similarities. The position of the wound, the general lack of blood at the scene—I understand not a tea cup of blood was found in the carriage. But I'd have a hard time being convinced they had much in common beyond that."

"Oh? And why is that?" asked the old doctor with quiet politeness.

"Well, in the dock case there was an obvious attempt to place the victim in a humiliating circumstance, sure to be found. An obvious warning, if you catch my meaning. The inspector, on the other hand was hidden away. And these two here…well, they wasn't hidden and beyond the circumstance of their relationship, they weren't in a particularly humiliatin' circumstance, as they might well have been, if you understand my meanin'."

"I see," Dr. Rudalac said, rubbing his long nose with his forefinger. "What about you, Mylo? How do you see the similarities?"

Strumm patted Murray on the shoulder. "I'd be likely to agree with Murray, if it weren't for a couple of details," he said, disagreeing with his partner without wishing to insult him. "Normally, like Murray was getting' at, when you have a string of murders, there's certain things that get done the same way. Maybe the same kind of victim, or same kind of scene, like that. But in this case, other than the lack of blood, there doesn't seem to be much to tie 'em together."

"Are you saying you too think these cases are unrelated?"

"I would, but the missing blood is so queer, it's that, no blood at any of the three scenes, that's the biggest point in favor of a connection in my mind. And the two cases down on the docks had wounds nearly identical to these. One was a dock worker, the other as you know, was curiously enough that inspector from Scotland Yard."

"Yes, and why is it we haven't heard more about those murders, do you suppose? A short article in some of the more salacious papers, then nothing. Perhaps the dock worker would go unnoticed, but an inspector from Scotland Yard? I would think his murder would be big news."

"It certainly would, if it had been reported as a murder."

"What do you mean?"

"Rudy, you know how things are on the docks. If there's a murder that looks like it could be a warning, the bosses fall all over themselves trying to excuse it or downplay it. In this case, with these two, the wounds were so extensive that it wasn't too great a stretch to create a beast to commit the crimes. A beast like a wolf or large dog could conceivably have made the wounds in all three cases. So officially, that's the way they been feedin' it to the newspapers."

"Besides," added Murray, "the commissioners don't wanna give the newspapers any more fodder for the Ripper angle."

"Yes, but it's not conceivable that the same animal could drain the bodies so thoroughly and without leaving a bloody, gory mess. There was only a single drop of blood discovered in the carriage where these two were found."

"Exactly, Rudy. It don't make sense that an animal would deposit the body of its victim in a sealed crate either."

"The inspector?"

"Yep, and it's also very unlikely any criminal element would take the time to so completely collect the blood. What possible reason could they have?"

"But if not an animal and not the gangs, Mylo, who do you think could do such a thing?" It was evident Dr. Rudalac was sure Strumm had already formed an opinion.

"I wish I knew, Rudy," he said, scratching his head, "I wish I knew…a madman perhaps."

"But your face tells me there is more. What is it?"

Strumm considered a moment, and then said, "Take a look at this, Rudy," Digging into his pocket, he pulled out a button.

"The button? The Holmes fellow has dispensed with its utility in this case, don't you think?"

"Take another look Rudy." Strumm held the button up in the light, where it sparkled. "This isn't the button I showed Mr. Holmes. That button was found near the body of the first victim. We don't even know if it has a place in this investigation."

"Are you saying that this button was the one clutched in the inspector's hand, Mylo?"

"Yes, that's right and actually, I'm the one who found it," Murray said.

"That's right. Murray found this one here. The inspector was clutching it when we found him. I found the other in the alley, nearby where the first guy was hangin'."

"So, if you can find the owner of this button, you find the murderer, eh?"

"Maybe." Strumm said as he scratched his head. "Perhaps this one is from a woman's dress too. Finding two buttons at two different murder scenes is a bit coincidental, don't you think?"

"I'd say they wuz both off'n a woman's dress, maybe it's a woman who's the murderer," interjected Murray.

"There is no way a woman killed the inspector, or the dock worker for that matter, at least not alone. Not only were their wounds brutally inflicted, but the bodies were in positions a woman could hardly be expected to have put them. The dock worker was hung from a wash line a good nine feet off the ground and the inspector was placed in a crate that was stacked on another crate. It would have ta'been lifted at least twelve feet off the ground. A woman simply don't have the strength to do that by herself."

"Yeah, yer right. It was just a thought."

"And what of the blood, Mylo?" Rudalac reminded him.

"You mean the lack of blood. I haven't figured that out yet. It just makes no sense for someone to savagely murder someone and then carefully remove all the blood from the body. It must be the act of a madman, or a mad woman, or both. It's an impossible case."

"Mylo, It's not like you to give up so easily. You will solve this case. I'm sure of it. But you must keep an open mind."

Smiling an embarrassed smile, Strumm asked, "But what could explain such a set of circumstances? For what purpose could someone murder four people in such a horrible fashion, and then steal their blood? What possible use could it be?"

"But you have a theory, do you not? Tell me."

"What? You have a theory?" Murray's face was a mixture of surprise and pique.

Strumm gave Murray an embarrassed look, "I didn't say anything because it's crazy, Murray. If I told you, you'd think I was nuts."

"Mylo," Dr. Rudalac said, "I've known you a long time, too long to think you are anything but a gifted investigator. What is your theory?"

Smiling but still obviously embarrassed, Strumm said, "Well, if I didn't know any better, Rudy, I'd think these murders were the work of a vampire."

"A vampire?" He scanned the detective's face. "What...what made you think of such a creature?"

"Ah, well..." scoffed Murray, "...I see why you didn't say anything. A vampire? Are you serious?"

"I knew you'd think I was crazy, Murray, but Doctor, I'm surprised by your reaction. I expected you to laugh, or ridicule the idea, but..."

"Ridicule you? Laugh at you? No, Mylo, not I." Dr. Rudalac closed his eyes and took a deep breath. After removing his glasses, he lifted his hand to his face and squeezed the top of his nose between his eyes using his thumb and forefinger. Opening his eyes again, he asked, "Mylo, have I ever told you how I came to be in New York, in America?"

"No, I don't think so. I just figured you came for much the same reasons thousands of other immigrants come, to create a better life for yourself."

"Yes, yes, of course, but beyond that, if not for a peculiar set of circumstances I would probably never have left my home country, Hungary."

"What circumstances, Rudy?"

"When I was a very small boy, my father became involved with a wealthy financier, a member of the Italian aristocracy."

"I thought you never knew your father."

"It's true, I never knew him. But I knew enough of him to know he was an evil man. My mother left him shortly after I was born. If she'd had the wherewithal, she would have moved far away from him. Unfortunately, she was a very poor woman."

"Evil's a pretty strong word, Rudy."

"I don't use it lightly, Mylo. Let me explain. You see, my father was in league with the devil, or if not the devil, the closest thing we're likely to find on this earth." Mylo watched the disgust in the old man's face. "My father obtained young women for the financier I spoke of earlier."

"Still, Rudy, while what you are suggesting may be immoral, disgusting even, evil still seems a bit strong."

"These women were not procured for carnal pleasures, my boy. If it had been only that, he might be forgiven. After all, that was commonplace in that era in Central Europe." He laughed, "In every era. No, what became of those young women was much more sinister. They were procured to satisfy the blood-craving of just such a creature as you have mentioned."

"A vampire?"

"What?!" Murray said. "Bah…!"

"Yes, in my country it is pronounced, Vámpír. The undead who drink the blood of their victims and walk the earth by night."

"Then, you believe such creatures exist?"

"Believe it? I know it!"

"How can you be so sure?"

The old man smiled, his wrinkled hands slowly unbuttoned the collar of his shirt. He turned his head to the side, "Here," he said. "Here is the mark of that beast." Near the base of the left side of his throat were two small purplish scars, like blood blisters.

Murray peered over Strumm's shoulder, "Christ on a crutch…will you look at that."

"I was fortunate. My mother hid me away, I almost escaped being found at all. By the time I was found, the beast had ravaged my entire village and had become so engorged with blood, the blood of every man, woman and child in that village, including my own mother, that he left just enough blood in me to keep me alive."

"You must have been terrified."

"Yes, I was, at first. But once his teeth pierced my flesh the only thing I remember was wanting the feeling to continue."

173

Murray asked, "Wanting it…to continue? Why?"

"Yes, why?" asked Strumm.

"Because it was the most intense feeling of physical pleasure I'd ever felt. Nothing to this day has matched its intensity. Nothing. They told me I teetered on the edge of death for weeks after, delirious, asking the doctors and nurses to please let me die. Such was my need for that feeling that I didn't think I could survive without it, nor did I want to."

"But you were just a kid. What makes you think it wasn't just a kid's imagination?"

"And so I thought it must be until years later when I came into possession of my father's estate, such that it was. He was fearful of being found out, so he maintained his important papers and artifacts in the Bank of Budapest. When I became of age, I received them, according to his will. In his papers was a journal where he went into great detail about his dealings with this financier, this vampire."

Strumm looked at him stunned. "Are you saying this could actually be a real vampire we're after?"

Dr. Rudalac looked at Murray.

"Don't look at me…I think you're both crackers," Murray said. He walked back out of the reefer and into the morgue office.

Addressing Strumm's question, Dr. Rudalac answered, "And why not? The fact that in every case the blood has been drained from the body is certainly unusual. You've said yourself the murderer must have tremendous strength to position the bodies just so. A vampire has the strength of ten men. Only our lack of imagination prevents us from coming to the logical conclusion. There can be no other."

"Rudy, I'm…I don't know what to say. I never dreamed…"

"To paraphrase Shakespeare, 'There are more things in

174

heaven and earth, Detective, than are dreamt of in your philosophy'."

"Then you don't think I'm crazy."

"No, I don't, but I wouldn't advise that you advertise these theories."

"I won't, but at least I know there is someone I can talk to who won't think I've gone over the edge."

"Indeed, but more than that, I'm a bit of an authority on the vampire, possibly the only such authority."

"That sounds like a pretty questionable distinction, being an expert on a creature most sane people relegate to the world of make believe."

"You would be surprised to know that there are a good many wise and learned men who are aware of this unholy form of being. It is, however, best not to discuss it too freely. Tell me, Detective, how did you come to this, this line of thought?"

"I'd like to say I came to it on my own, but I'm afraid I'm far too conventional. This line of thought would never have occurred to me if I hadn't run across another detective who it looks like was arriving at the same conclusion."

"Well, if there are two of you working in parallel I'm sure you'll discover the creature's whereabouts, and with my knowledge about vampires, we can destroy it."

"That won't be possible, Rudy. That other detective is lying on the table behind us. He must have gotten too close to the truth."

"That's a pity."

"I found out about his train of thought in some papers he had on him."

"You must proceed cautiously, Mylo. The vampire is an exceedingly clever creature with nearly supernatural powers. I would not like for you to fall victim to him."

"That makes two of us, Rudy."

Chapter 17

Linking witness...

With Christmas Day fast approaching, in point of fact it was to arrive the very next day, Holmes and I decided a call upon Dr. Tremaine was long overdue. The two trips we'd taken to meet with him at the hospital where he works met with failure. We'd begun to wonder if he was truly employed at St. Vincent's.

Once again we hired a growler for the day and headed north to upper Manhattan, but this time to the home of Dr. Alan and Julia Tremaine. The skies were gray and overcast with the promise of Christmas snow and the temperature had dipped so as to be absolutely frigid. We had timed our arrival for the early evening and as luck would have it, arrived just as another coach approached the house.

Holmes and I dismounted our carriage and directed our footsteps towards the door. We noticed the livery man coming out from behind the house and deduced the other arrival was either Dr. Tremaine or an expected guest of the house. We were soon to discover it was the doctor. "May I help you gentlemen?" a voice inquired from behind us.

Holmes and I turned to see a gentleman who seemed much too young to be a doctor of such renown as we had discovered was Dr. Tremaine. Holmes spoke in a jovial manner, "A most merry Christmas to you, but certainly you cannot be the venerable Dr. Alan Tremaine of the African expedition fame."

A smile broke out on Tremaine's lips as he said in return, "Guilty as charged, gentlemen, but I'm afraid you have me at a disadvantage." While he spoke he approached with his hand extended. "To whom do I have the pleasure of finding at my doorstep this evening?"

This time I spoke as I accepted his hand, shaking it vigorously, "I am Dr. John Watson, and this is my friend and associate, Mr. Sherlock Holmes." At the mention of Holmes name the smile dimmed but did not disappear.

"Your accents tell me you are a long way from home during this season. How may I be of service to you gentlemen?"

"I've come to inquire about a mutual acquaintance of ours," Holmes said. "But as it's frightfully cold here on your stoop, would you mind if we came in to chat?"

"Dear me, certainly, and please excuse me for leaving you out here. My wife will scold me for that, I'm sure. Please, come in and warm yourselves by the fire." He opened the door and guided us into the parlor where a beautiful young woman with golden hair, fair complexion and eyes of the most enchanting blue, was working most assiduously on a needlework sampler of complex design. "Julia, we've company," he said as we entered the parlor. Then, he called down the hall, "Annie, please bring coffee for four to the parlor. We have guests."

His lovely wife, for by then I was sure this was his wife, put down her work and stood to greet us most warmly. "Good evening, gentlemen," she said extending her hand. "Are you doctors as well? My husband rarely treats us with guests from his place of

178

employment."

"I'm afraid we aren't colleagues of your husband, although John Watson, my associate here, is a medical man as well, aren't you, John," Holmes said as he and I moved closer to the fire warming our hands.

"Well, yes, I am, although not of such distinction as your husband."

"Don't be silly, Doctor," Tremaine said. "I'm sure in your specialty you are certainly my match."

"Kind of you to say so, sir," said I.

"Well, then, I'm sure you are both giants in your field, as well I'm sure is Mr. Holmes," Mrs. Tremaine said with a wonderful little laugh, chiding us gently. "But if you aren't colleagues of my husband, what has induced him to bring you here for this visit?" Coming closer to the fire, she said, "Please, let me take your coats, gentlemen." Holmes and I handed her our coats, hats and scarves as we warmed ourselves. By this time the housekeeper, Annie, had arrived with a tray on which there was an urn of coffee and service for four. We each took a cup and saucer.

Tremaine said, "Actually, I only just met them at our door just now."

"Not that we hadn't tried to make your acquaintance before, though," said I.

"Oh? When was that, sir," asked Tremaine.

"We've dropped by your office on two occasions only to find you indisposed, or absent," Holmes said. I noted a curious look on Mrs. Tremaine's face when she heard that.

"Ah, well, the hospital is a very large building and I'm often out of the office. I'm terribly sorry to have missed you there."

"I'm certainly not," said I, "otherwise we might not have met this beautiful wife of yours."

Her face colored somewhat as she said, "Sir, you flatter, but surely you haven't come to trifle with me," she said, to direct the conversation back toward her husband.

"They were coming to see us in connection with, what was it now, Mr. Holmes? A mutual acquaintance?"

"Yes, quite right," Holmes said. "I believe you are acquainted with a man known as Antonio Barlucci. Baron Antonio Barlucci?"

"Why yes," Tremaine said without a moment's hesitation, but throwing a quick and telling glance at his wife. "He was a patient of mine while I was in London."

"Oh?" Holmes said. "I was unaware you were practicing in London. I thought you were there on a lecture tour."

"That's correct, I was, but the baron approached me to aid him with a most rare condition. I could hardly refuse." Tremaine motioned, inviting Holmes and I to sit down on a sofa, while he sat in a chair beside that in which Mrs. Tremaine was seated when we came in.

"Thank you," we said as we accepted his invitation.

"Do you mind if I smoke, Doctor?" Holmes said while patting the pocket of his jacket. "Never mind, I seem to have mislaid my cigar case."

"Here, have one of mine if you fancy a cigar," he said producing a walnut humidor from under the table. "I think you'll find these quite pleasing."

"Why thank you, Doctor," Holmes said as he passed the cigar beneath his nose. "Don José LaMadrid Piedra."

"Why yes," said Tremaine. "I'm astonished you know it. I

only discovered them myself recently."

"I've made a study of cigars, cigarettes, tobacco and the ash they leave."

With a smile, I interjected, "He's written a monograph on the subject."

Ignoring me, Holmes said, "I make it my business to know the unusual as well as the commonplace. Now, Doctor, what was the nature of the illness for which you were treating the baron?"

"I'm sorry, Mr. Holmes, but that is privileged doctor-patient information. I can't tell you."

"Besides," Mrs. Tremaine said, "we've recently discovered the baron is deceased. What possible interest could his disease be to anyone?"

"Ah, yes, the reported sinking of the *Animus Lacuna*."

"What do you mean, reported, Mr. Holmes?" asked Julia.

"Simply that the ship was never found, only some debris, and a longboat with the body of a young woman."

"Do you mean Abigail Drake?" Mrs. Tremaine asked, a question that appeared to make her husband uncomfortable.

"You knew Miss Drake?"

"Oh no, but I've met her sister..." Mrs. Tremaine stopped in mid-sentence as her husband gave her a stern look.

"This is an interesting turn. When did you meet Miss Emily Drake?"

"Well, I...I..." she stammered.

Before she could finish, Dr. Tremaine said, "Miss Drake visited us a few nights ago. She'd heard of me through her sister and was hoping I might be able to tell her some details of her sister's life in London before she sailed to America, her last weeks on earth, so to speak. Unfortunately, I could give her precious few details, having only briefly met her while I was in London. I did recall her to be a charming young woman."

"Yes," Holmes said. "A pity she died in that longboat." I was astounded by Holmes next question. I thought certainly he would pursue the doctor's connection to Emily Drake. "But tell me, Doctor, surely the baron's demise releases you from your vow of silence concerning his disease. It could be of great import in the case I'm working on."

"Well, I suppose I can tell you. He had a blood disorder, one so rare that I couldn't resist coming to his aid."

"Vampirism?" said Holmes.

Mrs. Tremaine nearly dropped her cup into its saucer. Dr. Tremaine looked at her with admonishment, and then said, "That' correct. But if you are thinking of the old wives tales you've heard as a child, that's all rubbish."

"Then vampires don't feed on blood, Doctor?" Holmes said. I was astonished at the way this line of questioning was developing. I was perfectly aware that Holmes had no more belief in the vampire legends than I and couldn't for the life of me figure why he was acting as though he did.

"Well, yes, it's true the vampire can gain sustenance most easily from blood, which is why of course they gravitate toward meat that is exceedingly rare to most tastes."

"I see," Holmes said. "And you have not been contacted by Barlucci?"

"Do you mean since he's drowned, Mr. Holmes?" Tremaine said with what was to my ear a condescending tone.

"Yes, since he's drowned, or has been supposed to drown,"

182

Holmes said.

"Really, sir. This is ridiculous. I've told you what you came to find out. Of course I haven't heard from the dead man. I must say, sir, your questions are getting rather tiresome."

Holmes arose. "Perhaps you are right, Dr. Tremaine. But if you would be so kind," he said, reaching into his waistcoat pocket and withdrawing a card. "Please take this card." He handed it to Tremaine. "I've written on the back where we may be contacted in the event you hear from Baron Barlucci." As he said this he moved his gaze from the doctor to his wife, "Or should you hear from anyone who may be associated with the baron."

By this time I was also on my feet and had retrieved our coats, hats and scarves from the coat rack on which Mrs. Tremaine had deposited them. "Come, Watson. We've troubled these good people with dour conversation quite enough on what should be a most joyous time of the year." Donning our coats, we followed Dr. Tremaine to the entryway where we'd come in.

"Glad tidings to you and Mrs. Tremaine," I said. "And I hope we didn't disturb your peace too heavily."

"I mirror my friend's sentiments, Doctor. May you and Mrs. Tremaine receive the blessings of the season." Then, in low voice so as not to allow Mrs. Tremaine to hear, he said, "The baron is quite mad, you know. Anyone who puts his, or her, trust in a mad man must in turn be mad."

#

"Come, Watson," Holmes said as we reached our cab. "I think it's time we paid Miss Drake another visit." He gave the cabman the address and admonished him to quicken the pace, instructing him to cross the park to save time.

"I must say, Holmes, I was beginning to think you might be slipping, going off on that vampire tangent like that. I thought surely you would pursue the Emily Drake connection."

"I'm afraid that course would have borne no fruit. Didn't you notice the way Dr. Tremaine tensed when her name was mentioned? He would only have denied anything other than his meager story of her asking after her sisters' last days."

"I see, and so before we can question Miss Drake, you think he will try and warn her?"

"I think that's a distinct possibility."

In just a few minutes we were again at the decaying edifice that is Mauldin Place. In the dull light of the early afternoon the grounds had an eerie feel. Holmes rapped upon the door.

"Strange, there doesn't even appear to be a glow in the window," said I.

"Yes, the place is deserted. I thought as much as we came down the drive. There was no smoke coming from any of the chimneys. Miss Drake may be spending the holidays with her Aunt Lucie."

"Well, then, let's speak to her there."

"No, if Dr. Tremaine is in communication with Miss Drake, he undoubtedly would know she would be there and not here. Hence, while we were hurrying here, he would be traveling to Mrs. Belmont's to warn Emily of our inquiries.

"Pity. Well then, I guess there's nothing more we can do."

"Hallo, what's this?" he said, bending down by the door. "Watson, look." Holmes was examining a small cast iron replica of the Brooklyn Bridge.

"Eh what," said I, "mud on a mud-scraper. What of it?"

"Not just mud, Watson, sandy loam," he said and scraped some into a small brown envelope he'd produced from his pocket. "There, the trip wasn't wasted after all."

Chapter 18

Strumm takes in the laundry...

Not taking the vampire story seriously, Murray was making the rounds of the hospitals and medical colleges on Manhattan on a hunch to see if perhaps anyone had been selling quantities of blood. It was a long shot, but needed to be checked out. Despite his partner's theory and the doctor's assertion there could be truth in it, Murray prided himself on being a practical man, and practical men didn't believe in fairy tales and ghost stories. He would let Strumm and Dr. Rudalac hunt vampires till the cows came home, but as for Murray, he'd hunt for a flesh and blood murderer.

This left Strumm to go from door to door, checking the seamstress shops and the laundries beginning in lower Manhattan, moving north, looking for the one that might have been used by the assumed murderer, or murderers. He concluded that there was a better than even chance whoever owned the dress or waistcoat from which the buttons came would launder their garments within a reasonable distance to the crimes from where they'd been found. Today was his fourth day of inquiries and Strumm was already becoming discouraged. Many of the shops he'd visited either had no knowledge of the buttons, or more likely, wanted nothing to do with the police.

Molly Flanagan had been taking in clothes to wash and mend

186

for twenty-three years, ever since her father died when she was the tender age of thirteen. 'Flanagan's Laundry and Seamstress Shop' was located on 43rd Street just west of the Bryant Park Reservoir, although shop might have been something of a misnomer. Molly's place of business was actually a residence converted into a business. The only distinguishing feature between this particular red brick residence and the ones to its right and left was the sign hanging above the door at a right angle to the building. In addition to having the words 'Laundry' and 'Seamstress' printed in bold, black letters there were also pictures of a washtub and a spool of thread alongside a threaded needle to guide those New Yorkers who could not read English, or more commonly could not read, to Molly's establishment.

He turned the bell on the door. Detective Strumm had been to a half-dozen independent laundresses in mid-town Manhattan already this morning. So far, he'd come up empty. After a minute, he turned the bell once again.

"Hold yer horses…I'm a'comin'" came a woman's voice from behind the door. It had a hoarse, strained quality to it. Seconds later he found the voice belonged to a stout woman of about forty years who opened the door.

"Good afternoon, Ma'am. May I speak to Molly Flanagan?"

"I'm Molly. What's yer business?" She looked down and around him to both sides. "I don't see no laundry bags," she said in a manner as gruff as her appearance, brushing a wisp of graying hair off her sweaty forehead with the back of her hand. Strumm noticed her forearms were raw and mottled from repeated submersion in lye-water.

"I'm sorry to bother you, Ma'am, but I'm Detective Sergeant Strumm. I have some questions I'd like to ask you. Can I come in?"

"You don't look like no copper," she said, resting her hands on her ample hips.

Strumm reached into his jacket pocket and produced his badge and identification.

Softening her manner a bit, she dried her hands on her apron saying, "Very well, then, you can come in, but I'm a very busy woman, Detective. Say yer piece and go. I don't have no time for idle chit-chat."

"I get that, Mrs. Flanagan. This won't take long."

"Miss Flanagan," she corrected him.

"Miss Flanagan," he repeated. The inside of her shop reeked of lye soap as he stepped through the door. Reaching into the pocket of his greatcoat he pulled out two small buttons. "Have you ever seen or had in your possession a garment with buttons like either of these?"

Looking from the detective's hand up to his face and back, she took the small buttons from his palm. She placed one back as she examined the other one. "I've seen that one for sure," she said as she carried the second button over by the window to get a better look.

"You have? When, where?" asked Strumm, both excited and irritated—excited she might have some piece of information that would prove useful and irritated that she ignored his interest and moved toward the window. But then he discovered why.

"Sure. I've sewn that very button on dozens of dresses. It's a very common wooden button with a wire ferrule. They're ten for a penny in any seamstress shop."

"I see," he said as his shoulders slumped a bit in disappointment, thinking that Holmes character might be more clever than he gave him credit. But he kept his eye on Molly as she held up the second button to the light.

"But this one," she went on. "Oh this one is special, it is…glass inlaid on ivory with a gold wire ferrule…can't be many like it around."

Again dejected that her interest seemed only due to professional admiration, he said to her, "That's nice, Miss Flanagan, but it's not the rarity I'm interested in."

She handed the button back to Strumm and said, "Not even if I told you I've only seen the like once, and very recently at that?" She seemed to be toying with him now, enjoying leading him on.

"You've seen a button like this one? When and where, Miss Flanagan, it's of vital importance. You can only imagine."

"Why, in my washtub this morning, Detective."

#

"This is not the person you seek, Mylo," Dr. Rudalac said shaking his head and wiping a bit of catsup from the corner of his mouth after Strumm told him of his visit to Molly Flanagan's seamstress shop. "This Emily Drake person is not the vampire."

"But the dress, it has identical buttons on the bodice as the one I found at the scene of Inspector Andrews' murder. Miss Flanagan even said it was missing a button when she got it. She was asked to replace it with as near a match as she could find."

"Ah, but Mylo, the woman who dropped off the dress, what time of day was it?"

"Mrs. Flanagan said it was about noon. She remembered because she said she was eating kippers and beer, her usual noon meal."

"Around noon, Mylo, that is the key. The vampire is a creature of the night. They don't venture forth during the day. Their powers are greatly diminished during the daylight hours. Some say they are paralyzed during the day and must seek the shelter of darkness. Others say that sunlight itself can kill a vampire. No, Mylo, this is not the creature."

"But she must have been at the scene, she must know who the vampire is."

"Perhaps. If the dress belongs to her, then yes, you are right, but tread softly, Mylo. If she is an accomplice of the vampire, then she could be nearly as dangerous as the vampire himself. It's not unusual for him to have one or possibly more accomplices."

"What kind of person would join forces with such a creature?"

"You are asking me?" Dr. Rudalac said with a wry smile, "Have you forgotten my father?"

"I'm sorry, Rudy, I didn't mean to…"

"Never mind, Mylo, I understand. It's difficult, even for me, to understand how my father could have aided such a beast. My father was, simply put, an evil man. But don't be fooled. The accomplice is not necessarily evil. The vampire is a trickster, an accomplished liar. He can be charming and gracious. He can wield a great influence on certain kinds of people. Don't forget he's of an ancient lineage who've spent centuries perfecting their skills."

"Skills? I'm not sure I follow."

"In my father's papers he made mention of a bodyguard, a large brute of a man who saw to the vampire's every need."

"Someone very much like your father, then?"

"No. No, this man did not act out of self-interest as my father did. This man acted solely out of loyalty."

"Loyalty? To a vampire?"

The old man smiled sadly. "Mylo, you have much to learn. The vampire is as cunning as he is deceitful. He uses this to dupe the unsuspecting into aiding him in his unholy enterprise, most often without their suspecting his true motives. My father wrote that the vampire had rescued this man from death at the hands of a band of gypsies who had raped and murdered his wife and two daughters. He had been left for dead. The vampire found him, nursed him back to health and buried his family. He told the vampire, though he did not know him as such, what had happened. The following morning he found a basket outside his front door. In it were the heads of the men who'd killed his family. From that day he swore his loyalty."

"Incredible. I can see why he would feel an obligation…"

"Yes, but what the man did not know, and what my father discovered only after his death was the vampire himself had arranged the entire episode. As I said, the vampire knows how to protect himself, and when needed, how to create loyalty. If the woman you seek is helping him it may be that he has convinced her that he can provide something that she desperately wants, something she can get from no other person. Perhaps it's revenge for a wrong or perhaps she is acting out of a sense of a debt he has manufactured."

"Diabolical."

"To us it would seem so, yes. But to the vampire he is merely using his skills, talents, and experience to ensure his own survival, as would any one of us, I'm afraid."

"How heartwarmin'…sounds to me like you're makin' excuses for this vampire of yours, Doc." Murray stepped into the room. "Some might think you almost sympathize with 'im." Murray put his hand down on the table, then jerked it back when it made contact with the corpse lying there. "Ieww…" he said, and then cleared his throat before continuing, "…let's not forget this fella's killed at least four people we know of."

"I don't think that's what Rudy meant…?"

"Certainly not. I'm merely pointing out that every coin has two sides and it's where you stand in relation to the coin that governs which side you can see."

"So, Murray, any luck with your blood peddling angle?"

"Nah…most of the hospitals laughed at me when I asked 'em. Said they don't have no use for blood, actually. There was a doc by the name of Crile they told me wuz doin' some kind of experiments, but he wasn't workin' there no more, moved to Ohio."

"Well, then, that puts a hole in that theory."

"I still say all this vampire business is just a lot o'gas."

Dr. Rudalac sneered at Murray as he said to Strumm, "There are some that wouldn't believe in a vampire if it bit them on the nose."

"Ahhh…" Murray said and with a wave of his hand, he walked out of the morgue.

Chapter 19

A doctor's deceit…

With holly garland around the windows and a large evergreen wreath hung on the door, complete with an oversized, gold-trimmed, red bow, the house of Charles Edward Cabot looked as festive this Christmas as it had in many Christmases past. The traditional Cabot Christmas dinner, always the highlight of their holiday season, was a time when the entire family gathered to celebrate the season's tidings. But this year, they would be gathering without the youngest Cabot, Charles, Jr.

Although Julia sorely missed her brother, Charles, or Chuckles as she called him, a new British Army officer stationed in Africa, she was confident the myriad cousins, uncles, aunts, etc., would keep the house bustling and prevent her from dwelling too much on his absence.

Julia and Alan Tremaine were among the last to arrive in the late afternoon, just as dinner was being brought out from the kitchen and placed onto the long dining table. The aromas of a traditional Christmas dinner met them as they entered the house—the smell of roast turkey and roast goose mixed with the steamy delight of a variety of vegetables and above it all, the sweet, spicy aroma of pumpkin pie.

"Oh, Mama," Julia said as she removed her coat and gave her mother a kiss on the cheek. "Everything looks and smells so wonderful."

"Thank you, dear. I was afraid we might have to start without you."

"I'm sorry we're so late. I hope you're feeling better. Papa said you've been a bit down lately." She looked at her mother's care-worn face with concern as she kept hold of her hand.

"Don't you worry about me, I'm just fine, and as far as being late," she said in a conspiratorial whisper with a twinkle in her eye, "newlyweds are famous for being late, if you understand me." She nudged Julia's arm and gave her a knowing smile.

Julia fought back a blush and said, "Oh no, mother, it was nothing like that. Alan had to go in to the hospital this morning. Father's been working him so hard." She laughed. "I told him I wanted to get here in time to help with dinner, but he insisted it was important."

"Don't bother about that, dear, I wasn't wanting for help in the kitchen." As she said this two of Julia's cousins came laughing out of the swinging kitchen door, their hands filled with steaming bowls of potatoes and green beans.

"I can certainly see that," Julia said as she dodged another cousin on her way into the kitchen.

"But what was so important that Alan had to go to the hospital on Christmas morning?" she asked Julia as they moved into the formal dining room. "He's the head of his department, not a practicing physician."

"Oh, well, you know how dedicated Alan is," she said with more than a touch of pride in her voice.

Mrs. Cabot raised her eyebrows just a bit, "Yes, dedicated indeed." A pensive furrow ingrained itself on her brow, but vanished quickly and she said, "Pshaw, it's Christmas, Love, let's think nothing more about the hospital," and she led Julia to her seat beside her husband, calling the family to the table.

Julia knew her mother too well not to recognize there was something she wasn't saying. She'd seen that look on her face before. It was the same look she'd had when Julia was thirteen and her grandmother lay dying in this very house, the same look she got when Charles, Jr., left for Egypt, the same look she has every time more than three weeks goes by without hearing from him. It was the look she had whenever something was bothering her that she didn't wish to talk about, as if the act of not talking about it, ignoring it, would somehow make it go away. Julia couldn't get her mother's look off her mind all through dinner. It put a shroud over the joyousness of the occasion.

After dinner Julia helped clear away the dirty dishes. They'd laid on extra help for Naomi, the housekeeper, to wash the dishes, but all pitched in to clear. As the family gathered in the parlor for the traditional singing of Christmas carols and exchanging of gifts, Julia pulled her mother aside.

"Mama, something's been bothering me all through dinner."

"What is it, dear?" she asked, but the look on her face made it clear she knew what was on Julia's mind.

"When I told you Alan was at the hospital, you almost said something, but stopped yourself. What was it, Mama? What did you want to say?" She stood looking expectantly at her mother.

"It was nothing, dear, nothing at all. I'm just a bit tired, that's all. Not myself lately. Oh, to be sure, I'm well enough to tend to dinner with a houseful of guests, but in all honesty, I did very little. Your cousins did most of the work. The holidays can be very taxing on a body, especially one as old as mine," she smiled, but it was a sad smile. "But I do wish you'd speak to your father about not working Alan so hard. The two of you are too young to let work come before your marriage. I sense you're being left alone far too much for a young bride."

"Oh, Mama, how do you always know?" Julia looked down, her fingers worrying the frill on her Christmas dress.

"Know what, dear? Know when my child is unhappy? You'll understand when you have children one day." She took Julia's hands in her own.

"It's true. Alan has been working night and day. He says he's doing it for our future, but it just seems there's so little time for the two of us now," she said as she looked down at her hands in her mother's, "so little time to plan a family."

"Then you must speak to your father. Today." She gave Julia a serious look.

"Yes, you're right. I will," she promised.

"Good," she said, and then she smiled. "He's in the den, darling, waiting for you."

Julia gave her mother an incredulous look, her hand rising to her mouth.

"Go on dear, I'll stall the others, but don't be too long. Join us in the parlor when you're done."

Julia was often amazed by her mother's intuition. She seemed always to know what was on Julia's mind even before Julia knew herself.

As she entered her father's den she was overcome by the same feeling of awe she had as a curious little girl, a feeling that lessened as she grew older, but never entirely went away. This was her father's sanctuary, where he went to get away from all of the daily routine of a busy household. She loved the smells within—tobacco, rich leather, and wood paneling.

In his overstuffed chair, her father was sitting beside, and not behind his desk, with his back to the door. He was staring out the window at the falling snow as it danced in the sphere of light surrounding the gas lamps in the street. The room itself was darkened, but she could smell the sweet, acrid smoke that hovered above his head, like a great cloud over the Olympus that was her father.

She entered the room noiselessly, closing the door behind her. Tentatively, she broke the silence of his reverie, "Father?"

As he turned, his face went through a metamorphosis from a look of such concern that it would have frightened Julia had she seen it in full light, to one of a supremely loving and indulgent parent. While the low light of the room softened the lines of worry on his face, his smile and the light in his eyes seemed to visibly brighten upon seeing his only daughter, even before he turned up the light of the table lamp. "Ahh…Julia. Your mother said you wished to speak to me?" He held out his hands, beckoning her to come closer.

She went to him and kissed his forehead. "Yes, Father." She continued with a little laugh, "She knew even before I did."

"Doesn't she always?" he agreed, no stranger to the insightful ways of his wife. Jokingly he said, "I always tell her it's the gypsy in her blood." Gesturing for her to sit, he asked, "So what can I do for my favorite daughter?"

"Your only daughter," she said, smiling at his little joke.

"It's the same thing, my dear," he said with a chuckle. So,

what's troubling you?"

"It's Alan, Father."

"Alan?" he asked in an even tone that seemed incongruous with the way the tip of his eyebrow jutted up as he repeated the name.

"Yes, Father, he's been working so hard at the hospital these past weeks, too hard…"

"Too hard? I don't understand."

"Oh, please, Father, don't think we…don't think I am being ungrateful. It's just that…well, Alan has been spending so much time at the hospital that I…we have had precious little time together." She stopped, seeing a quizzical look come over her father's face. "What is it, Father?"

"Well, I'm just a bit perplexed is all. You see, Julia, actually Alan's attendance at the hospital, or I should say his inattendance, has been brought to my attention on more than one occasion these past few weeks. Oh, to be sure he makes a show of getting to the hospital early, but he disappears at long stretches during the day and habitually leaves early, I'm told."

"He does?"

"Yes. It was becoming so prevalent that I had a little chat with him. He led me to believe he'd been meeting you for lunch and…well, let's just say I dismissed it as a case of 'newlywed' syndrome. And with your mother so looking forward to grandchildren…well, I was inclined to indulge him a bit."

Julia blushed. "Oh, father."

"As a matter of fact, he's asked me if it was absolutely necessary that he make the Baltimore trip. And now, you are telling me he's been working too hard? I'm afraid I don't know quite what to think."

"Nor do I," Julia said, taken completely by surprise with her father's revelation. With her womanly instincts bristling now, she added, "But I intend to find out."

#

The carriage ride from the Cabot home to that of the Tremaines was unusually quiet. Although Julia was seated beside her husband, they might as well have been in different coaches. She sat stonily silent, her hands folded on her lap as she watched the snowflakes dance in the light of the passing gas lamps.

As they pulled onto their street and neared the house, Alan finally broke the silence, "Julia, you've hardly said a word since dinner. Didn't you like the bracelet I gave you?"

"It's lovely, Alan. Of course I like it," she said in short, clipped sentences. She then resumed sitting quietly again, contemplating whether she should continue. At last she said, "Alan, I spoke to Father about—"

"Your father? Oh, dear, that reminds me," her husband interrupted. "I must go to the hospital this evening. I hope you don't mind."

"The hospital? Again? Oh, Alan, it's Christmas and you were just there this morning," she hoped her annoyance showed in her tone. Silently she wondered what could possibly be so important that he would leave her now, on Christmas night, but she decided to bite her tongue and bide her time.

"Yes, I know, dear, and I wouldn't go if it weren't of vital importance and it shouldn't take too terribly long, I'm very close…" he stopped in mid-sentence, looking away, fearing he'd already said too much.

"Close to what?" She turned to look at him.

"I'm close to...to finishing the report on my department's operations. Your father has been screaming for them for over a month now. I promised him I'd turn it in before I leave for Baltimore tomorrow."

"Oh, I see," she said, becoming silent once again at his obvious lie.

"Please, Julia, don't be sullen. I promise, once I've completed what I'm working on I'll take some time off and you and I will take a little trip."

"Oh, Alan, do you promise? Do you really promise?" she asked hoping that whatever it was that was keeping him away would be over soon.

"Yes, yes of course I promise," he said as he drew her to him and gave her a kiss.

"All right, but please try not to be too late." She decided she needed to do something to discover what it was her husband was doing while he was supposed to be working. She was determined, but afraid at what it might be. Nevertheless, she intended to discover whatever secret he was hiding. But she didn't quite know how she would do it.

"I won't, dear. I promise." He stopped the carriage in front of their home and stepped around to help Julia down. After he climbed back into the coach, she stood watching as her husband snapped the whip above the head of their chestnut mare, startling it into a spritely gait down the road. For the first time in her life she stood alone feeling absolutely helpless.

Then, as she turned to walk up the steps to her door, a familiar voice hailed her, "Julia." She turned to see a carriage coming from the same direction she'd just come with her husband. "Julia," the call came again.

She could see Uncle Ralph's red and smiling face. "Julia, dear, I must say, do you mind putting up your old uncle for the evening?" He pulled the carriage up alongside her on the street. "When I started for home I felt quite all right, but now I must admit perhaps I've had a bit too much merrymaking this evening."

With a kind smile, she answered, "Oh, Uncle, of course, come on inside, you can use the guest room." Thinking quickly she said, "Say, Uncle Ralph, I wonder if I might borrow your buggy. Alan has just now gone to the hospital and I'm afraid he's forgotten his keys. I need to take them to him right away." She intended to take advantage of her uncle's arrival to get to the bottom of Alan's secret.

"Why, yes, yes of course, dear. Perhaps if you hurry, you can catch him before he gets too far. Don't worry about me, I know my way."

"And Uncle," Julia said with a smile as she climbed into the seat of the buggy, "I won't tell Mother."

"Ooh..." he said and then laughed, "There's a good girl. You know how your mother fusses over her little brother, don't you." But Julia had already snapped the reins and the buggy was moving quickly away.

Her uncle's gelding fell into an uneasy trot in the direction of the hospital where her husband had just headed. As she turned the corner, she saw Alan's carriage about two blocks ahead of her, but instead of continuing toward the hospital, he turned the carriage away from the hospital's direction and towards the park. Although her heart sank, she knew she'd made the right decision in following him. If he was going to lie to her in such a bold fashion, what else might he do? She was going to find out just exactly what he was hiding from her and she was going to find out tonight.

She maintained her distance without losing sight of the carriage. She was shocked and a bit heartbroken when he turned the carriage into Central Park. She had heard of the goings on there at night and it distressed her to think her husband might have any such inclinations. She remembered reading something in the papers just this morning about an acquaintance of her father's being found in this same park, murdered—and in a very scandalous fashion. When Alan continued through the park, emerging on the east side, Julia breathed a little easier.

There were scarcely any coaches in the streets at this hour once they turned off Park Avenue and onto 71st Street. In order to prevent Alan from seeing her, she maintained a more than discrete distance. The snow was falling harder now, which aided Julia in her efforts. Many of the houses they passed were dark, the holiday revelers having long since retired.

Julia was beginning to wonder if, perhaps, she were just a bit foolish following her husband like this. Perhaps he was merely taking a circuitous route to the hospital in order to collect his thoughts. He'd often told her how relaxing and peaceful a ride along the river was. Just then, Alan turned down a long, tree-lined drive. Julia slowed her horse's pace in order not to reach the entrance to the drive before Alan had reached the house. When she was even with the drive, she stopped her carriage. She watched him as he approached the door. As she sat, hoping a colleague might answer his knock, she saw the door open and a silhouette, the silhouette of a woman, was framed by the light within. As Alan entered, the woman turned and Julia could see her face—it was Emily Drake.

#

A lone figure sat huddled against the cold, his frock coat pulled up tightly to his chin, in exactly the same spot he'd sat at this time last Christmas night, and the Christmas night before that—the same spot he'd sat each Christmas night since they'd passed away. A casual observer driving past the cemetary might not even notice the man sitting there as still as the night. By now, snow was beginning to collect on the shoulders of his coat and on his hat. He moved only occasionally, his gloved hand bringing a dark bottle to his lips from which he drank deeply. The gravestone said simply "Millicent Eliza Strumm and infant" giving the date of Millie's birth and death. No dates were given for the child, the daughter that was never born.

Somehow Christmas was even harder than their anniversary or Millie's birthday. It was on Christmas that she had told him they were going to have a child. On the night Millie died, the doctors had made a vain attempt to deliver the premature baby girl. But now, his wife and daughter both lie in the cold grave beside him. Mylo Strumm took another long drink from the bottle of spirits as tears tumbled down his cheeks, freezing against his skin. Crawling down onto his knees, he stretched out on the top of the grave, his fingers tracing Millie's name on the gravestone. He whispered her name just before he passed out.

That's how Murray found him three years ago—passed out and nearly frozen to death. Since that time it had become an annual ritual. Murray would come by each Christmas night, wait for Strumm to pass out in his drunken grief, and then trundle him off home so that he wouldn't die of exposure to the elements. Each morning after, Murray would scold him for being so foolish and secure his promise that it wouldn't happen again.

Murray scooped Strumm up in his massive arms and gently

placed him in the back of his carriage. On the way to Strumm's apartment, he quietly wondered if Strumm would ever have peace in his heart again. It saddened the big man to think what would become of Strumm if he weren't around.

Chapter 20

Two trips...

It was well past midnight when Alan returned home. Carefully and quietly, he entered the front door. He wanted very much not to awaken Julia. Trying to remember which steps squeaked, he ascended the stairs and tiptoed down the hall to their bedroom. Slowly, he turned the knob and eased open the door to their room. Emily heard the hinges squeak but waited until he was well inside the bedroom before saying his name in a low, quiet tone, "Alan?"

"Julia, what are you doing up? You should be asleep."

"I've been waiting for you, Alan. I want to know where you've been tonight. And please, keep your voice down. Uncle Ralph is sleeping in the guest room." She sat upright in their bed and turned up the lamp on the nightstand.

"I don't understand. You know where I've been. I've been working at the hospital."

Julia could see the look of surprise on her husband's face— and guilt. In a tone colder than she'd ever used with Alan she said, "Don't lie to me, Alan. It's bad enough you've been unfaithful to me, but..."

"Unfaithful?" Alan raised his voice. "What are you saying?" He removed his jacket and unbuttoned his shirt.

205

"Yes, unfaithful," she said in a hushed tone, "and I told you, keep your voice down."

Lowering his voice to match hers, "But what's given you such a ridiculous notion? Unfaithful...? Julia, please..." There was a plaintive, petulant tone to his voice. She wondered how he could lie so convincingly.

"I followed you, Alan."

She could hear him gulp. "You..." Seeing the stunned look on his face she felt ashamed and hurt, ashamed that she'd followed him, and hurt by his look of abject guilt. "What's the meaning of this?"

"I followed you. I saw you go into the house of that...that...woman." She wanted to tell Alan what she really thought of the woman who was having an affair with her husband. But she wanted more to be proven wrong, for it all to be some kind of terrible mistake.

"It isn't what you think, Julia. Not at all...not at all," he said, his voice trailing off.

"Oh? And what am I to think? My father told me you've been shirking your responsibilities at the hospital. You tell me you've been working late and my father says that when he spoke to you about leaving work early you lied and said you were with me...and last night, when I followed you, you drive straight to a house where that woman welcomes you at the door. What other explanation is there, Alan?" She dabbed at her eyes with the handkerchief she'd been clutching in her hand.

"My work," Alan said, his eyes pleading to be believed. "You must believe me, Julia."

"Oh, Alan," she said, succumbing at last to the tears she'd been so bravely holding inside. "I want to believe you, but how can I when you tell me once again that it's the hospital keeping you from me, when…when…" her voice gave way to sobs of despair.

"No, Julia, not my work at the hospital…" he said with a sheepish look.

Julia paused. She looked at Alan through her tears and asked, "Not the hospital? Then what?"

"I'm working on the cure." His expression brightened when he said the word as if he expected saying it would make everything all right.

"Cure?"

"Yes, of course, the cure for vampirism. I've been able to think of little else since she came. I simply had to complete the experiment I was working on before I go off to Baltimore tomorrow."

"Since who came?"

"Abigail Drake, of course," he answered before he could stop himself.

"Abigail Drake? But wasn't she the woman in the…don't you mean Emily? Emily Drake?"

"Yes, yes, of course, Emily. She is financing the continuation of my work in England. That's who you saw last night. She's set up a laboratory for my work in her home."

"Oh, Alan, none of this makes any sense. You know yourself the baron's ship was lost at sea. He's gone, Alan, and good riddance. That should be the end of it, the end of this vampire business. What reason could you possibly have for pursuing a cure to a disease for which there are no victims?"

"Yes, of course you're right. And that's exactly what I told her. But Miss Drake reminded me that the baron is no ordinary man, that simply because he was involved in a shipwreck, did not necessarily mean he was dead," he lied. The truth was that Abigail Drake demonstrated the baron's power over death. If he could save her from perishing in the freezing water when their ship was lost, certainly he would survive.

Julia, unable to believe her ears crumpled on the bed sobbing. "Get out," she said, her voice somewhat muffled by her pillow. When Alan only stood at the foot of the bed, she raised her head and with it her voice as she pointed to the bedroom door, "Get out!"

Alan left, and having thrown her husband out of the bedroom, Julia cried herself to sleep.

The following morning Julia was up early. She went directly into the kitchen to make a handsome breakfast for Alan, who'd spent the night in the overstuffed leather couch in his den, as the guest room had been occupied by a snoring Uncle Ralph.

When Alan emerged from the den the aroma of frying sausage and fresh muffins met him in the hall. Disheveled and bleary-eyed, he entered the dining room. There, Julia was waiting for him. She set his place at the table without saying a word.

Uncle Ralph arose upon Alan entering the room, "Dear God, old boy, you look as if you haven't slept a wink all night. Sit down, I was just finished myself." With a twinkle in his eye, he said, "I'll leave you and your lovely wife to have breakfast alone." Winking at Julia, Ralph chided, "You should really take it easy on him, Julia. After all, he's only a man," and he left the room laughing at his own brand of levity.

As Alan sat down in his normal place at the head of the table, Julia poured him a hot cup of coffee. She placed a plate filled with his favorite breakfast foods in front of him before sitting down gingerly at his left side. "What's this?" he asked. "I must say, I didn't expect you would…I mean after last night…" Completely rattled, he didn't seem able to complete a thought.

Silently and with a serious look on her face, Julia took the napkin from the table, spread it carefully on her lap, and then folded her hands, placing them on the white linen. In a quiet voice that amplified her seriousness she said, "It's very simple, Alan. You must choose."

"Choose? But I told you, Julia, it's my work. I've not been unfaithful to you."

"So you said. But your work now is at the hospital."

"This is ridiculous." His tone was one of confusion. "I told you it's the carrying on of the work I began in England."

"Yes," she said, now leaning forward, her forearms flat on the table for support. "Then you must choose, either your work at the hospital, or your…," pausing as if searching for the right word, finally settling on, "…your other work, your work with Emily Drake."

"You aren't making any sense. I don't understand what you mean."

With a calmness in her voice that was at odds with the fire in her eyes she said, "As I said, it's simple, elementary, really. You have to choose between your *work*," as she said the word she was unable to stop the invective in her voice from showing through, "or your wife." She paused to allow the words to sink in before continuing, "Whichever choice you make, you will also reap all that comes with it. With your work comes Emily Drake, but little else. Your position, your income, and your reputation will be forfeit, for who would hire a doctor who's on a mad search for a cure to a disease that exists only in his mind."

She could see the discomfort written across his face as she

paused once again to allow him to consider her words. "Choose your wife," she continued, smiling a smile that was somewhere between smug and loving, "and you will have the love and respect I know you crave." Pausing yet again, she patted his hand. "If you choose your wife, we will forget all about Emily Drake and all this vampire nonsense. Life will continue as if she'd never come to visit us at all." She gripped his hand and looked hard into his eyes, "But mark me, Alan, you must never see or speak to Emily Drake again."

She could see by the blank look on his face that Alan was quite stunned. Julia rose from her chair saying, "Now, run along to Baltimore," as she retrieved his hat, greatcoat, and suitcase. "You can give me your answer when you return. I believe that should give you ample time to consider the situation." She waited for him to stand, and then handed him his coat and hat. Turning away from him, she went to the front door and opened it to see him off. Alan, dumbstruck, donned his hat and coat, picked up his suitcase and walked to where Julia was standing. He took his walking stick from the umbrella stand, gave her a kiss on the cheek and went out the door.

Julia smiled. It was obvious she'd achieved what she set out to do. She'd never spoken to him, or anyone else for that matter, in such a manner. She felt quite proud in spite of herself.

#

Just a few blocks away, another trip was beginning. Emily Drake was feeling a bit uneasy leaving her Aunt Lucie, even for just a few days. When she'd first arrived from Chicago she was taken aback at how much her aunt had declined since last she'd seen her and how confused she appeared to be. But in the short time they'd been together, Emily had seen her aunt steadily improving. She didn't wish to do anything that would interfere with that. But she had to go to

Boston, to find out what she could about the *Animus Lacuna*.

"Are you quite sure you'll be okay if I leave for a few days, Auntie?" she asked as she packed her bags for the trip to Boston.

"Yes, dear, truly you don't need to bother yourself about me; I'll be just fine, I promise."

"Oh, Auntie," she stopped packing to give her aunt a hug. "I wouldn't be leaving, but I promised." She paused and turned away from her aunt. "I promised Elizabeth that I would visit her there."

"I know...I know, but honestly, Emily, I'll be all right. I'm feeling better and more like myself every day. It's been such a blessing having you back home. I'm afraid I was beginning to unravel a bit since your Uncle Cedric passed. And to know that Abigail is going to be fine again soon too...it's just been so wonderful. I wish I could see her."

"I'm afraid that's impossible just now, Auntie, but once she's cured..."

"Of course, dear, I understand."

"But Auntie, you must be careful. No one must know about Abigail until she's completely recovered."

"Yes, yes, you told me all about that. I wouldn't dream of telling anyone." She laughed, "Besides, who'd believe me anyway?" Again she laughed, this time a bit more forcefully, putting her fingers to her lips. "I can just see the looks on the faces of my bridge club, 'Oh, yes, my dears, this evening I'm having dinner with my niece, she's just returned from the dead.'" She chortled. "They'd have me over in the looney bin on Blackwell's before we'd completed the rubber."

Emily laughed along with her aunt. "Oh, Auntie, I love you," she said as she put her arms around her and kissed her on the cheek.

Grand Central was bustling with travelers as Emily boarded one of the few express trains to Boston. She sat looking out the window of her private compartment in the day car thinking about Abigail. The train pulled out of the station while a steady snow fell, layering New York with a clean blanket of white. The snow reminded her of her mission, to meet with Mandible Pierce, the only man who knew the *Animus Lacuna* wasn't truly lost at sea.

The Carney Hospital in Boston was run by the Sisters of Christian Charity, Daughters of the Blessed Virgin Mary of the Immaculate Conception. It was the post to which Sister Elizabeth had been traveling when she and Emily rode the train together from Chicago, and Emily was very happy to see her friend again. It was she who showed Emily to Mr. Pierce's room. The room, however, was empty, as it was getting close to noon when she arrived. "Mr. Pierce must be in the dining hall. If you'd arrived much later, you might have missed him altogether," Sister Elizabeth explained. "Truth be told, I suspect he is well enough to have left a week ago, and good riddance to him when he does."

"Sister, I must say I'm a bit surprised at your attitude," Emily teased.

"You haven't met Mr. Pierce," Elizabeth said with a sly grin. "Come, we'll join him in the hall with the others. I suspect lunch is being served just about now."

Just as they arrived at the door to the dining ward, one of the nuns came scurrying out, followed closely by a tray of food narrowly missing her. "You call that slop food? Tryin' to poison me, you are," called a voice from within.

Sister Elizabeth raised her eyebrows as she turned to look at Emily, "That's Mr. Pierce," she said. Smiling, she added, "And in an unusually good mood today, too." Stepping around the spilled milk, she led Emily through the door. There were a number of patients crowded at various tables. Mr. Pierce, however, sat alone. It was obvious no one wished to dine with Mandible Pierce.

"Mr. Pierce, you have a visitor," Sister Elizabeth said in a cheerful voice. "This is Sister Emily. She's come all the way from New York to make your acquaintance, though I can't for the life of me understand why." With a wink she leaned over and said to Emily, "Don't be afraid to call if you need anything," as she turned to leave the ward.

Looking Emily over with rheumy gray eyes, he said, "Sister? Why ain't you wearin' your frock, then?" His voice was nearly as grizzled as his beard-studded face. His dirty-blonde hair hung loose and thin across his forehead and over his collar.

"Well, Mr. Pierce, I'm still a novice," she lied, "and I'm on a leave of absence to attend my sister's funeral." She didn't feel it was necessary to discuss her recent decision to leave the order with him.

Casting his eyes downward, he said, "God rest her, I'm sorry," out of a politeness that was as short-lived as it was automatic. "What brings you here to see me? I don't know yez, does I?" His right eye squinted as he considered her.

"No, Mr. Pierce, we've never met. I've come here on behalf of someone who would very much like to speak to you."

"What about?" he asked, squinting both eyes now with his head turned to the side, suspicious once more.

"About what you saw when you found the *Animus Lacuna*," Emily said as she sat down in the chair opposite him.

Pierce crossed himself three times when he heard the name. "No," he said simply and turned away.

"But you are the only witness."

"Damn my eyes, dear God, that ship was the devil's own."

"Nevertheless, Mr. Pierce, the person I represent will make it worth your while to tell what you know."

Twisting his frame in the chair to look at her again he asked, "What's he want to know and why didn't he come himself?"

"This person finds travel a great inconvenience."

"Ha. So do I," he growled.

"As I said, Mr. Pierce, we shall make it worth your while. How much do you think would be a fair price for you to travel to New York?"

He thought for a moment. Emily could see he was trying to judge what would be safe to ask and still maximize his take. Finally, he said, "Twenty, no thirty dollars."

Emily opened her purse.

"Fifty dollars and...and you pay for the train and a hotel, a good hotel...with soft beds."

"Of course," she said as she handed him five ten dollar notes and an envelope. "You'll find the train tickets inside, as well as the name and address of the hotel where you will stay. The tickets will be good for one week. I'm sure you'll find everything satisfactory."

Pierce was busy inspecting the bills.

"Did you hear me, Mr. Pierce? The tickets are only good for a week." Handing him a small card, she added, "Wire me at this address."

He looked at her in disbelief, "What makes you think I won't just spend the fifty dollars on whiskey and bangtail...er, ahh, pardon sister, on entertainment."

"That's all right, Mr. Pierce, I've heard worse," she said as

214

she rose from the chair. "I'm quite confident you'll come to New York. I'm a very good judge of character. Besides..." she said, smiling.

"Yes?" he asked, fully attentive now.

"After you've spoken to my...associate, you'll receive an additional one hundred dollars, for your inconvenience."

Chapter 21

...and a fall

Once she was certain her husband was on his way to Baltimore, Julia Tremaine put on a very striking, but sensible dress, and then called for a hansom cab. From her home on West 73rd Street she directed the driver to take her through the park along Terrace Drive, the same path in which she'd followed Alan on the previous evening. As she got closer to her destination she could feel her ire rising.

The hansom exited the park on East 72nd Street, cutting over to 71st Street at Park Avenue, then east once more until she arrived at number 104, the home of Emily Drake. As her cab pulled up the drive to the estate, Julia rehearsed in her mind what she wanted to say. Stepping down from the cab, she asked the driver to wait. She couldn't imagine what she had to say to Miss Drake could possibly take too long. Setting her face in a serious expression, she rang the bell.

Emily opened the door. "Yes? May I help you?"

"Good morning, Miss Drake, I trust I haven't come at an inconvenient time."

"Not at all. How may I help you?"

Julia was all the more incensed that Miss Drake apparently

didn't know who she was. "I should think as my husband has been a frequent visitor you might at least invite me in rather than leaving me standing here like a common peddler or charwoman."

"I'm sorry, did you say your husband?"

Julia could see she appeared genuinely puzzled. She looked at her closely. There was something different in her eyes, and her voice didn't sound exactly as she'd remembered it. "Yes, my husband, Dr. Alan Tremaine. I am Mrs. Tremaine. Surely you remember coming to my house."

"Oh dear, I'm so sorry, Mrs. Tremaine," Emily said with a reassuring smile. "Please, come in won't you?" She stepped back, allowing Julia inside the door. "I hope you'll forgive the looks of the place." Julia stepped through the door, looking at every corner with a woman's discerning eye. "I've just been tidying up a bit. The cleaning lady is ill, and I'm afraid we've gotten a bit behind. Please," she said, indicating a settee, "sit down, won't you? May I take your wrap?"

Julia sat down without removing her coat, keeping to the edge of the settee as Emily sat down beside her. "Don't worry yourself, I'll be brief," she said, endeavoring to keep her voice businesslike, devoid of emotion. There was something in Miss Drake's manner that took Julia by surprise. She'd expected to feel both anger and hatred. She felt neither, but still knew she needed to say her piece. "I've come by this morning to let you know my husband will no longer be assisting you in your quest for a..." she paused as if tasting the next word before spitting it out, "...a cure, was it?"

"Is your husband ill?" Emily asked with real concern, ignoring the question.

"Of course not. He's perfectly healthy."

"Then, I don't understand. Is his compensation inadequate? If

217

so, I'm sure it can be increased."

Julia's eyes widened. Now she could feel her rage returning. "His compensation, as you call it, is at an end. I've forbidden him from seeing or speaking to you again. That's the end of it."

"Oh dear...oh...OH," a look of realization passed across Emily's face. In an earnest and quiet tone she said to Julia, "I assure you, Mrs. Tremaine, my...my association with your husband has been on a completely professional basis."

"Ah, yes, the cure for vampirism," she scoffed, her eyebrow rising accusingly as she gave Emily a humorless smile. "My husband has told me all about that fantasy." She straightened her coat front. "No matter. That delusion is over also."

"Delusion? Mrs. Tremaine, I don't understand." Once again Julia noted a look of innocent confusion on Emily's face. She might even be taken in by it, were she not on her guard.

"Miss Drake, it was one thing when Alan was duped by this baron, thinking he could cure him of vampirism, a foolish notion to be sure. But now, with the baron dead, this charade must come to an end." Julia stiffened her back as she continued, "I'm sure you realize my husband is a brilliant man, Miss Drake. But even brilliant men can be fooled, blind to what's obvious. And I simply will not allow you or anyone else to take advantage of the fragility of his mind in this area." She leaned forward slightly, "Miss Drake, I don't know what your game is, but you will not be allowed to further whatever enterprise you are engaged in at our...at my husband's expense any longer." Julia stood abruptly. "I believe I've made myself clear. Thank you for your time." With Emily hurrying to catch up, Julia strode to the door.

"I do wish you'd reconsider, Mrs. Tremaine."

Julia didn't answer. She opened the door, stepped through it, and only when she was safely outside of the house did she turn and look directly into Emily's deep blue eyes to say, "That's out of the question. My mind is made up." Then, with a smile, more of relief than of comity, she extended her hand, "Good day, Miss Drake."

As the cab moved smartly down the drive Julia swallowed hard, a light sweat breaking out on her brow. Her knees felt weak, her legs heavy, and her head light but she was proud of herself and the way she handled the matter. For the second time that day she had achieved her goal and as the hansom drove back across the park she felt a quiet satisfaction in the knowledge that she'd faced down her rival and successfully defended her marriage. Now she was quite confident everything would be all right.

Julia spent the rest of the day well into the evening with her parents. They had such a good time, with Julia in an ebullient mood, that before they realized, it was almost midnight. Julia's mother wanted her to spend the night, but she insisted on going back to her own home, the home she defended so ably earlier today. Over her strenuous objection, Julia's father insisted Winthrop the butler drive Julia home.

As her father's landau ambled along Eighth Avenue, a black coach pulled by two coal-black horses sped out of the park, careening past Julia. Only Winthrop's steady hand on the reins kept their dapple from spooking. Julia said a silent prayer thanking God for her father's doting concern for his only daughter.

Minutes later, they arrived at Julia's home, safe and sound. Julia thanked Winthrop for escorting her home and especially for his skill in handling the horse during their brush with death. She laughed gaily when she said this, but she squeezed his arm as she left the coach, letting him know she was truly appreciative. Quickly, she walked from the coach to her house. As she opened the front door, Julia turned and waved to Winthrop, her signal that all was well. Upon seeing this, he cracked the whip behind the mare's ear, startling her into a trot. As he turned the coach back down the street, Julia watched him drive away.

Before going to her parents house, Julia had asked Annie to make up a fire in the bedroom and to leave the parlor fire roaring in order to keep the downstairs warm until she arrived back home, but that had been hours ago. There remained only a warm glow from the parlor as Julia passed by on her way up the stairs. A falling ember caused a flame to burst to life, the flicker of light painting shadows in the hall. Julia shuddered as she imagined one of those shadows passing by her on the stairs. "Oh dear," she cried to the empty staircase, "that carriage must have unsettled my nerves." Then she laughed at her own foolishness.

This was the first time since she and Alan were married that she'd spent the night alone. As she thought about it she realized it was the first time she could remember ever spending the night completely alone. She found herself wishing she'd asked Annie to stay the night, or better, wishing she'd stayed over at her parents' home. Her mother had asked her, but she wanted very much for her parents to treat her as an adult. She felt staying with them would be a step backward in that regard. But that didn't seem quite so important now. She decided the only thing to do was to put all those thoughts of being alone out of her mind and climb directly into bed. The sooner she fell asleep, she knew, the sooner the gloom of night would give way to a new and brighter day.

Immediately, she started the fire in the bedroom fireplace. Annie had done a good job of setting it up. As she undressed for bed, she got the uneasy feeling of being watched. She knew better. The curtains were drawn, the door was shut. Still, she could not shake the feeling and hurriedly slipped her nightgown over her head. As the flames painted shadows of demons on the walls, she climbed into bed, onto the side Alan usually occupied, pulling the bedclothes tight up to her chin.

She lay there for a long time, listening to the night, her eyes wide open as if she expected someone or something. The only sounds were the crackles and pops of the fire. She counted each pop and each crackle. She remembered a trick her father had taught her years ago, to keep her mind off being scared. At night, whenever she'd become afraid, her father told her that if she counted each pop and each crackle of the fire, the sandman would take her off to sleep before she knew it. As a little girl, she'd never been able to count more than fifty before the hypnotic sounds of the fire and her own meditative concentration combined to put her to sleep. It had been years since she'd needed to employ this nocturnal tool, and she was able to count more than fifty now, but before she reached seventy-five, she'd fallen into a peaceful sleep and dreamed.

Her dream began with her and Alan are in a small row boat on a lake. Through a misty-gray haze, she can see her house in the distance on a far shore. Alan is rowing towards it, but the more he rows, the further in the distance their house becomes.

Suddenly the sky is dark and Julia is alone in the boat. The water beneath the boat turns blood red. It begins to seep through the deck boards. Julia is frozen, unable to move. The red liquid, now looking more like blood than water, begins to wick up the hem of her dress, filling the bottom of the boat. She closes her eyes, terrified, still unable to move. She feels the boat melt away from beneath her and she's swimming, swimming, swimming. She's swimming toward a figure on the far shore where her house had been. But now the house is gone. A figure stands there in its place. As she swims toward the figure, her arms grow increasingly tired and leaden. It feels as though she will never reach the shore. Once again, she closes her eyes. When she opens them she's back in her home, lying in her own bed. The figure, now standing beside her, is obscured by darkness and a hooded cloak. Julie looks up, reaches out, and squeezes the figure's hand, cold and hard, but is unable to see its face.

The figure leans down and kisses Julia's cheek—a kiss with no warmth—and then whispers into her ear. Julia turns her head to the side, obeying the command. She feels a sting. Then, a warmth fills her with an intense, burning pleasure, unlike anything she's ever experienced. As the warmth courses through her, she falls into a deep, dreamless sleep.

Chapter 22
Mandible Pierce...

"Thank you, Miss Flanagan, and thanks again for finding a button to replace the one missing on my dress. It looks almost like new."

"I'm afraid it's not a perfect match, Dearie, but it's a barely noticeable difference, if I do say so meself," Miss Flanagan said as she counted the money she'd just been given.

Strumm watched as Emily walked out of the shop and made her way back to the cab carrying the dresses he'd seen several days before in Miss Flanagan's laundry room. He and Murray had been taking turns watching Flanagan's Laundry and Seamstress Shop waiting for the owner of the dress with the missing button to turn up to claim it. Today was Strumm's turn. Miss Flanagan pulled the shade halfway down in her shop's front window, the agreed upon sign that the customer just leaving her shop was the owner of the dress in question.

As he watched from his carriage across the street, parked in front of the tobacconist, he thought to himself that Miss Flanagan had failed to remark on how beautiful Miss Drake was. Even from this distance he could see how her eyes sparkled. He followed at a discreet distance as Emily's cab made its way along the streets of Manhattan to her sister's estate on East 71st St. Strumm pulled his brougham into a narrow lane not far from the drive where Emily turned in to the estate. He settled in, planning to keep an eye on the house until it was dark and the interior lights were all extinguished. He and Dr. Rudalac had decided it would be prudent for him to watch Miss Drake from a distance for a while before confronting her. They hoped to discover whether she was in league with anyone. They hoped she would lead them to their vampire. Once they knew for certain where he was hiding, they could deal with him, they could destroy him.

#

After retrieving Abigail's dresses from Miss Flanagan, Emily had been in a hurry to return to her sister's home. Tonight Mandible Pierce was due to arrive. The hotel had contacted her this morning, letting her know he had checked in at about ten o'clock. She knew she would need to be there, to stand in for Abigail until after the sun had set. She could have arranged for the visit to take place later, but was concerned that given Mr. Pierce's rough manner, a late night engagement might have given him the wrong impression.

Emily carefully put Abigail's dresses in the large armoire in the nearly empty master bedroom, and then set about titivating the parlor. The habitual state of disarray in which Abigail had left it was quite a surprise and a little distressing to Emily. It was Abigail who had always been the tidier one of the two. It seemed quite unlike her to allow her parlor to get into such a condition and Emily was growing increasingly concerned about the changes she'd noticed in her sister. Her disposition appeared to change with the direction of the wind. When first she'd spoken to her about Julia Tremaine's visit she could see that she was quite distressed and agitated. However, the very next day she dismissed the whole affair with a laugh, saying that once Dr.

Tremaine returned, she was certain the situation would right itself. She thought perhaps she and Abigail should have a talk, to make sure Abigail was all right.

At about 5:30pm there was a knock on the door. Emily knew this must be Mr. Pierce. She also knew it would not be long before Abigail would be joining them. She opened the door to see Mandible Pierce standing there looking at her, his hat in his hand.

"Good evening, Miss. I'm here just as I promised," he said, shifting his weight, first on one foot and then on the other as he stood in the cold portico entry.

"So you are, Mr. Pierce." Stepping back and opening the door in a welcoming if not terribly friendly manner she said, "Come in. I'm so glad you've come," even though there was something about him that made her skin crawl. She was careful to maintain a formal and businesslike demeanor.

"Thank you, Miss. Where's the gent what wants to ask about the *Animus Lacuna*?"

"In due time, Mr. Pierce. May I take your coat and hat?"

Pierce hesitated, looking at Emily suspiciously. After a few seconds, apparently satisfied Emily did not have designs on his battered bowler and pea coat, he handed them to her. She hung them on a coat rack near the door.

"Now, why don't you sit down. Would you care for some coffee while we wait?" she said, showing him into the parlor.

"Thanks, Miss, but would you happen to have something a tad stronger? There's a bit of a chill wind out tonight and I was hoping you might have something to take the bite off."

"Very well, Mr. Pierce, I'll sweeten your coffee with a bit of whiskey, then," she smiled as she twisted the cap off a dark bottle of

225

spirits. She'd seen her late uncle sweeten his coffee just that way many times.

"That's the ticket, girl," Pierce said as he licked his lips and held out both hands, still encased in fingerless gloves, to receive his prize. After a sip he looked up at her and said, "But you didn't bring me all the way from Boston to feed me coffee and fine liquor, did ye?" The leer he gave her made her blood run cold.

"No, Mr. Pierce, we did not," came the reply from directly behind his chair. Emily was visibly relieved to hear her sister's voice.

Startled, Pierce nearly dropped his cup as he spun around to see Abigail Drake. His eyes widened as they lit upon her, then his head snapped around to look back at Emily. "Dear God," he said, "twins," and then he laughed. "I'll be damned. I almost didn't come, hundred dollars or no."

"Why is that, Mr. Pierce?" asked Emily.

"I had a dream, I did."

"Oh? And pray tell us, what did you dream, Mr. Pierce?" This time the query came from Abigail.

"It was a horrid dream, Miss. A nightmare. It filled me so full of dread that I nearly gave up the chance to earn the two hundred dollars you promised," he said, upping the ante.

"And what has relieved your dread?"

"Aw, well, I knew it couldn't be real...I mean, he couldn't really..."

"He?" interjected Abigail. "Who is he?"

"That devil in the ice, of course. I dreamed it was him what sent for me, that he wanted to drink my blood now." Emily shot a glance at her sister who stood staring intently at Mr. Pierce.

"Tell me about this 'devil'," asked Abigail in a voice both

226

sweet and commanding. "What did he look like?"

"He was a frightful figure, he was, with wild hair and a wilder eye."

"Was he tall?"

"Aye, he towered over the bosun, what was a big man himself."

"Tell me what you saw, Pierce. Tell me everything." Abigail's voice was calm, but the sweet, soothing tone took on a hard edge that had a menacing undercurrent.

Emily watched as a strange look came over the face of Mandible Pierce. He looked neither at Emily nor Abigail, but rather at a scene only he could see, a scene that caused a look of terror to come over his features. His voice was low as he recounted his encounter with Baron Barlucci. "I'd gone back to the launch to fetch some line to use in lashin' the remains we'd found…those poor devils…we were going to wrap them in their blankets to transport them back to the ship. That's when I heard O'Brien scream. I turned and saw the steaming jets of thick red blood shooting from O'Brien's neck as he lay dying in the pink snow."

Emily shuddered at the description, but Abigail only looked intently at Pierce as he continued, "then from behind the shelter he came. He was dragging the bosun, his mouth fixed upon the bosun's throat. I drew my pistol and took aim at this beast of a man. He looked straight at me…clean through me…and he dropped the lifeless body of Bosun and just stood staring at me with those eyes…" Pierce closed his own eyes and covered them with his fists, "…eyes from the pit of hell, Bosun's gore smeared over his mouth. He came towards me…I took a step back. Lucky for me, I slipped on the ice. So terrified was I that I'd forgotten about the pistol in my hand, but as I fell, I must'ave squoze the trigger. The report from the gun jostled me awake from the terror and I fired the gun again and again until it was empty."

"And what of the man? What happened to him?"

"I don't know. The next thing I remember was waking up on the ship. They said I'd been senseless for days."

"But you know what happened next, Pierce. You saw it." Abigail's voice was cold and commanding.

"Please, Abigail, I think poor Mr. Pierce has…" But Abigail ignored her sister, inching closer to Pierce, her gaze burning into him.

"Yes…I was there," said Pierce, his voice taking on a dreamlike quality. He stared, wide-eyed, at Abigail as he spoke.

Emily watched as the look on Abigail's face became a mask of concentration, her eyes wide, peering at Pierce. "Tell me," she commanded, "tell me what you saw."

"As I emptied the pistol into that devil's chest, I heard a rumble. It was low at first but quickly became so loud it filled my ears and I couldn't hear my own voice screaming. I felt the freezing cold rush of air as the ice and snow came roaring down from above, covering everything before me, the bodies, the camp," he paused, "and the beast. Had I been any closer, it would have covered me as well."

Abigail moved between Pierce and Emily, the hatred on her face concealed from her sister, who said from behind her, "My God, that's dreadful. You poor man."

"Yes, you poor man," agreed Abigail, "how…horrible." She turned around, her eyes softened as she spoke to her sister, "Perhaps you should take Mr. Pierce back to his hotel on your way home. He's been through quite an ordeal," she said, barely able to control her rage at the man she knew had taken her Antonio away from her.

#

Strumm had just finished his sixth cigarette when he saw the front door open. He'd been watching the house since he followed Emily home, trying to decide his next move when, just before sunset, a visitor arrived with coach and driver, a man. Perhaps this was the elusive vampire. He decided to wait and see what developed.

The driver waited while his passenger was inside. Now, over an hour later, he watched from his hiding place as the man and Miss Drake exited the house. Miss Drake appeared to help the man into the waiting cab, it was difficult to tell as the clouds had covered the moon and from his hiding place he couldn't see clearly and wasn't sure if Miss Drake had re-entered her house. He thought perhaps she'd entered the cab with the man, but as the cab started down the drive, the door to the house opened once again. This time he clearly saw Miss Drake silhouetted in the doorway. She walked quickly around the side of the house toward the stable. After the cab exited the drive, Strumm hesitated in deciding whether to follow the man or wait for Miss Drake to reappear. His mind was made up for him when a second carriage, a trap, emerged from the drive. It was obviously Miss Drake, her hair blown by the wind. He wondered why she would choose to follow, rather than ride with her gentleman caller. Strumm took his place behind the trap, at a discreet distance, and followed Miss Drake's carriage as she followed the cab through the streets of upper Manhattan.

The three carriages moved among the sparse traffic along the light-lined streets from upper Manhattan south to the less affluent and more sparsely lit midtown area, arriving finally at the Front Street Hotel, a respectable but definitely not an upscale establishment. When he saw the cab stop, Strumm pulled up short, stopping directly beneath a street lamp to put the interior of his coach in shadow. He watched as the gentleman stepped out of the cab and the cab turned around to retrace its route through the city. It was not until the cab passed by the stationary trap that Strumm realized the trap was empty. He'd been so intently watching the gentleman who exited the cab he hadn't noticed when the trap pulled up to a darkened building and stopped that Miss Drake had moved out of the trap and into the shadows. Then he saw her step from the shadows and walk the short distance to the hotel, entering only moments after the gentleman had disappeared inside.

He lit a cigarette in anticipation of another lengthy wait, trying to fathom why they moved from meeting at her house to the hotel, and why they traveled separately. There must have been a reason, if he could only figure it out. Just as he finished his second smoke, crushing the ember onto the floorboard of his carriage, he saw Miss Drake emerge. Why she'd followed him all the way back to his hotel only to stay a mere fifteen minutes became even more a mystery to him. Perhaps he'd left something behind during his visit and she was returning it. But if that were the case, why not overtake his carriage and save herself from following all the way to his hotel. No, there must be another explanation. Strumm sat motionless, the collar of his frock coat turned up to hide his face, as the trap and Miss Drake passed by. As it did, the glow of the street light shone upon her making her lips glow an almost iridescent red against her pale skin.

Strumm waited until she'd turned around a corner before turning his carriage around and following her back to her estate. He wanted to be sure she would make no further calls tonight. In the morning he would seek out the mysterious gentleman to question him about his relationship with Miss Drake.

Chapter 23
A match and a murder...

"What are you doing, Holmes," I said as I came upon him in our room dressed in an apron wearing goggles of the kind one sees on a horseless carriage operator. I had been down in the lobby enjoying a fine Cuban cigar and reading the paper as I observed the other guests at the hotel. When I'd left, Holmes had been taking a nap, or so I'd thought, but as I think of it now, perhaps the nap was a ruse to get rid of me in order for him to work undisturbed. Scattered across the bureau were several small bottles and vials containing various chemicals.

"Ah, Watson, right on time, I've something interesting to show you." He held up two glass tubes with about an inch of purplish liquid in each. "Do you see this?"

I said, "Yes, I see it, but I'll be hornswoggled if I know what I'm looking at."

"My dear Doctor, you are looking at the last of my experiments establishing a soil match. These have the same pH values, identical phosphorus content as well as available potassium and organic material. They are the same in every detail," he said with a pride that caused me to believe he expected some congratulations, but I had none to offer.

"I'm afraid I don't understand the significance," said I.

"The significance…" he paused as he looked at me as though I'd suddenly grown a second head. But then his eyes crinkled and he laughed most boisterously, "Of course you don't, old boy, of course you don't. You don't know from where the samples were taken. That makes all the difference." He was quite excited and took me by the arm as he pointed out a small bit of earth at one end of the bureau. "This," he said, "was taken from the scene of the park murders. I scraped if off my shoes as you recall and on a whim, I retained the small amount you see before you, less that which I've tested."

"I see, but surely there must be a good many places with similar chemical composition in New York."

"Ah, similar, perhaps, and that is exactly what I thought. But while I'm not as familiar with the soils of New York neighborhoods as I am of London…"

"Oh yes, I'd nearly forgotten that monograph you wrote. What was it called again? A Cleaning Woman's Guide to London?"

Holmes glared at my little joke disapprovingly as he corrected me, "'A Treatise on the Soils and Mineral Content of London and Vicinity.' As I was saying, I'm not as familiar with the soils of New York but I reasoned I could make a study by collecting samples from nearly everyplace we've gone. There have been near matches in one test or another, but none with the exact composition as that from the park, except…" He walked to the distant end of the bureau. "…except this sample. It is too exact a match to be a coincidence."

"I see…and from where does this matching sample come?" said I with increased interest.

"This sample was collected from the mud scraper at the home of Miss Emily Drake," he announced in triumph.

"You don't mean to say you suspect Miss Drake of these horrible murders."

"Certainly not. I do, however, believe she knows the murderer and has in fact some kind of relationship with him."

"With him? You know who the murderer is?"

"I think we've both known all along, Watson. It cannot possibly be anyone other than Barlucci."

"Then you don't believe he is dead."

"I postulated as much while we were still in London. But as I have told you on more than one occasion, once you eliminate the impossible..."

"And you have eliminated the impossible?"

"Precisely."

"You mean to say you think he has visited Miss Drake and that she is helping him?"

"I know it. Didn't you notice in the corner of the parlor in which we spoke to Miss Drake there was a walking stick behind the coat rack?"

"No, I'm afraid I did not," cursing myself silently for my lack of attention to the small details that my friend habitually notices.

"Whatever remains, Watson, however improbable, must be the truth. In this case, the truth is that Barlucci is still alive and plying his murderous trade here in New York and has duped Miss Drake into assisting him?"

"My God, Holmes."

"Poor Watson, you see but fail to observe."

"Yes, so you've *observed* more times than I care to count. But what about the cane?"

"It was of Italian design, very expensive and, as you recall, Barlucci carried a cane."

"Ah, yes, the trail of blood from the tip...you followed it down Berner Street."

"Exactly. The cane in the corner of Miss Drake's parlor may have been the very same cane. The light was not good, so I could not be sure, but it suffices to say the fact it was of Italian manufacture gives a strong indication it belongs to Barlucci."

"What shall we do? We can't very well take this evidence to Detective Strumm and expect him to arrest her."

"No, no, we can't do that. I doubt Detective Strumm possesses the sophistication required to understand the significance of my little experiments here."

"Then what do we do, Holmes?"

"We observe, Watson...we observe."

#

The scene inside Room 221 was the most horrendous Strumm or Murray had ever seen, and that was saying much. If not for the hotel registry and the whale tattooed across his chest, it might have been a much more difficult job to identify Mandible Pierce as the victim. After having his throat savagely ripped out, it appeared his head was literally torn from his body and suspended on the bedpost as if on a pike. At some point one of his arms too had been ripped from his torso and tossed into a corner of the room, muscle and ligaments stretched and hanging. Both of his eyes had been plucked from their sockets and stuffed into his rectum. But for all the savagery of the scene, there was less than a tea cup full of blood anywhere in the room.

"Good God, Mylo. What do you make of this?" asked an obviously affected Murray.

"I don't quite know what to say. It's not possible that Miss Drake could have done this."

"What makes you so sure. You followed her here yerself, didn't'cha?"

"Yes, but for God's sake, Murray, look around. No woman could have done all this, not in the five minutes she spent in the hotel."

"I thought you said you waited fifteen minutes before she came out."

"Five, fifteen, what difference does it make? That little wisp of a woman could not possibly have done all this—not even if she'd had all night."

"I'll give ya'that all right, but surely she's mixed up in it, right up to her arse...every time a body shows up, there's somethin' that ties her to it."

"Now who's exaggerating...she only has a tie to this murder and the inspector's. There's nothing that ties her to the docks or the Park cases."

"My achin' arse... Nothing except the savagery and the lack of blood at all four scenes." The grizzled detective's tone showed he was now convinced all four cases were undeniably connected. Murray scratched his head under his battered homburg and said, "If I remember my arithmetics, that would be the transitive property, if you catch my meanin'."

"All right, all right...I still say she's either an innocent bystander or a victim herself."

Murray laughed, "Very well, have it your own way. But I hope you're basing that on your intuition from here," he said, pointing to Strumm's gut, "and not there," pointing lower.

Pulling Murray aside, "Very funny, but this has got to be the work of the vampire Dr. Rudalac was talkin' about."

"That, again, eh? You and that doctor friend of yours can go lookin' for vampires till bees fly backward if you've a mind to, but I'll be watching for a powerfully built man of human qualities, if inhuman habits."

Among the possessions of Mr. Pierce, Strumm found a scrivener's tool, three small bags of Shipley's Rough-Cut shag tobacco and a knife and fork inscribed with the name, 'Carney Hospital'. Strumm had Murray wire the hospital to try and get a line on Pierce and to attempt to discover his connection to Emily Drake. Although he'd found Emily to be irresistibly attractive, Strumm instinctually knew she was somehow, most probably principally, involved and that the key to solving this murder, as well as the four others, rested with her, even if he didn't want to admit it to Murray.

After completing their examination of the crime scene, Strumm commandeered a trap from one of the officers at the scene and he and Murray went directly to the home of Emily Drake.

The house was dark and quiet. Strumm knocked on the front door. No answer. They walked around to the back of the house, where they encountered a heavily locked door to what would likely be the root cellar. Murray raised his foot and was about to kick in the door when Strumm stopped him. "We can come back here later, when she comes back. It'd be difficult to explain why we'd kicked in her back door, don't you think?"

"Wouldn't be the first time," Murray said with a grunt.

"Besides, I have another address I've been meaning to run down. We'll come back here later." He didn't tell Murray that the address was one of the last entries in Inspector Andrews' notebook, and one of the few items that Andrews had failed to encode.

Technically, Strumm and Murray were off the Andrews murder case as it was not officially connected to either the Parks case, or now the Pierce case, but Strumm knew that the inspector's notebook could be the key to all three cases. What he did not know was what could possibly tie all three cases together, other than the perpetrator, other than the vampire. Were they all merely random victims of a malignant vampire? While that was certainly possible, surely, at least, the young inspector was murdered with purpose. It was nearly certain he was in pursuit of the vampire, a pursuit that had brought him all the way from England. This fact made the supposition of some of the newspapers somewhat plausible. If the newspapers were to get wind that a Scotland Yard detective had been one of the victims every newspaper in Manhattan would be running with the Jack the Ripper story in no time. Panic would almost certainly grip the city.

Strumm counted five victims thus far, the first being the dock worker they'd initially chalked up to a union warning; next was the inspector, then came the two Park cases and now, Mandible Pierce. Certainly some of these could be of no real value in finding the vampire and were mere casualties of the vampire's requirement for fresh blood, while others might be more intimately associated. Thus far he could only find a plausible motive for the inspector's murder. But Pierce had a connection to Miss Drake, having visited her on the night he was murdered. Miss Drake appeared to be the one tangible connection between the Andrews and Pierce murders. Each murder had a unique feature about it, and yet all were essentially the same. He

237

would need to ruminate on the matter, perhaps over a bit of spiced rum.

Strumm and Murray hardly spoke as they traveled along Madison Avenue. Strumm stopped the carriage just a few blocks south of the Park. 103 East 54th Street was a typical home for the area, with ornate trim and wrought iron gate across a narrow walk. It commanded the corner lot and wrought iron also adorned the main roof and corner tower.

Murray rang the bell. As they waited, Strumm surveyed the street and the convent just across the intersection. He was somewhat familiar with the convent. It had been the sisters from the Sacred Heart who were so kind in attending his wife while she lay dying in St. Vincent's, making her final hours as comfortable as possible. It was a bitter remembrance for him, one that never failed to darken his mood.

"May I help you?" The voice of a young woman snapped Strumm out of his reverie.

"Yes, Ma'am," Murray began, tipping his hat to her, "I'm Detective Murray and this is my associate Detective Sergeant Strumm…" he stopped short when he saw the stunned look on Strumm's face.

Recovering, Strumm continued, "Yes, I'm Detective Sergeant Strumm of the New York Municipal Police, Miss. We'd like to ask you a few questions, if it's not too inconvenient." Murray looked at Strumm with a bewildered expression. Strumm looked from the young woman to Murray and raised an eyebrow. His mood, only moments before dark as dung, now appeared to lift, as if by magic. Murray had no way of knowing the reason for the change was that the young woman standing before them was Emily Drake.

"Yes, Detectives, how may I help you?"

"Who is it, dear?" a voice from inside inquired.

"A detective, auntie," Emily called over her shoulder.

"Another one?"

Strumm was thrown a bit off his guard. First, he wasn't expecting to find Emily Drake at this address, and second, she was even more beautiful close up than she had appeared at a distance. Recovering his composure, "I wonder if I, er," he paused remembering his partner, "we might ask you a few questions, Miss…Miss…?

"Drake, Emily Drake." Murray's eyes widened in recognition when he heard her name.

"Miss Drake, as I said, I'd like to ask you a few questions. I'm investigating a murder."

"Oh dear. Won't you come in?" she looked around to see if her aunt's neighbors were about. "Come into the parlor, I'll get us some coffee." Emily showed Strumm into the quaint little parlor in the front of the house. "Auntie, this is Detective Strumm and Detective Murray was it?"

"That's right, Miss," Murray said, removing his hat.

"Detectives, this is my aunt, Lucie Belmont."

"It's a pleasure, Mrs. Belmont," Strumm said extending his hand.

"Thank you, Detective. Oh dear, aren't we becoming popular with you investigators of late. How may my niece and I be of service this time?" shaking his hand. "Please, sit down, we were just about to have some coffee."

"Thank you," Strumm said taking a seat and accepting a cup from Emily. Murray sat down stiffly, watching Emily closely as he took the cup from her hand. "I take it you've had another detective visit recently? May I ask on what business?"

"Well, nothing quite so morbid as a murder." She paused, "But then again..." Mrs. Belmont said, "...I guess in a way it's even more morbid now that I think of it. They were here about the theft of my niece Abigail's body."

Strumm looked at Murray. "The investigator's name wouldn't happen to be Sherlock Holmes, would it?"

"Why yes, I believe it was. He had a very handsome doctor with him too. Watson, I think his name was." She smiled as she sipped her coffee. "So, what are you investigating?"

"Detective Strumm says he's investigating a murder, auntie."

"Oh yes, that's right. Dear me, no one we know, I hope."

"That's what I'm here to find out. Anytime a person is murdered in the city, it's routine to interview relatives, acquaintances..."

"Relatives? Dear God, Detective, who has been murdered?" asked Mrs. Belmont, now visibly concerned.

"I assure you, Mrs. Belmont, the murder victim is not a relative of yours."

Fanning herself with her hand Mrs. Belmont appeared calmer as she said, "Oh, goodness, that's a relief. You gave me quite a start, Detective."

"Who is the victim, Detective?" asked Emily, raising her cup to her lips. She looked from Murray to Strumm over the rim.

"A merchant seaman, name of Mandible Pierce," Murray said. He watched Emily's eyes behind her cup of coffee. They darted back to look intently at him, but told him little.

"Ha, there you have it. We know no one of that name,

Detective, and we certainly don't consort with any merchant seamen, do we Emily."

But Emily was silent, her cup still at her lips. Quietly she placed her cup back in the saucer on the table. "I think you two should leave, Detective."

"Emily?" Aunt Lucie put her cup down and looked at Emily, her mouth agape.

"Miss Drake, I must insist…"

"You've upset my aunt, Detective. I think it would be best for you two to go."

"I can come back with a warrant, Miss Drake."

"Are you planning to arrest me, Detective?" asked Emily, raising her voice even as she rose from her chair.

Strumm hesitated. He knew he didn't have nearly enough evidence to make an arrest.

"You?" she asked, looking at Murray who set down his cup and gripped his hat with both hands. "I thought not," she said. "I'll see you both out."

"I think it only fair to tell you, Miss Drake," Strumm said on the way to the door. "You were seen entering Mr. Pierce's hotel on the night he was murdered."

Aunt Lucie followed a few paces behind. "Emily? What's he talking about? You? Visiting a seaman in his hotel? Your uncle would not approve, that is, if he were still alive."

"Preposterous, Detective," Emily said, opening the door as she tried to understand what could have happened, refusing to believe what came to mind. "Who would make such a ridiculous claim."

"I saw you, Miss Drake. I followed you from your home on East 71st Street."

241

"Oh, but that's not—" Aunt Lucie began.

"You are mistaken, Detective," Emily interrupted, motioning behind her back for her aunt to remain silent.

"Where were you last night, Miss Drake?"

She looked back at her aunt before answering. Then Emily said simply as she closed the door, "I was visiting a sick relative."

#

The ride back to the station began as quietly as the one to the address on 54th Street. About halfway to their destination Murray decided to break the silence, "Well Mylo, now what do you think about your little girl friend, eh?"

Mylo only sat, quietly brooding.

"If ya asks me, she acted guilty as sin." He wasn't sure Strumm was listening. "And you, I never saw you at such a loss for words. She gave us the bum's rush and you didn't do nothin'."

Finally, Strumm broke his silence, "What did you expect me to do, Murray? We got nothin' on her. Nothin'."

"Nothin'? You saw her go into the dead man's hotel on the night he was butchered."

"Yeah, and saw her come back out again five minutes later."

"Fifteen. Besides, she don't know you saw her leave. You could've sweated her good over that. The Mylo Strumm I know would've sweated her." Murray then mumbled to himself, "Never thought I'd see ya go soft, Mylo...never thought it."

Mylo slipped back into silence. He couldn't believe Emily Drake could have anything to do with a cold blooded murderer. Everything in his gut told him something was wrong, something didn't fit with this, but every fact seemed to point to Emily as an

242

accomplice in the murders. Mylo sat going over in his mind all the little bits of fact, each piece of evidence, trying to come up with a picture that didn't have Emily Drake with bloody hands in it. But he could not.

Chapter 24
Twin convictions...

When Abigail entered the parlor, Emily was awaiting her. "Sister, I heard you come in. I apologize for the wait. I find it so very difficult to arise before the sun is fully set."

When she heard her sister's voice, Emily turned toward her and asked, "Did you murder Mr. Pierce?" There was no pretension of politeness in her voice.

"Pierce is dead? Is that why you've been pacing incessantly this past hour? To accuse me of murder?"

"Did you kill him?"

Walking around the room Abigail picked up a fireplace poker and idly stoked the fire, sending sparks and tiny embers dancing up the flue as she contemplated how best to answer her sister. "While I can't say that I'm sorry the reprehensible Mr. Pierce is dead, I'm surprised you could think I'm capable of being responsible. Surely, someone of his ilk must have more than his share of enemies," she said. Placing the poker back in its holder she turned and looked Emily in the eye. "No, sister," she said without emotion, "I did not murder Mr. Pierce. I wasn't even aware he was dead."

Emily, who'd been holding her breath waiting for her sister's response exhaled in great relief. "Oh, Abigail," she said, her voice cracking with relieved tension, "I knew you couldn't have done it, but when the detective told me he'd seen me enter Mr. Pierce's hotel…well, I…"

"Detective? What detective?" Abigail asked, her antennae up, wondering if this new detective had any connection with Inspector Andrews, thinking perhaps she'd misjudged him.

"Detective Strumm. He came to see Aunt Lucie and me this afternoon. He told us that he followed me from here to Mr. Pierce's hotel last night, and that he saw me enter the hotel after Mr. Pierce. So I thought…"

"So you thought I must have followed you and after you departed, I went into Mr. Pierce's hotel and murdered him?"

"I didn't know who else he could have seen."

"It didn't occur to you that your Detective Strumm might have been bluffing? That he didn't see anything at all?"

"But how would he have known Mr. Pierce visited us if he hadn't been watching the house."

"Come now, Emily. Let's think it over, shall we? Put yourself in the detective's position. He is called in to investigate a heinous murder in a respectable hotel. Obviously, the first thing he would do is to question the staff and management to discover what they might know about the victim. Management would naturally tell them that the reservation was placed not by Mr. Pierce, but by a young woman, by you. You were the one who all made the arrangements. It was you who purchased his train tickets. You even arranged that the bills he accumulated were to be sent here, to this address. Isn't it logical for this Detective Strumm to assume you had a connection with Pierce? And isn't it equally logical that someone at the hotel could have seen you when you took Mr. Pierce back to his hotel? That would give him both your name and this address, as well as your presence near the scene of the murder. From that, even a dull-witted detective could put two and two together."

"I suppose the doorman might have recognized me, but who would kill poor Mr. Pierce."

"Of course the doorman saw you. He would obviously be one of the first people the detective would have questioned in investigating a murder at a hotel. As for who would kill Mr. Pierce, I'd say we wouldn't need to look further than the gin mills in which he's been spending the money you gave him. I'll wager your Detective Strumm didn't find the two hundred dollars Pierce left here with last night."

"That's true. Of course it's true." Emily looked thoughtful and said, "I should have thought of that."

"Besides, Emily, why on earth would Detective Strumm be watching this house *before* a crime had been committed?"

"I hadn't thought of that." Emily smiled as the logic of what Abigail was saying eased her concern. "You're absolutely right, Abigail, he'd have no reason at all."

"It's all too obvious he concocted the story in an effort to get you to confess to a murder you had nothing to do with. These detectives…they are quite good at taking bits and pieces of factual information and filling in the gaps to a make a complete story. If something doesn't fit their scenario, they ignore it…if there's something missing, they make it up, regardless how ridiculous the outcome."

"Or who they upset in the process." Emily laughed. "I should think they could make a steady living writing penny-dramas."

"Poor Emily, you've been the victim of a cruel police trick. First, he throws you off guard by saying he has the evidence on you, then invites you to confess. I'm told it's a common piece of police subterfuge."

"Oh, poor Abigail. I'm so sorry. I nearly accused you…"

Abigail put her arm around her sister, "There, there, sister. I know my present condition is strange to you, but…"

"Yes, it's just, well, it's just that when you first heard of the fate of the *Animus Lacuna* you showed such a fit of temper the likes of which were so unlike, so foreign to the sister I know…"

"It's true, my condition has put my nerves off balance a bit," she said turning away from Emily. "But a show of temper, even violent temper, is a far cry from a cold, calculated murder."

"Yes, of course…I see that now."

Turning back to face her sister, she said, "I'm glad. I don't wish to be rude, dear, but you should probably leave now. I'm expecting Dr. Tremaine this evening and it wouldn't do for him to see us together."

"Of course, sister," said Emily as she pulled on her coat and pinned her hat. She looked at Abigail with earnest eyes, "Can you ever forgive me for doubting you, sister?"

"Of course, Emily. After all, we're sisters, and sisters always forgive.

#

The past four days had been absolute torture for Alan Tremaine. While he attended the conference in Baltimore, representing the hospital, he'd been thinking of little else beside the choice Julia had given him.

He hadn't told Julia the whole truth concerning the baron and his unusual powers as he'd come to know and witness them; he didn't wish to frighten her. In fact he had downplayed the disease to Julia, explaining it as a disorder that affected the metabolism making normal sustenance impossible, creating a need to subsist on blood and blood alone. He told her that its very rarity caused folktales and superstition to arise around it. What he failed to mention was the lack of a pulse or heartbeat, saying only that the victim's circulation was restricted, causing their body temperature in the extremities to be lower than normal. He also failed to mention the preternatural senses and the greatly enhanced physical strength characteristic to the condition. Instead, he told her that the baron was hypersensitive to sunlight and rarely ventured out in the light of day. He knew if she was aware of the truth she would be horrified. Even his truncated description of what he termed "clinical vampirism" was met by her with disbelief. He had hoped to gain the support of Julia's father shortly after he and Julia were married, but when Alan mentioned the disease and his wish to find a cure to him, he was met with outright derision.

So now Julia had given him an ultimatum. But this ultimatum was more far-reaching than Julia could possibly know. If he chose to continue his research for a cure, he would lose the love of his life, the only woman he had ever loved. Along with losing her, he would lose his career, his reputation—Julia's father would see to that—not to mention his standing in the community, and any hope he ever had of the kind of fame and fortune of which he'd always dreamed.

Those dreams now seemed insignificant in comparison to reality. If he chose the path his heart now truly desired, the alternative would be exponentially worse. A vampire, Alan knew, was not a creature to be crossed lightly.

The baron, he knew, had been ruthless in his pursuit for a cure, but there was always a bare trace of humanity. What he'd seen in Abigail was different, frighteningly so. The baron had lived with his affliction for centuries. Although the powers and acuteness of senses it brought with it were astounding, Dr. Tremaine was aware that the baron had grown tired—tired of existing at the edge of reality, tired of being forever wary of being discovered, tired of the senseless slaughter that purchased his immortality.

Abigail, on the other hand, had only recently awakened to her new existence, she'd been a vampire mere weeks. But Abigail was quickly adapting to her new reality, thriving on it, it seemed. As Dr. Tremaine had seen, she was already adept at intimidation, a talent that hardly seemed probable in the fragile young girl he'd remembered from London. He remembered how she'd clung to her uncle's side as though afraid if she let go she'd be trampled underfoot in the Grand Ballroom on the night they both met the baron. Now she seemed every bit the baron's equal in confidence—confident in her own security and confident in her ability to get whatever she wanted. Unlike the baron's, it was a cold, ruthless confidence, one not tempered with conscience or pity.

And now she wanted Dr. Tremaine to find a cure for vampirism. His own desire to find that cure was, at first, fueled by an overpowering sense of ambition. Now fear of Abigail's wrath drove him forward as much as ambition, perhaps more. He feared for his life if he failed. But more than that, he feared for Julia. What would become of her? What might Abigail do to Julia should he refuse her will? It was too terrible to contemplate.

As the cab took him from the train station to his home, Alan was torn, still unable to make up his mind. He didn't wish to lose Julia, but he didn't dare deny Abigail and risk losing Julia in a much more final way.

As he retrieved his bags from the cab's boot, he decided what he must do. Walking up to his front door, he looked more a man walking to the gallows than a newlywed returning to his bride. He decided that he would have to sit Julia down and make a clean breast of everything. He must tell her the complete truth about the baron and his ailment, and about Abigail. He must convince her that his only hope, their only hope, was to cure Abigail and the baron, should he materialize as Abigail was convinced he would; then and only then would they cease to be a threat.

"Julia," he called as he opened the front door. The first floor of the house appeared deserted. "Julia," he called again as he looked first in the parlor and then in his study. As he returned to the entryway Annie appeared at the top of the stairs.

"Oh, Doctor Tremaine," she said, and then she burst into tears.

"Annie, what is it? What's happened? Where's Julia?" He ascended the stairs two at a time until he confronted Annie, taking her arms in his hands forcing her to look at him. "Is she all right?" The look on Annie's face told him she was not. Letting go of Annie's arms, he sprinted the short distance to the bedroom. Julia was lying upon the bed, as pale as the sheets in which she was wrapped. Her mother sat beside her, holding Julia's frail, near lifeless hand. "Julia," he said softly, staring in disbelief.

"Thank God you're home, Alan," Mrs. Cabot said as she turned upon hearing his voice.

"Is she…?"

"No…only asleep," she said as she placed Julia's hand beneath the sheet.

"What's happened to her?"

"We aren't sure. I saw her the day you left for Baltimore. She

250

visited with her father and me in the evening and was in an exceptionally good mood. She appeared to me to be completely at peace with herself, and happy, happier than I'd seen her in a long time."

Alan immediately thought that perhaps she'd been putting on a front for her parents.

"Then the next day I came by to see her. I thought perhaps we would go to lunch together. When I arrived, she was lying on the divan in the parlor, just lying there. Annie said she arose complaining of fatigue and had barely moved all morning from that spot. I put her to bed at once and summoned her father. He said she was showing signs of anemia, and recommended she eat something, but she could keep nothing down. He prescribed a powder to be mixed into her milk, something with iron I believe. She drank it down and after a while seemed to perk up a bit. I asked Annie to stay with her overnight and make sure she stayed warm."

"Why didn't you wire me? I'd have come home at once."

"Julia wouldn't hear of it. She insisted she would be all right, that she only wanted a good night's sleep. But she made me promise not to send for you."

"Still, you should have let me know. Did she give you any clue as to what could be wrong?"

"I know it seems silly, but she complained of having bad dreams."

"Bad dreams?" Tremaine felt certain he was probably the source of those dreams. "Did she tell you what was troubling her? Did she tell you about the dreams?"

"No, she said she couldn't remember the dreams once she awoke."

"And she is no better today?"

"No. Annie slept last night just down the hall in the guest room. She said she was awakened in the night by voices."

"Voices? But who was here?"

"That's just it. They were alone. Annie became alarmed and went to Julia, thinking perhaps she'd had a dream or nightmare. When she opened the door, she said the room was frigid and the window unlatched. Annie swears she checked every latch in the house, most especially Julia's window latches, and everything was tightly locked up before she went to bed. Julia must have been sleep walking and opened the window herself."

At the mention of her name, Julia stirred in the bed. "Alan...?" she said as her eyes tried to focus on who was in the room.

Alan knelt down beside her, taking her hand from beneath the sheets, "I'm here, my love."

"Alan, I'm so sorry...I've been so foolish."

"Shhh...don't. It's all right. Whatever it is, it's all right."

"No, I...I..." she struggled to sit up in bed and with some effort and Alan's assistance, she propped herself up on the pillows behind her. "I have to speak to you, Alan...I have to tell you..."

Julia looked past him at her mother, "Mother, I need to speak to Alan alone. Would you mind leaving us for just a moment?"

Mrs. Cabot looked from her daughter to her son-in-law, "Are you sure, dear? I'm sure Alan doesn't mind..."

"Please, Mother, I need to speak to my husband. It's all right." Her voice was quiet but determined.

"Of course, dear," Mrs. Cabot answered, though obviously uneasy. "I'll just be outside."

After Mrs. Cabot closed the door, Alan asked, "What is it,

Julia? What's wrong?"

Julia took a labored breath, "Oh, Alan, I've been absolutely miserable since you left. I was horrid to you."

"No, Julia, you were right…those things you said…"

"But Alan, I'm your wife. I should never have sent you away like that, especially not now. I never should have…"

"It's all right, my darling. The important thing is I'm back."

"But I was so unfair, telling you that you must choose either your work or me. You must think me the worst kind of beast." She pouted and for just a moment looked her old self again.

"Of course I don't, but none of that's important now, Julia. What is important is for you to get well. We'll discuss it all when you are better."

"But don't you see? I'm ill because I was such a beast to you. Say you'll forgive me and I'm sure I'll be better," she said with a weak smile.

"There's nothing to forgive."

"Then you'll continue your work?" she asked with an almost desperate intensity.

"You mean…you mean you want me to continue?" he asked her. He thought perhaps he'd misunderstood.

"Oh yes, you must…you must. I had no right, Alan, no right at all, don't you see…?"

Alan could see she was becoming quite agitated. "Very well," he said, "I shall continue, just as before. If you are sure that is what you want."

"Yes. Yes it is. Do you promise?" she asked, smiling up at him like a little girl.

It made him happy to see her smile, even though it didn't

appear to have all of its former sparkle. "I promise," he said.

She sighed deeply as in great relief. "That makes me very happy. Now…" she yawned covering her mouth with the back of her hand, "…I'm a bit tired." She slid down beneath the sheets and closed her eyes. "I think I'll rest a little," she said and he could tell she was already asleep.

He patted her hand and placed it back beneath the sheet, leaving her to rest peacefully.

Alan went downstairs to the parlor where Mrs. Cabot was waiting for him. Annie had recovered her wits enough to make coffee and Mrs. Cabot was having a cup. "She's sleeping peacefully now," Alan told her.

"Thank goodness." As he took a seat beside Mrs. Cabot's, she poured him a cup of coffee.

"Mrs. Cabot, you say she became ill the day after I left?"

"Yes. I thought at first it was only morning sickness."

"Morning sickness? Why would…"

"Julia didn't tell you she's pregnant?"

"No. I had no idea. When did you find out?"

"She told her father and me the same day you left. Of course I knew when I saw her at Christmas dinner, but I assumed then she hadn't had a chance to tell you, what with you spending so much time at the hospital," she brought her cup up to her lips as she said this and peered at him over the rim.

"Yes. I've been such a fool," he said, staring into his own cup. "And you say she was taken ill the next day?"

"Yes, but today is much worse. I told her I would look in on her first thing. When I arrived, she was so weak she couldn't get out of bed. I didn't wish to say anything in front of Julia, and I don't wish to intrude, Alan, but you should know that Julia's been terribly upset since you left, though she didn't say anything to me until yesterday."

"Yes, I know. That's what Julia wanted to talk to me about just now. I think she'll be all right now." He took a sip of coffee. "Did she tell you what was troubling her?"

"Only that the two of you had a tiff and she was desperately afraid of losing you."

"Losing me? That's ridiculous, Mrs. Cabot," he said but he knew his face was less convincing than his words.

"Alan, forgive a mother-in-law's intrusion, but is there…" Mrs. Cabot averted her eyes and sipped her coffee. "I'm sorry, I don't mean to pry."

"Is there what, Mrs. Cabot? Is there another woman?"

Mrs. Cabot placed her cup down on the table, looked Alan directly in the eye and said in clipped syllables, "Yes. Is there another woman, Alan?"

"Of course not. Please, Mrs. Cabot, I assure you there could never be anyone but Julia for me," he said. This time his face was more convincing.

"Well, I'm very glad to hear you say it, Alan, and I'm sorry to have to ask, but your actions recently have led us all to wonder. Julia too I'm sure, though she's never said as much."

"Exactly what actions are you referring to? I don't understand. What has Julia told you?"

"Not much, I'm afraid. She's said only that you've been working too hard. In fact, she asked my husband if he could arrange for you to not have to work quite so hard or such long hours."

"I see," Alan said, realizing he hadn't been quite as clever about concealing his absences from the hospital while working on his experiments at Abigail's as he thought. Apparently, they were common knowledge.

"So you can well imagine my husband's surprise. He thought that he was being quite generous in looking the other way at your meager attendance, marking it up to a newlywed's enthusiasm for his new bride."

"Yes, Julia told me."

"He even told me that once the holidays were past, he'd have to speak to you. So when he told Julia this, I would imagine it quite naturally caused her concern. It certainly did her father and me." She sipped her coffee before asking matter-of-factly, "Tell me, what has been stealing your time, Alan?"

"Mrs. Cabot, I assure you—"

"I wouldn't normally be so bold, Alan," she interrupted, and then lifted her eyes in reference to Julia lying in bed above them.

"Very well. I expect in view of present circumstances you have a right to be curious." He placed his cup down in the saucer on the table. "Mrs. Cabot, I am engaged in trying to find a cure for a rare blood disorder. A wealthy benefactor has set up an independent lab and I've been asked to collaborate on a cure for his ailing son. Once I heard the facts of the case, I could hardly refuse. It's very similar to another case on which I'd worked and achieved some success." Retrieving his cup from the saucer, he drew it to his lips, wondering how convincing he was and feeling miserable for the lie.

"But why didn't you just come to my husband and explain? I'm sure he'd have been sympathetic. It sounds like the kind of thing with which the hospital would be most interested in being associated."

"I wanted to, truly I did. But as I said, the man who'd engaged me is very wealthy. What I didn't tell you is that he is also a well known public figure, a man of great power and influence. He insisted on complete secrecy. Should his enemies discover his son is ill, he was afraid they might use the information to their advantage. It's all very political, I'm afraid."

"Oh dear, I see."

He hated having to deceive Julia's mother, but under the circumstances he had no other choice. If he mentioned vampirism he knew Dr. Cabot would have him sacked and divorced before he could spit. And now, with his child to think of, it was more important than ever to cure Abigail Drake quickly to remove her as a threat to his family. "I didn't tell Julia because I know she would have insisted I tell your husband. Apparently I wasn't as clever as I thought and she got a contrary notion in her head about our marriage. I think she's been worried and that's why she's…she's ill."

"Julia has always been a very sensitive child. Once she found a sparrow that had broken its wing. She was convinced she could nurse it back to health. When it died, she was in bed for a month," taking another sip of her coffee. "A broken wing is a small matter compared to a broken marriage. A worry like that can take quite a toll on a woman's nerves, Alan, believe me." With a more hopeful tone, she added, "But I'm sure now that you're home and can assure her she has no need to worry, she'll get better, and quickly."

"I hope you are right, Mrs. Cabot. Truly I do."

After Mrs. Cabot left, Tremaine went back in check on Julia. He pulled the bed sheets up around her, tucking her in. Julia sighed, closed her eyes, and then turned her head, falling into a deep sleep. At first, in the darkened room, he wasn't sure he saw anything at all, just a shadow, perhaps. But to be certain, he took a candle from the dressing table and stepped into the hallway where he lighted it from the gas lamp. Alan went back to Julia's bed, sitting down on the edge, and held the candle closer. There, on the side of Julia's throat, he saw two neat little tear-drop-shaped holes, two holes that wept a thick reddish plasma—the mark of a vampire.

When Dr. Tremaine left England a lifetime ago he'd taken, at the baron's insistence, numerous volumes from Barlucci's personal library on vampirism. In practical terms Dr. Alan Tremaine knew more about vampires and vampirism than any man alive. Still, as he left Julia to rest, ensuring her windows were bolted tightly shut, he went into his study to re-read sections from those volumes dealing with the victims of vampires and victimization. In several references he found passages suggesting that victims who die of a vampire's bite become vampires themselves. These the baron had lined through the entire passage writing in the margins 'ridiculous' or 'nonsense' or some other dismissive. What he did not line out were passages saying that the victim, once bitten, comes under the vampire's power, becoming a slave to the will of the vampire, yearning for the vampire to bite them again. As he read each passage confirming his worst fears he became increasingly enraged. When he'd closed the last volume, *Carmilla*, he knew what he had to do.

Chapter 25
Secret confidences...

"Come in," Holmes said in reply to the second knock on the door. When no one entered, I crossed the room and opened it myself. There, standing outside, with a look of hesitancy on his face that resembled embarrassment was Detective Murray.

"To what do we owe the pleasure of this visit, Detective Murray?" said I with perhaps too much formality considering the look on his face.

"I come to see Mr. Holmes, is he in?" Holmes was sitting in a straight backed chair at a small desk just out of Detective Murray's view, reading newspaper accounts of the now five murders.

"Yes, Detective, I am in, and soon so shall you be. Watson, please show the detective in."

I acceded to my friend's request and allowed Detective Murray to pass by me into our inner sanctum. "You can take that chair, there," said I, indicating the overstuffed chair by the fireplace.

"Thank you, Doctor," he said in a quiet and, what I thought, a humble voice.

"Now, Detective Murray," Holmes said turning towards our visitor as he lighted his pipe and blew a large cloud of smoke in the space between them. "What brings you here without your partner, Detective Strumm?"

"I'm catchin' the night train to Boston, but I wanted to speak to you first. He wouldn't like it at all if he knew I was here, and if you tell 'im, I'll call ya a liar to yer face."

"Come now," said I, "you must have cause to come and if so, why would you wish to deny it?"

"Look, first you gotta understand a few things."

"Go on," Holmes said.

"Mylo and me, er, Detective Strumm and me go back a long piece. We been partners ever since he got kicked outta—" He paused and looked as though he obviously had not meant to use that particular phraseology, "...ever since he came to the First Precinct, after his wife was murdered."

Holmes said, "We'd heard she was hit by a train in a tragic accident."

"That weren't no accident," Detective Murray said, his voice rising and becoming tough-edged, like the blade of an Elcho bayonet. "It nearly ruint Mylo. He ain't been the same man since."

"Yes, we understand he's become addicted to the bottle. But you didn't come here to tell us of Strumm's shortcomings. They're quite obvious on their own," Holmes said in a more mean-spirited way than I can ever recall hearing. But it didn't appear to have the desired effect. Murray simply sat in the chair, twirling his hat between his meaty hands.

"Don't I know it, Mr. Holmes. But if you'd a'known Mylo before...well, I think you an' he'd be good friends...sorta' kindred spirits, so ta' speak."

"Oh? How so, Detective?" Holmes said without looking at him.

"I know what you'se'r thinkin', 'big dumb cop like Murray, what's he know'. But I been readin' up on you, Mr. Holmes. My cousin runs a periodical shop and when I mentioned your name to him, he gave me a stack of the *The Strand* magazines. It was like I was readin' about the old Mylo, the Mylo from before."

The look on Holmes face went through a metamorphosis from one of disdain to one of genuine interest, if not compassion, almost as if he'd suddenly remembered he too was human.

I said, "I understand," partly because I didn't think Holmes was going to say anything and something definitely needed to be said, and partly because I did understand, perfectly. I'd spent many hours alone contemplating what my own loss would be, let alone the world's loss, should Sherlock Holmes addiction to stimulants and opiates wreck what I often thought was his frail constitution. I also contemplated my own part in aiding and abetting his loathsome habits. God knows I spent many a sleepless night mulling it over in my thoughts and prayers.

The big man looked at me with what I thought were the most gently intelligent eyes I'd ever seen, eyes I'd barely noticed before. "Thank you, Doctor. It ain't easy for me comin' here like this. I...I feel like a bit of a traitor. But, Mylo's my friend and I can see he's lettin' his feelings cloud his judgment."

"Nonsense," Holmes said. "It's only natural for a true friend to want his partner to be understood rather than misunderstood." His voice had softened and lost some of the rancor it formerly contained.

Murray's eyebrows lifted a bit as he said, "Oh, it ain't that, it's…it's what I come to tell ya…what Mylo is chasin' and what he's ignorin' and what that damned fool Rudlac's put it in his head."

"Please, take your time and explain. Do you mean what line they are taking concerning the murders?"

"Yes, yes, the murders." He seemed quite agitated so I got him a glass of water to calm him. "Thanks."

"Now, then, take it easy and tell us what's on your mind, what is Detective Strumm investigating in relation to these murders. I take it he's come to the conclusion, as I have, that they are all related, all committed by the same fiend."

"Yes, except…that Drake girl, she's mixed up with this thing up to her bustle, but Mylo's been makin' allowances for her, how she couldn't be the one. That's easy enough t'see but it don't mean she ain't involved."

"Certainly not; as an accomplice, you mean," Holmes gave him an agreeing nod.

Yeah, and, well, you know how there ain't been hardly no blood at any of the murder sites?"

"Yes, we are aware."

"Well, at first I figured the bodies was moved after they was murdered. At least up 'till the parks case, anyway. But I never had an idea that…" Murray suddenly went silent, examining the band on his hat.

"Come on, Murray, you didn't come here tonight to stop now. Tell us what Strumm is up to."

Murray looked first at me, then at Holmes. Suddenly he blurted out, "He thinks he's after a vampire."

There was a stunned silence in the room. After a moment, I laughed and said, "A vampire? Poppycock. That's absolutely ridiculous."

"Yeah, that's exactly what I tole 'em. A vampire...that's crazy, I says. But Mylo and Rudlac, they both are dead-right convinced of it."

"That's the most laughable, the most preposterous thing I've ever heard of, eh Holmes?" said I, thinking back to the related case we'd so recently been involved in. "Eh, Holmes?" I said once again. But Holmes just sat puffing on his pipe, his face frozen in a pensive stare.

#

Strumm could see the warm glow of a fire in the window of Emily Drake's house as he approached. The snow that had fallen glistened as the moon shone between the clouds. It crunched beneath his heavy boots as he walked from his trap to the door, fingering the piece of lace he carried in his pocket. He listened before knocking, thinking he'd heard the muffled sound of raised voices, but then nothing. He knocked. He could hear no movement inside as he waited. After what must have been a full minute or more Emily Drake opened the door a crack and peered out.

"Yes?" she said.

Strumm removed his hat and was immediately lost in her eyes. They seemed so deep with an almost aqua quality even more striking than they had appeared before, if that were possible.

"Detective Strumm? May I help you?"

"I'm sorry to call on you at this hour," he said after he'd regained his voice. "I just have a few more questions, if you don't mind. May I come in, or is it too inconvenient." He scanned what little of the room behind her he could see remembering his impression of voices and wondering if Miss Drake might have other company.

Miss Drake looked quickly behind her into a corner of the room Strumm could not see before answering, "Of course, Detective, please come in."

"Are you sure I'm not interrupting anything?"

"Interrupting? No, not at all, why do you ask?"

"You'll forgive me, but as I arrived, I thought I heard voices," he said, watching her face, looking for any trace of apprehension. Those eyes, he thought, my God, they're beautiful, they're like…then he snapped himself out of it. He was here on official business and despite her beauty and grace, she was suspected of being involved in a series of murders, though as he looked at her gentle features and graceful movements, he could not imagine this creature could be involved in anything so heinous as murder.

"Oh, dear, I do sometimes mutter to myself, but as you can see, Detective, I'm quite alone," she said, her delicate hand extended in a sweeping movement indicating the empty room. "Please, let me take your coat. Make yourself comfortable by the fire." He handed her his coat and hat, which she hung on an empty coat rack by the door.

Strumm found a seat on the canapé by the fire. Miss Drake sat close to his left, just a bit further from the fire, on the matching chair. "Good, then. Now, Miss Drake, I just wanted to ask you some questions that we didn't," he cleared his throat, "have time to get to when my partner and I spoke to you at your aunt's."

"Yes, Detective, and I owe you an explanation," she said in voice as gentle as an evening snowfall. "My aunt, you see…well, how shall I put this? My aunt is a bit delicate of mind. My uncle passed away a little over a year ago and she took it very hard."

"I'm sorry to hear that."

"Thank you. I wouldn't burden you with that bit of knowledge except that since his passing, Auntie's been a bit…well, sometimes she gets…"

"Confused?" he offered.

"Yes, confused, that's it exactly," she smiled. He was pleased that he'd shown both compassion and understanding. It had been some time since he'd practiced either. "When she gets…confused…she also gets upset, and I, well I only wanted…"

"You only wanted to spare your aunt any embarrassment or agitation, isn't that right?"

"Why, yes, Detective. You're very understanding." She reached out and touched his hand. "Thank you."

Strumm looked down at the delicate hand touching his and thought immediately how much it reminded him of his dear, sweet, Millie. He looked from her hand up into her face, the guileless face of an angel he thought, how could she have anything to do with murder. But he had come here to discuss the things that made her appear deeply involved in these crimes, and he had to do it, no matter his personal feelings, feelings that were growing each time he saw her. He reached within his jacket pocket and held the piece of lace within it. It had been so long since he'd had any feelings at all. His hand hesitated.

Snapping back to himself he said, as gently as he could, "But Miss Drake, you must realize there are certain things that have come to light…things that bear on not only the murder of Mandible Pierce, but also that of Inspector Walter Andrews of Scotland Yard."

"I don't understand, Detective. I told you I don't know anyone by that name. Perhaps you are mistaken," she said, her voice calm and soothing, like velvet. No, he had to put his feelings aside. He wished he hadn't opened that bottle of vodka before coming here tonight. He needed all his wits about him, especially now, especially at this time of year.

"I suppose he might've given you a different name, perhaps, but yours was in his notebook, Miss Drake." It was too much for him. He knew he had to leave. He was making excuses for her now, giving her imagined alibis instead of pursuing the truth as he was trained to do.

"What's wrong, Detective?" she said. He looked at her, there was a look of genuine concern in her eyes. Or was it something more?

"I'm sorry, Miss Drake, please excuse me," he said as he got to his feet. "I shouldn't have come here like this." She followed him to the door.

"It's perfectly all right, Detective," she said, as she moved between him and the coat rack. "I'm glad you did."

"No...no, I should go." He stretched out his hand for his coat, but she placed her hand on his arm, staying his reach. Unable to resist any longer, he pulled her to him and kissed her lips gently but deep, the scent of her body filling him with desire.

#

It was after midnight when Strumm returned to the precinct house to see Dr. Rudalac. "Rudy, don't you ever sleep?" Mylo asked, announcing his entrance into the morgue.

Dr. Rudalac didn't at first appear to hear Strumm as he stood examining a tissue slide in great detail under a microscope. But then he said in an annoyed tone, "If I did, Detective, who would you..." He stopped as he focused on Mylo, the scowl he'd initially had on his face vanished. "Oh..." he said, startled. "It's you, Mylo my boy. I'm sorry; I mistook you for that fool Detective Wilson. He wants me to prove that poor devil there was poisoned," gesturing toward the cadaver that he had sectioned for the tissue sample he'd been examining when Mylo came in. "But to answer your question, I find that the older I get, the less sleep I require." He looked around expectantly, "Where's your friend, 'doubting Murphy'?"

"Murray," he said, smiling at Dr. Rudalac's obvious disapproval of his powerful partner. "And don't be so hard on him. He's saved my bacon more times than I care to mention, I'll tell you."

"Well, I suppose if I were in his place, I'd have my doubts too. He must think I'm an old fool and you're a young one, chasing vampires. Has he asked to be taken off the case?"

"No. As a matter of fact, he's on a train to Boston to interview the nurses at the Carney Hospital. Our latest victim, Mr. Pierce was a recent guest."

"Mr. Pierce. Yes, that was a particularly nasty job. He must have crossed the vampire in some distinctly personal way. That murder went well beyond satisfying a hunger. Our vampire appeared to be settling some score." He looked up at Mylo, studying his face, scanning his features with the practiced gaze of an alert investigator. "What is it, Mylo? Is something troubling you?"

Strumm sighed and gave a weary grin, "How is it you always know, Rudy? Every time I'm troubled with something, you seem to…there are times I'd swear you can read minds." He looked at Dr. Rudalac and as he reached inside his jacket, he continued, "I'm afraid I've been holding out on you, Rudy, and that Holmes character too." Strumm said solemnly.

"Oh, really? How so?"

"Look at this," Strumm said, holding several worn pages. "I tore them out of that Andrews guy's notebook before I gave it over to

Holmes."

"What's this?"

"I knew I'd have to give up the notebook at some point. Captain Cortright and Murray both knew about it, so I took these pages out. The answer to this riddle is in them, I'm sure of it."

"So, these were the few loose papers, eh?" He fanned the pages with his thumb. "I'm confused, Mylo. Why wouldn't you think it important to share this knowledge with me?" He raised his eyebrow asking, "Does Murray know about the pages?"

"No," he said shamefacedly. "I think the inspector may have been onto this vampire character and paid the price for his trouble. I haven't said anything about it till now because I wanted to study it a bit, first. But after the Pierce murder..."

"What makes you believe the inspector was aware of the vampire, Mylo."

"Well, for one thing, there's this," he said pointing to a page in the notebook that had the word written in capital letters with a question mark after it. "At first I thought like Murray, that 'Oh yeah, sure, a vampire.' But then I began to examine the case from the perspective of 'What if it were a possibility.' Once I did that, a lot of the things about the case that didn't make sense at first began to fit. That's when I first mentioned the possibility to you, to get your reaction."

"Yes, I see, and now we are investigating with that in mind. But what else?"

"Take a look for yourself. A lot of what's in the notebook is in code. I've made a kind of study of codes over the years. It's good mental exercise, relaxing, and this code is a good one. I've been unable to crack it as yet."

"So, the late inspector writes his notes in code. What does that prove?"

"It doesn't prove nothing, I suppose, but much of what's in the notebook is from cases back in London and very little of that is in code. It's only since he's been in America that he's used the code routinely. So, I figured that if I was a foreigner and suddenly found myself investigating a vampire in a country where no one knew me, I might want to keep a lid on it too, just in case it fell into the hands of someone who might think I had squirrels in the attic, so to speak."

"I see. I suppose you could be right, Detective."

"Yes, I'm sure whatever he's encoded here will help us solve the mystery, and clear Emily, but I haven't gotten anywhere in breaking the code. I thought I was pretty good at codes before this. Would you like to have a look?"

"So it's Emily now, is it?" Dr. Rudulac thumbed through the notebook. "Yes, I see." He noted on the pages were written a series of letters, in groups of five:

"HECYY   QKEBI   GVMSP   BURKO   HIECI
PSLKR FVROQ
DIKKF OVCYM QTINI QTE"

"Have you tried using substitution in breaking it?"

"Of course, that was my first thought."

"Caesarean?" offered the doctor.

"No, the method for cracking a Caesarean code is pretty much the same method as substitution. It doesn't fit this code. This is something else, something I've never seen before."

"I see…" Dr. Rudalac flipped through the remaining pages of the notebook, and then he looked at Mylo thoughtfully, "Hmmm…have you ever heard the name Giovan Belaso?"

"No, the name doesn't sound familiar to me. I don't think I've heard it before. Is it someone you know, someone who might help us with the code?"

"Yes, perhaps he might, but no, I don't know him, at least not personally. He's been dead for three hundred years." He laughed. "He was an exceptional mathematician and cryptologist in the Italy of the sixteenth century." He paused, and then as if another thought suddenly came to mind, "Perhaps you have heard of Vigenére?"

"Hmm…yes, it certainly sounds familiar. Another cryptologist?"

Dr. Rudalac shrugged, "So they say. Vigenére is the name associated with the cipher developed by Belaso, through a most detestable miscarriage of justice." He looked as though the name left a bitter taste in his mouth. "But that story is for another time, perhaps. The cipher, though, was considered an unbreakable code for many years. It has been used for diplomatic communications as well to carry military plans during time of war. In practice it was used with a device invented by Leon Battista Alberti, the Alberti code wheel."

"Yes, I'm very familiar with the wheel and its use in encoding substitution ciphers, but I told you, this code doesn't follow the form of either letter substitution or alphabetical offset."

"Perhaps it does, if you know what to look for."

"What do you mean?"

"Belaso used a key word in which to encode his messages, changing, or shifting the alphabet by an amount determined by the number of each letter in the keyword. Essentially, if his key word was seven letters long, he used a repeating combination of seven separate shifted alphabets, complicating the substitution code by a factor of seven."

"Then unless you have the key word, it is unbreakable. It's hopeless."

"I'm surprised at you. That doesn't sound like the Mylo I know. Perhaps you aren't the gifted detective I'd always thought you were after all," Dr. Rudalac said turning his back on Strumm.

"Aw, come on Rudy, you know what I've been through. Don't you start treating me like a has-been, a, a washed up drunk."

"Bat guano. I know better than that. You may have become a bit lazy but you still have one of the finest investigative minds I've ever seen, logical and deliberate. Just because you've spent the past few years trying your best to pickle it hasn't changed things. You certainly got to the bottom of the Knickerbocker murders quickly enough."

"That was an easy case, Rudy, not like this. There were so many clues..."

"Bah...clues are where you find them. Does that sound familiar? You told me that yourself, Mylo. Don't you remember?"

"That was a different time, Rudy...and I was a different man."

"Nonsense."

"But Rudy, the only clues in this case have all led me to Miss Drake. She's certainly not the murderer and I'm going to prove it."

"What makes you so sure, Mylo? Her pretty face?"

"I never told you she was pretty."

"You didn't have to. I can see it in your eyes whenever you mention her. I imagine it's why she's not under arrest right now."

Mylo stood silent, knowing that even with his back turned Dr. Rudalac could see right through him.

"So, Detective...my advice to you is, detect," Dr. Rudalac said, once again facing Strumm, cleaning the lens of his glasses on his tie. "I've given you two names, Mylo. And I'll give you just one more. Kasiski."

"Kasiski? Who is Kasiski?"

"The man who can provide you with the answer to your code."

"Where do I find him?"

"That's easy. You will find him in the library."

Chapter 26
Revelation and retreat...

Built in 1854 as a free reference library funded by the will of John Jacob Astor, the Astor Library stood at 425 Lafayette Street in lower Manhattan. Within its three stories were more than 200,000 books on topics ranging from ancient history to transcendentalism. It was the logical choice to research cryptography and indeed contained a section dedicated to the topic.

Strumm spent most of the afternoon following his visit to Dr. Rudalac perusing the volumes of books written on the subject in the central main floor of the library. Normally it takes a reservation and a pass to gain entry and the books are never loaned, but Strumm had solved a case involving the theft of several rare hand-scribed copies of the Bible some years before and had enjoyed the favor of Superintendent George Henry Moore ever since. On more than one occasion he had taken advantage of this relationship to gain immediate access to the library's treasures.

Today, he read and re-read the descriptions of Alberti's wheel, Vigenére's cipher (he found no reference to Belaso) and discovered that Kasiski, a major in the polish infantry, devised a method for discovering the length of the key word to the cipher, a discovery that was key to decoding the cipher. Painstakingly Strumm copied the passages he thought he would need, as borrowing the volumes in which the descriptions were found was forbidden, even for a friend of the Superintendent.

On his way back to his apartment, knowing he was in for a long night, Strumm stopped to purchase two packages of Old Judge cigarettes. He stopped on the corner near his apartment and gave the newsboy there the trading cards from the cigarettes. "Here you go, Richie," he said, handing the boy the cards.

"Thanks, Detective. Yowza, King Kelly."

"I didn't know you were a 'Beaneater' fan, Richie," he said.

"Not me, but Billy Thompkins is nutters for 'em and he's got a Tim Keefe I'm ripe for and this should get it from him if nothin' will. Thanks, again."

"Sure, kid."

When he got back to his apartment, he fashioned a crude version of Alberti's wheel from two circular pieces of stiff butcher's paper, one slightly smaller in diameter than the other. He settled in at a small table in his kitchen with several other pieces of paper to work on the code. Strumm first set to work applying Kasiski's method for determining the length of the code's keyword, the first step to breaking a poly-alphabetic code. Kasiski reasoned that if a message were sufficiently long there would appear segments that would repeat at some multiple of the key word length. Once the length of the keyword was determined, it should be a relatively simple task to decode the message by the same method used to decode the simpler letter substitution or alphabetic shift ciphers.

Taking the longest message, he underlined the repeated segments of two or more letters, counting the distance between them.

WIAS PRI<u>B</u> <u>Y</u>HB<u>K</u> <u>H</u>SII CIDX HIEN AL<u>KH</u>

LPRF DVIV JROQ
DZNC XZFM SRHI SKRG RYYY QX<u>BY</u>
CZYA DGRL LNLD MELI
FFMO SI<u>KH</u> OFOF ONMU ZTZS VJIL PHSA
BPXT CSMV RLSZ
HFRE RGVA NXKR TRIL JROW SFNC MECE
PSUJ HIQL JSSR
JDIC WGIA UI

The interval between the repeated segments "KH" were fifteen, sixty, and forty-five. The common factors between those three numbers are three, five and fifteen, meaning the keyword should be either three, five or fifteen letters long. The second repeating section he found was "BY". The interval between these was thirty-five. The factors here were seven, five and thirty-five. The length of the key word must be the common factor between the two. The key word, therefore, was made up of five letters.

The next step to breaking the code was to line up the letters in five columns, one for each letter in the key word. Each column was a different code with a different alphabet, based on the amount of shift introduced by the key word. On Alberti's wheel, devised by fifteenth century philosopher and cryptologist Leon Battista Alberti, the encoder would take each letter of the keyword, place the "A" of the inner wheel beneath the first letter of the keyword, causing a shift in the alphabet. He would then find the letter to encode on the inner wheel and transfer the letter above it into the encoded message. Laborious to encode, the Vegenére cipher was even more laborious to decode.

Mylo's task now was to take each column and decode the letters via the simpler common letter method. This would allow him to deduce the amount of the alphabetic shift and thereby discover the keyword. This is normally done by determining which letter has been substituted for the "E". Mylo knew that the letter "E" is by far the most common letter in the English language. By finding the most common letter in each column he could determine which letter was substituted for "E" and thereby deduce the shift, that is provided the sample of letters he worked with was sufficiently long. An hour and a half of working each column in turn provided a key word, "DBWOE". A very unsatisfactory result.

A bit disappointed, Mylo continued to work on the code, substituting the second most common letter in those columns where the first and second most common letters were nearly equal in frequency. After two more hours, his search for the code's keyword yielded "DGAGE". Three quarters of the way through his box of Lone Jack cigarettes, and after two pints of Jersey bitters he'd found no keyword that made any sense. His latest attempt, making no more sense than any of the rest was "DRAXE".

Dejected, disillusioned, and disappointed he decided to cash in for the night and get some sleep. Perhaps a new perspective in the morning would help his work. If not, perhaps Dr. Rudalac might be of some assistance. As he rubbed the sleep from his eyes, his gaze became transfixed on the crumpled paper with the latest attempt at a keyword written on it. He'd spilled a bit of the bitters on the table and it had caused the ink to run on the paper. What he now saw was no longer "DRAXE". He opened his eyes wide as he stared at the brown scrap of paper and exclaimed, "DRAKE!" He mouthed the word quietly to himself as he contemplated it. There was no doubt this was the key word. "Dear God," he said to no one.

He cleared the table with a swipe of his arm, lit another

cigarette, he had three remaining, and began to work. His head throbbed as a result of the bitters. He tried to cure it with a combination of tobacco and strong black coffee as he worked Alberti's wheel. In half an hour he'd decoded the first section of the first message:

> "The trail of the body thief littered with bloodless remains; two miners and a young boy…"

Mylo realized this proved what he'd suspected all along, that Inspector Andrews had been on the trail of a murderer, a trail that would end in the inspector's own demise. But if he'd suspected a vampire, he had yet to specifically mention it in his notes.

He continued to work. After another three cups of coffee, interrupted by the use of his facilities, two more cigarettes and forty-five minutes, he'd decoded the rest of the first message and all of the second and third. They read:

> "Is it possible Barlucci is still alive? or undead? That he is responsible for the missing Miss Drake?"

And,

> "Encountered Emily Drake; resemblance remarkable; coincidence? Sister?"

And finally,

> "Suspect Miss Drake involved in theft of sister's body; fear she may be mad—or worse."

Mylo sat back in his chair, contemplating what it all could mean. He was certain the reference to 'undead' meant that he believed Barlucci was the vampire and somehow connected to Emily Drake. It was apparent Andrews believed Emily might have something to do with stealing the body of her dead sister, that she is mad. Could it be true? Could Emily Drake knowingly have something to do with what was by now eight horrendous murders as well as the theft of her sister's corpse? No. Mylo didn't want to believe the frail and beautiful, genteel woman could possibly be a cold, calculating murderess and ghoul. But this last piece of the puzzle pointed inexorably in that direction. Murray was right. They should have arrested her on the spot. He needed to talk to Rudy. But first he needed a drink, badly. He searched the cupboards for the fifth of Burke's Irish Whiskey he knew was there somewhere.

#

Murray returned to New York from Boston on the afternoon train. He was anxious to tell his partner about his very illuminating conversation with Sister Elizabeth at the Carney Hospital where Mandible Pierce had been a patient. There was no way now that Strumm could deny Miss Emily Drake was integrally involved in the string of murders they'd been investigating. On the train Murray sat organizing both his notes and his thoughts. He knew he would need to tread lightly when he confronted Strumm with his findings.

Although Murray knew of Strumm from before by reputation and by hearing of his exploits, it had only been since Captain Cortright had teamed them together shortly after Strumm's arrival in the First Precinct that he really got to know him. There were few policemen in the city of New York, or in the state, who didn't know how he'd brought down Danny Fitz, but none who knew him like Murray.

Their relationship had been rocky at first. Murray was a tough, no-nonsense cop who believed in using muscle, in getting to the heart of any investigation by finding the likely culprits and then sweating them until they either confessed or turned on their compatriots and he wasn't hesitant about twisting a few arms in the course of an investigation, literally as well as figuratively. He had little time or patience for a cop that couldn't be relied upon during an investigation. And from past experience he'd learned a partner with a weakness for drink could not be relied upon when it counted.

But as time went on, and Strumm made at least some attempts at staying sober, Murray began to appreciate Strumm's talent. He also became more adept at reading Strumm's moods and seeing ahead of time those incidents and times of the year that might set him off on a bender. He also grew to genuinely like his partner and began to look on him as a younger brother. He had every reason to believe the sentiment struck both ways.

All of this made him understand he'd need to tread very carefully. He'd seen the look on Strumm's face while they were questioning Emily Drake. Strumm was smitten. Looking back, Murray knew he should have guessed as much when Strumm first described her to him. And now, with what he'd learned in Boston, it looked as though Strumm would have no choice but to arrest Miss Drake, an arrest that could well lead to her being hanged. Murray knew that added to the guilt he still felt over his wife's death, this new guilt at being the instrument of death for Miss Drake could very well push Strumm over the edge. If he got the opportunity, Murray might need to take matters into his own hands and spare Mylo that burden.

After arriving at Grand Central, he took a cab directly to the station house. When the desk sergeant told him Strumm hadn't been in all day, Murray knew there was something amiss. He didn't bother making the trip down to the morgue; he'd had his fill of Dr. Rudalac and his charnel house. He left his canvas travel bag with the desk sergeant and hired another cab to take him to the squalid rooms

279

Strumm called home.

When he arrived, the streetlights were just coming on, but Strumm's apartment appeared dark and empty. He strode up to Strumm's door and knocked loudly. Getting no response, he tried the knob. The door was unlocked. As he opened it, he saw Strumm. Apparently passed out, he was sprawled across his bed fully clothed, an empty bottle of Burke's Irish whiskey on the night table.

Murray clucked his tongue to his teeth as he raised the bottle to swirl what was left of the contents. A torn sheet of butcher paper was stuck to the bottom of the bottle. He pulled it off and was examining the scribbles on it when he noticed several other sheets lying on the floor beside the bed. In a small alcove that served as Strumm's dining room there stood a table illuminated by a bare bulb hanging down from the ceiling. Gathering up the scraps of paper, he carried them to the table and put them down. The scribblings made no sense to him whatever, random arrangements of letters as far as he could make out.

As Strumm lay snoring, Murray looked around for more. In Strumm's left hand he saw a ball of wadded paper. Taking it to the kitchen table, he smoothed it out with his hand. It read:

> "Is it possible Barlucci is still alive? or undead? That he is responsible for the missing Miss Drake?" Then, "Encountered Emily Drake; resemblance remarkable; coincidence? Sister?" And, "Suspect Miss Drake involved in theft of sister's body; fear she may be mad—or worse."

"Hmmphh," he snorted, "I wonder what all this is...Mylo's come to the same conclusion, although from a different direction? No wonder he's gone and gotten himself drunk," he said in a low voice to himself. He shook his head as he gazed over at his partner. He knew it would be no use trying to rouse him now. Perhaps he could spare his partner further heart ache. Leaving the paper on the table, he walked over and pulled a blanket up over the sleeping Strumm. "By the time you come to, chum," Murray said quietly, "the hard part'll be over."

Murray sent a message to Holmes by the late post and hired a rig of his own rather than taking a cab. He expected he'd have a passenger to ferry to the station house. Confident he would catch her in as it was getting on to evening, he went directly to Miss Drake's home. As he approached the house, he passed a trap going the opposite direction that had just turned out of Miss Drake's long drive. He watched as the pale young gentleman passed, apparently without noticing him.

When he reached the house, he tied the reins onto the brake handle and approached the door. The dusting of snow from earlier in the day crunched beneath his feet as he walked to the front door. His breath streamed in white jets from his mouth and nose. He could see a cold glow of light coming from the window, a good sign that someone was home. He wondered to himself if vampires needed a fire to keep warm. The moon alternately illuminated and then fell dark as the clouds passed before its face, making strange shadows jump about. Murray shivered, and then looked about him as if embarrassed to be frightened even for a moment by the talk of vampires. He knocked on the door.

#

Before leaving, Dr. Tremaine ensured the serum and the full syringe were safely locked away in the supply cabinet. He wanted to take no chances they would be disturbed before he retrieved them the following afternoon. Abigail smiled at the good doctor's care and diligence with every detail. He couldn't know that Abigail had no intention of beginning the curing process just yet.

Once she heard his trap start down the drive, she went directly to the supply cabinet. Placing her index finger over the hole into which he'd inserted his key, she closed her eyes in deep concentration. After a few seconds, there was an audible 'click' and the cabinet door swung open. She reached inside the cabinet and withdrew the syringe containing the serum. From her pocket she took a second syringe, one she'd prepared herself, with a mixture of her own blood diluted with a bit of saline solution to mimic the color and consistency of the serum. She placed it inside the cabinet and closed the door, allowing it to lock once more.

So intensely had she been concentrating on the cabinet, its lock, and her business with its contents that she failed to hear a second carriage arrive at her front door. The knock startled her. Thinking Tremaine must have forgotten something, she slipped the syringe with the serum in it into her dress pocket, intending to dispose of it later, and opened the door. "Did you forget something—" she stopped in mid-sentence when she saw it was not Dr. Tremaine.

"You might say so, Miss," Murray said, pulling out his notebook. "I've a few more questions to ask, if you don't mind. May I come in?"

Abigail realized instantly this must be the partner of the detective who had visited Emily. Smiling sweetly she stepped back, opening the door wide enough to allow Murray's passage. "Yes, of course. Please come in, Detective. You must forgive my lack of candor the other day. I didn't wish to upset my dear, sweet aunt. I'm sure you can understand, what with all those questions." Abigail remembered what the baron told her about the susceptibility of some minds to suggestion and reached out with her own in an attempt to lull the large detective into a sense of security.

"Well, Miss, I suppose I do understand...you wouldn't want to upset your aunt," Murray said behind a kind smile.

"No, I really wouldn't. She's been through a good deal recently." She sensed something was wrong. He seemed sympathetic, but she couldn't feel a connection.

Still smiling, Murray said, "For example, you certainly wouldn't want to tell her you'd just murdered Mandible Pierce and left his head on a pike, if you catch my meaning." His smile disappeared.

"W-what?" said Abigail, feigning fear while she tried to fathom how much he knew.

"That's right. I know you murdered Mandible Pierce, not to mention Inspector Walter Andrews of Scotland Yard and Mr. Josephson in the park with his whore. I even know about that poor steeve down on the docks."

Abigail put a stunned look on her face, sensing the confidence of her accuser, a confidence that would work to her advantage when the time was right.

"Or should I say, your accomplice murdered them folk. You just helped set 'em up, didn't'cha, Miss Drake? But what I can't figure out is why. But maybe we'd need to talk to your accomplice to find that out, eh?"

"I'm sure I don't know what you mean, Detective," said Abigail, now certain that whatever knowledge he had was woefully incomplete.

"Please, Miss, don't play dumb. An accomplice...someone powerful enough to carry a body atop two crates and dump it in a third…powerful enough to hoist a man onto a washline…" Murray's eyes narrowed as he continued, "…powerful enough to rip a man's head and arm clean off'n his body. Someone like, say, Barlucci." Murray watched for a reaction. He wasn't disappointed.

"What do you know of him?" asked Abigail, her eyes narrowing into dark slits before she regained her composure.

"Then it was Barlucci. Come now, Miss Drake, we know you couldn't be responsible for all these horrendous murders, and we'd hate to see that pretty little neck of yours stretched by a hangman's noose for the likes of him. A woman as attractive as you could get herself off fairly easy, I'd wager, if she cooperated and rolled over on her partner. If, however, you insist on protecting this Barlucci fella…Italian, is he? If you continue to protect him it'll go hard on ya'." He stood there in her parlor, his feet apart in a stance that was practiced to show he was tough, but not implacable. Abigail looked back at him, the very picture of vulnerable femininity. "So, what'll it be, Miss Drake? If you cooperate, we can see to it you only get thirty years for your part. No more, maybe less. Just tell me, where is Barlucci?"

Abigail slowly turned away from Murray, put her head down and said, "You…you could do that? You could arrange it?"

Murray stepped closer, "I'm certain a judge would take pity on a young, pretty woman such as yourself. All you need to do is tell us where we can find Barlucci."

Abigail turned to face Murray. The corners of her mouth formed a malignant smile. In a quiet tone she said, "But I'm afraid I don't know where he is, Detective."

Murray's voice took on a harder edge as he said, "Miss Drake, if you know what's good for you, you'll give up your accomplice. I don't know how or why a refined young lady such as yourself has come to let this madman involve you in these heinous crimes."

"But Detective," she said in a seductively sweet voice. "I didn't have an accomplice." Abigail, who'd been dabbing her eyes with a handkerchief, brought it down to reveal a menacing smile.

"Ridiculous," Murray sputtered, unnerved by her sudden change of demeanor—and a smile that would be at home on the face of old Scratch himself.

Abigail looked directly into Murray's eyes and with a voice so low that Murray heard the words inside his head rather than with his ears she asked, "Why, Detective, because a woman is too weak?"

Murray was about to reply when Abigail caught his massive forearm with her left hand and snapped the bones like matchsticks. Murray howled in pain. Confused, he struck at her with all his might using his left hand. It met nothing but air as Abigail deftly stepped out of the way. She laughed and her laugh echoed in his head.

"That's the trouble with men," she said, taunting him. "They think of their women as the weaker sex."

Murray reached under his coat for his revolver. He drew it out and fired, but while he'd clearly seen her standing before him as he pulled the trigger, when the muzzle flashed, she was gone. He looked about the room and saw the curtains being ruffled. He fired a second time, and then a third, into the curtains. He stood there motionless, waiting. Then came the low blood-curdling laughter, directly behind him. Before he could turn or move she'd seized both his arms just below the elbow. Hot flashes of pain shot through his right arm like a searing poker. "Aaagh!"

Just before sinking her teeth into his throat, Abigail whispered into Murray's ear, "Didn't you ever wonder what became of all that blood?"

Chapter 27
The vampire...

When Dr. Rudalac read the name on the piece of paper Mylo handed him all the blood drained from his face and he looked as though he were going to faint.

"Rudy...Dr. Rudalac, are you all right?" he asked as he caught the doctor's arm and guided him to a chair. Getting a cup of water from the cooler, he put it to the doctor's lips.

As he sipped, some of the color returned to his cheeks. He took a deep breath, and then spoke softly, "Mylo, you are after a dangerous adversary, one even more dangerous and evil than you can imagine."

"Yes, I know...a vampire."

"No, you do not. This is not just a vampire. This name, Barlucci, does it mean anything to you?" Dr. Rudalac asked as he read the decoded passages.

"No, should it?"

"No, probably not. Even if it did, it would likely be only in a carefully cultivated context, an unassailable personage."

"What do you mean, Rudy? Who is he, this Barlucci character?"

"Antonio Barlucci, the world knows him only as a great

financial power, one of the premier banking houses of Europe. It is said the Barlucci family has been the banker of kings and popes for over five centuries, more wealthy than the Medicis in their native Italy, more powerful than the family Rothschild."

"You talk like you don't believe it."

"That Barlucci is rich and powerful there is no doubt. He has financed nearly every war in Europe for hundreds of years, loaning money to both sides, then squeezing whichever interest would maximize his gain." As he spoke, Dr. Rudalac's countenance took on the appearance of someone remembering something from long ago, a trancelike glaze fixed his gaze.

"You mean 'they'," Strumm said.

The interruption appeared to bring Dr. Rudalac out of his reverie, back into the present, "What's that?"

Mylo repeated, "You said *'he'* financed wars; you mean *'they'*…"

"Yes, *he*, there is no mistake. The family is the lie."

Confused, Strumm asked, "What do you mean?"

"Oh, to be sure, there once was a Barlucci family. But that was many centuries ago. Now, there is only one. Him. Baron Antonio Barlucci. The same Antonio Barlucci that my father aided so many years ago. Certainly he takes wives now and again, but he lives on."

Strumm sat in stunned silence. Finally he said, "Rudy, what are you saying? That this is the same vampire that destroyed your village? Can that be?"

"Why not, Mylo?"

"For one thing he'd have to be over a hundred years old."

"He is much older than that—centuries. He is the same vampire that my father aided in Hungary. Vampires do not die, Mylo, at least not like you and I will someday die. I told you my father became involved with a wealthy financier, a member of the Italian aristocracy. That was…is Barlucci. And he was very old then."

"Rudy, this is an incredible story. I'm not sure…I'm…I don't know what to say. I never dreamed…" Although Strumm felt a closeness to Dr. Rudalac that was akin to a father figure, he wondered if it might be possible that Rudy could be having delusions. "But I still can't take that theory to the Captain, they'd lock me in a rubber room. You too. It's too fantastic."

"Fantastic, yes, but unfortunately true, and it is imperative you believe me, for it is only armed with knowledge that you can hope to defeat him. Evil in this world is more hideous than many would care to accept, my boy, but a reluctance to believe does nothing to ward off evil. You cannot act as if the evil does not exist."

"But I can't believe Miss Drake could be involved with anything so hideously evil as a vampire, Rudy."

Don't be fooled, Mylo. The vampire is evil, to be sure, but he can appear to be as appealing as he is sinister. Through the ages he's charmed men as well as women, gaining their confidence only to ultimately betray their trust, to destroy them. You must convince Miss Drake of the danger she's in and get her to show you where the vampire is nested."

"Nested?"

"Yes, where his coffin lies, or crate, or whatever he is using to rest. It will be a container in which he can fully recline, a container into which no light can reach. Only in pitch darkness can a vampire rest fully. It is most likely located in a cellar of the mansion you mentioned. If you can locate the nest before the sun has set, you can destroy him."

"But you said he can't die."

Dr. Rudalac walked over to a chest with a heavy pad lock. He took a chain from around his neck. On the chain was a small silver key. As he spoke, he placed the key into the lock, "And it is true, a vampire cannot die. The fact is he is already dead. You cannot 'kill' a vampire in the ordinary sense." Turning the key there was an audible click. "But he can be destroyed." He reached both his hands inside the chest. When he withdrew them, in one he held a small sledge hammer, in the other was what appeared to be a piece of wood a little over a foot long. One end came to a vicious point. Dr. Rudalac turned to Strumm. "A stake."

"Rudy…what the…?"

"To destroy the vampire you must find his nest, and then, before the sun has set, when he is in his deepest state of rest, when he is most vulnerable, you must drive the stake into his chest, piercing his heart."

"Rudy, that's…that's barbaric."

"Yes…, barbaric," Dr. Rudalac said, once again a far off look in his eye, "but quite effective."

"And that will destroy the vampire?"

"No, but it will allow you to destroy him." Dr. Rudalac reached back into his chest. "After the stake has pierced his heart he will be immobile. Then you must take this," he said, pulling out a short blade with a serrated edge and a stout handle.

"A bone saw?" Mylo asked, having seen Rudy use an instrument like it during autopsies.

"Yes, with this you must remove the head of the vampire. Then you can either burn it and the body, or you can bury them, in separate graves."

"Rudy, what you are suggesting is horrendous. Is it absolutely necessary?"

"It is the only way, aside from total immolation, you can be sure he is completely destroyed."

"Aren't you coming with me?"

"I'm sorry, my boy, I'm afraid I'm getting too old to be of any use to you on this quest. I would just hold you back. I wouldn't want you to falter in trying to see to my safety. No, take your partner, Murray, if you can convince him. His strength may come in handy." He patted Strumm on the shoulder. "Remember, if you wait too long, if you hesitate or shrink from your duty, he will have no mercy on you. Of this I can attest," he said, touching fingers to his throat. "You will die a most horrible death."

"You paint a bleak picture, Rudy."

The old man smiled at his young protégée, "Don't worry. Do as I have instructed and all will be well."

Staring back at Dr. Rudalac, Strumm looked unconvinced.

Chapter 28

The pieces fall together…

Holmes and I had just returned to our hotel from an uneventful visit to Miss Emily Drake's home. There appeared to be no one about. In fact, the condition of the house gave the impression perhaps Miss Drake had decided the old mansion might be a bit too much for a woman alone after all. The windows were dark and the shutters were closed up tight, as though awaiting a storm.

As we entered the hotel lobby, Abel Jenkins called out, "Mr. Holmes? Dr. Watson?" He was waving an envelope above his head.

"Yes, what is it, Abel?" said I as we walked over to the front desk.

"This came for you by the evening post last night. It fell down behind some packages and we only found it this morning, just after you left. I thought it might be important. It's from one of those detective fellows."

Holmes took the envelope, ripped it open and read it in silence, his brow creased in concentration.

"Come, Watson, the game's afoot and there's not a moment to lose."

#

It was mid-afternoon when Strumm left Dr. Rudalac in the

morgue to find Emily Drake and convince her to lead him to the vampire. Strumm first tried Emily's mansion hoping she would be there, but it was dark and empty. He was tempted to search for Barlucci's nest on his own, but he knew many of the houses in this community had been built before and during the Revolutionary War and a random search could take hours if not days. Many of these colonial mansions were honeycombed with secret rooms and passages. Instead he went back to the home of Emily's aunt, Lucie Belmont, where he'd run across Emily when they first questioned her.

As he walked up to Mrs. Belmont's door, he said a silent prayer that Emily would be there and that he could convince her about the danger she was in. Instead, Lucie Belmont answered the door. "Why, Detective, this is a surprise. I didn't expect to see you again."

Strumm was too agitated for pleasantries, "Where's Miss Drake? I have to speak to her, now."

Mrs. Belmont hesitated, making a slight movement of her head, "I'm…I'm afraid that's impossible, Detective, she's not in right now, but I do expect her back shortly. What's this about?"

Now it was Strumm's turn to hesitate. He had to restrain himself from shaking this foolish woman. Didn't she know what was at stake? It took him a minute to calm himself enough to speak without yelling at her. At last he asked, "I must find her and speak to her immediately. If you're sure she will be here soon, then I must wait for her. Do you mind? I can't stress enough that it's extremely important I speak to her, for her sake as well as others."

"Certainly, Detective, please come in. Perhaps in the meantime you can tell me what it is you want with Emily." Mrs. Belmont showed Strumm into the parlor, and then rang the bell for the maid. "Uhmm…just a minute, please," she said to Strumm. She then addressed her housekeeper who had come into the room, "Hannah, please bring the detective and me some coffee." Once Hannah exited, Mrs. Belmont said, "Now, what's this all about? I can see you are quite agitated."

"You're going to think I'm completely crazy, Mrs. Belmont, but I assure you I'm sane and I've never been more serious in my life."

"Oh, I doubt that, Detective. Please, go on."

Strumm felt a strange mixture of embarrassment and desperation. Knowing how crazy it was going to sound saying it out loud, but realizing it was the only answer that made sense, Strumm lowered his voice, "It's about your niece. I'm afraid she's gotten mixed up with a vampire."

Mrs. Belmont's eyes widened, "What do you mean, 'mixed up with a vampire', Detective?" The corners of her eyes crinkled with a nervous smile and she saw the look of surprise come across Strumm's face. "Detective, are you having fun with me? Really, you don't need to make up such nonsense to see my niece. I could tell you were attracted to her when first you met."

"But I…" Strumm reddened a bit in confusion, not quite knowing what to make of Mrs. Belmont's statements and demeanor.

"It's all right, I'm sure. She's a beautiful young woman, but your sense of humor might be somewhat of a concern."

"I only wish I were joking, Mrs. Belmont, truly I do. But I'm afraid if I don't speak to your niece and make her realize what she's gotten herself into with this, this man, this monster, great harm will come to her."

The smile fell from Mrs. Belmont's face. "I must say, Detective, your little joke has taken a rather cruel turn. I know nothing of any monster and I'm sure neither does Emily."

"Please Mrs. Belmont, this is no joke," he said slowly, hoping to make an impression. "This same vampire may very well have murdered Emily's sister, then stolen her body." He noticed Mrs. Belmont stiffen, and then relax when he mentioned Abigail. There was a different look in her eyes now.

Hannah brought in two cups of coffee on a tray and placed it on the sideboard, serving them to Strumm and Mrs. Belmont, who motioned for Strumm to remain silent until Hannah had exited.

With sudden coldness, Mrs. Belmont said, "Detective, Abigail died in a shipwreck, her body was found adrift in a longboat. She wasn't murdered. And yes, her body disappeared, but what has that to do with a monster?"

"Mrs. Belmont, that ship belonged to Baron Barlucci, who I have reason to believe is a vampire, a vampire who has left a string of murder victims from the fishing village where your niece's body was taken to the very streets of New York."

Mrs. Belmont placed her cup carefully in its saucer and said, "Of what victims do you speak, Detective?"

"The first was the mortician who tended your niece's body, then a young boy, no more than eighteen years old. If that weren't enough, before leaving Newfoundland on a ferry bound for New York, he murdered two others, a couple of copper miners. A dock worker was his first victim in the city, and then there was an Inspector from Scotland Yard…"

"Scotland Yard?"

"Yes, Inspector…" he consulted his notebook, though he knew the name well, "Walter Andrews."

Mrs. Belmont appeared to be quite shaken by the news, "Oh

dear, that's the name mentioned by that Mr. Holmes, the young man who was investigating Abigail's disappearance. But still, what has all this to do with Emily?"

"I saw Emily on the night Barlucci murdered his fifth victim since coming to New York, Mandible Pierce."

"I…I can't believe it…Emily would never…"

"She was going into Pierce's hotel. I have reason to believe she knows where I can find this monster."

Mrs. Belmont took a handkerchief from her sleeve and dabbed her eyes. A sob escaped her throat.

Suddenly there began a mad ringing at the door.

When Holmes and I arrived at the home of Mrs. Lucie Belmont it was evident by the growler parked on the street that someone had arrived there before us. We leapt down from the trap we'd hired and hurried up to the door where Holmes unmercifully twisted the bell in such a vicious manner that I was sure it would come off in his hand.

My friend didn't wait for pleasantries saying instantly when Mrs. Belmont had opened the door, "Mrs. Belmont, it is of dire importance that we speak with your niece."

"Holmes," came a voice from behind Mrs. Belmont. "What the devil are you doing here?"

"I might ask you the same question, Detective."

Strumm now stood beside Mrs. Belmont. "I came to warn Miss Drake about a very grave danger to her life," he said.

"Ha," Holmes said. "I believe the danger is not to Miss Drake, but from her."

"That's ridiculous," said Mrs. Belmont who'd been watching the two men go at it. "My Emily wouldn't hurt a fly."

"Not Emily, Mrs. Belmont, Abigail…" Holmes said.

"You're mad, Holmes," Strumm said.

"Am I? Tell me, Detective, where has your partner gotten to?"

"Murray? I'm not sure, he went to Boston to check on the Mandible Pierce case, but he should have been back by now."

"Yes, he came to see Dr. Watson and me before he left. He told us that Pierce had been a patient at the Carney Hospital there, before coming to New York." He looked at Strumm with the steely glare of which I was well aware.

"She must have met him while she was visiting her friend, Elizabeth," Mrs. Belmont said looking somewhat confused.

"No, Mrs. Belmont, she went to Boston to see Mr. Pierce. It was merely a happy coincidence that she had a friend working in the same hospital."

"Why would a woman like Emily travel to Boston to see a man like Mandible Pierce?" Strumm said. "So what if she visited a friend in Boston who happened to work at the same hospital where Pierce was a patient. It proves nothing."

"Murray warned us you had a blind spot when it comes to Miss Drake," said I.

"In itself it certainly doesn't prove Miss Drake was involved," Holmes said. "But what you don't know is why Pierce was in the hospital. He was recovering from trauma when the ship he was working on found the remains of a ship wreck—the *Animus Lacuna*, the ship that carried Abigail Drake and Antonio Barlucci."

"Barlucci's ship?" Strumm said.

"Yes, we received a post from Detective Murray this afternoon. Pierce was raving about a vampire from that ship killing his mates when he was admitted to the hospital. He apparently escaped when an avalanche buried the vampire, when it buried Barlucci."

"Barlucci? But Barlucci is here. It's he who murdered your detective and Pierce."

"Vampire or no," Holmes said, "if he was buried in snow, he could not have committed the murders in Manhattan, nor could he have stolen Abigail Drake's body."

"Are you saying...?" Strumm said.

"...that Miss Abigail Drake's body was never stolen. Abigail Drake is the vampire."

"My God, but if you know all this and Murray is back, why hasn't he contacted me?"

"He came by your rooms last night, but you weren't in a position to know, apparently. He said he'd discovered your notes about Miss Drake's involvement and was going to save you the burden of having to arrest her."

"You mean..."

"Yes, Murray left you last night to arrest Miss Emily Drake. The fact that we have neither seen nor heard from either since does not bode well, I'm afraid. Mrs. Belmont, if you know where Emily Drake is, it's of paramount importance you tell us. Her life could be in very grave danger."

"Emily is here. She's in the kitchen, but I'm certain she nor Abigail could have had anything to do with the death of Mr. Pierce or Mr. Andrews. Emily will tell you." She called out to her maid, "Hannah, have Emily come into the parlor, now. We must tell Mr. Holmes and Detective Strumm the truth."

Hannah came in and said, "I'm sorry, Mrs. Belmont, Miss Drake has gone. She left just before Mr. Holmes arrived. She said she must speak to Abigail."

Mrs. Belmont suddenly looked as though she was about to faint. "Oh dear," she said, tottering with one hand going to her head while the other reached for something to steady her. I took her by the arm and led her to a chair in the parlor. Holmes and Strumm followed. I poured her a glass of water from a carafe on a nearby side table. "Thank you."

Holmes was up and on his way to the door in an instant. "She's gone to see her sister. She's gone to see Abigail Drake."

"But that's impossible," Strumm said.

"No, not impossible, but so improbable as to seem impossible, which is why I overlooked it. I was blinded by my own conceit." He looked at me and said with a sad smile, "Watson, this will make an interesting corollary to my most prized idiom." He made long strides to the door, saying, "Strumm, we'll take your growler, quickly."

The four of us left Mrs. Belmont's house. While Holmes and Strumm sat up front, Strumm at the reins, I rode in the back with Mrs. Belmont and an ominous looking canvas bag.

Chapter 29

The treachery of Dr. Tremaine...

Dr. Tremaine removed the vial from the cabinet, along with the hypodermic syringe he'd prepared earlier, and placed them on a small cellarette at the head of the treatment table he'd constructed. The table was long and narrow, built of solid oak reinforced with steel hardware. He'd bolted it to the floor and fastened padding to the top. In addition, taking heed from what he'd learned from the baron, he fastened a series of specially made straps at strategic points so that he might restrain his abnormally strong patient. Each strap was constructed of two layers of leather stitched together around the outer edge. Between the layers were sewn twisted strands of tempered steel. He was taking no chances with Abigail.

Before drawing the heavy curtains over the windows, he turned up the gas jets to illuminate the room. He waited until the afternoon was waning before going down into the cellar to arouse Miss Drake. He wanted to ensure her energies were at their lowest ebb before beginning the treatment as an added measure of precaution. When everything was ready he took an oil lamp and walked down the stairs to the cellar. At the bottom of the stairs he knocked on the heavy, oaken door. "Miss Drake," he called. "It's time."

When the door swung open, Dr. Tremaine was somewhat shocked by the sight of Abigail. He'd never seen her while the sun was still in the sky. He remembered how frail the baron appeared when he'd first administered the serum to him, but Abigail looked much worse. Even in the dim orange glow of the lamplight her skin appeared a sickly pale, nearly translucent. Thin blue veins could be seen on her cheeks and throat. Her eyes were yellowish-red and watery, the whites criss-crossed with spidery red capillaries. He could scarcely contain his shock.

"You look startled, Doctor." She smiled weakly, "I'm afraid I'm not at my best at this hour."

"Not at all, Miss Drake."

Ignoring his attempt at gallantry, "Please, lead on." Her voice was uncharacteristically meek and small.

As they reached the top of the stairs, Dr. Tremaine took her arm, leading her into the laboratory. In spite of the way she looked, he noted that her arm felt solid and strong beneath the material of her dress.

"I've padded the table for you and placed a cushion for your head.'

"Thank you, Doctor, but you needn't have bothered." She sat on the edge of the table.

"Please, lie down while I strap you in."

As she lay back, she looked up at Tremaine with an amused look on her face, "I do believe you enjoy seeing me in this weakened condition, Doctor."

"Nonsense," he responded, hiding his smile as he fastened the straps over her arms and wrists.

Her eyes went to the draped windows, "I sense the sun will soon be setting. Even now it rushes towards the horizon."

"We have time, Miss Drake, don't fret. All is going according to schedule." He continued securing the straps across her chest, waist, and hips.

"I'm not worried, Doctor, not at all. But tell me, how long will it take before my symptoms subside?"

"You should notice a lessening of your most noxious symptoms almost immediately. Your sensitivity to sunlight will take somewhat longer, perhaps a few weeks."

"I assume by noxious you mean my proclivity toward certain forms of nourishment?"

"Yes, that's right."

"And how often must I inject myself? After this first one, I mean?"

"Twice daily. I shall have to prepare more serum once we've made sure there are no complications," he said as he strapped down her legs, both above and below her knees.

"What sort of complications?"

"Nothing to worry about, it's merely a precaution. I don't anticipate any difficulties. The serum is nearly identical to the one I prepared for the baron, and all the tests have been equally successful." Tremaine drew the last strap across her forehead, fixing her gaze toward the ceiling.

"That's reassuring," she said, closing her eyes.

"I trust that's not too uncomfortable?"

"Not at all. Thank you for your consideration."

Abigail's uncharacteristic show of appreciation surprised him. "You're welcome, of course. Now, if you will test the strength of the bonds, we can proceed."

Abigail strained at the bonds in a futile attempt to break free. Tremaine was relieved he'd had the foresight to specially order the straps. The steel reinforcement made them far stronger than the restraints he'd used on Barlucci.

Initially Tremaine had planned to let her know she was going to die and why, even as he was injecting the liquid death into her veins, but as she lay on the table before him he reconsidered. Her manner and courtesy demonstrated to him that she still had human qualities and wasn't quite a monster after all. Besides, the sudden knowledge she'd been betrayed might trigger a violent reaction beyond that which the medicine would invoke. It would be enough to kill her. There was no turning back and he had Julia to think of after all, and their baby. But for the first time he now contemplated that what he was about to do might be considered murder.

"I'm at your mercy, Doctor."

Tremaine took the Pravaz syringe from the tray. Turning to Abigail he said, "Miss Drake, the baron was able to will his median cubital vein, this one here," he pointed at the inner bend of her elbow, "the vein that crosses just here. He was able to will it to distend that I might have a suitable target for the needle. If you are unable, I shall have to inject directly into your vena jugularis, the jugular vein."

"I shall try, Doctor."

Tremaine watched her bare arm as Abigail attempted to will the vein to distend enough to become visible. After about a minute Tremaine said, "I'm afraid we will have to move…"

"Wait…" Abigail interrupted. She closed her eyes and Tremaine could see the strain register across her brow. Then he looked back at her arm and saw the vein standing out clearly, as if blood were coursing through it.

"Very good, Miss Drake," he said as he poised the needle. As he pushed the needle forward, he was pleased the resistance, unlike with the baron, did not cause the needle to break. Slowly he pushed the plunger in, transferring the deadly liquid into the arm of Abigail. When he completed the injection he removed the needle from her arm. Turning to the vial on the cellarette, he prepared a second injection before placing the syringe back onto the tray. Taking his watch from his waistcoat pocket he waited.

After nearly two minutes, Abigail asked, "Is there something amiss, Doctor? I don't feel anything."

"Don't worry, Miss Drake. I'm sure you'll feel something shortly," he said, marking the seconds as they ticked by. "Because your heart no longer beats the serum must diffuse through your bloodstream. It may take some time."

Abigail began, "Are you quite sure—" when her eyes opened wide and her words were cut short as she gasped for air. Shortly after her entire body convulsed violently, straining the steel reinforced straps, her body contorting in a hideous manner within the confines of the bonds for what seemed like minutes. Then, as suddenly as they began, the convulsions stopped. Abigail lay completely still. The convulsions lasted twenty seconds, no more. When he was sure they were over, Dr. Tremaine began a slow methodical examination.

From Abigail's mouth and nose a small amount of translucent pink viscous liquid dripped. Her skin was pallid and there was absolutely no movement. He knew there would be no need for the second injection. The reaction overall appeared similar to what he'd experienced with Baron Barlucci, but with the baron he had immediately attempted to stimulate a recovery by repeated blows across his face. It had been effective for the baron, but then, the baron received pure serum, not the cocktail of serum and strychnine—enough to kill ten men—that he'd prepared for Abigail. Besides, he had no intention of attempting to revive Abigail. He knew only her complete destruction would guarantee Julia's full recovery, so he planned to burn down the house with her in it, destroying not only Abigail, but any evidence of her malignant existence and his involvement with her.

He sat beside Abigail for a full five minutes waiting for the least little sign of movement, heartbeat or respiration. Finally, he said to her almost in a whisper, "I wish there could have been another way, Miss Drake. You should never have made my wife your vassal. You left me no choice. I sincerely hope the poison was painless."

He gathered his notebooks and loose papers, placing them haphazardly into one of the large packing crates filled with excelsior and then he placed the crate beneath the table on which resided the bulk of the chemicals that had once occupied the crates. He planned to be rid of Abigail, the baron, and all evidence of his association with them as well as any evidence of his work on a cure for vampirism. Although he was certain Abigail was dead, he knew from the books he'd received from the baron that the only sure way to prevent a vampire from ever being revived was to have its body totally consumed by fire.

He sprinkled oil from the lamps around the laboratory, on the curtains and furniture, in the boxes filled with paper and excelsior, and was getting ready to set it on fire when he glanced back at the treatment table. It was empty. The straps were shredded and hanging from the table as ineffectual as decorative ribbons. Terror gripped him as he realized he'd been duped. His eyes darted about the empty room.

"Ha ha ha ha ha ha ha…" the sinister laugh seemed to come from all directions at once. "Doctor," she said, directly behind him. He jerked around only in time to see the curtains rustling as if someone were behind them. He ran to the door of the laboratory, but it slammed shut before him, revealing a smiling Abigail Drake standing behind it. "Why, Doctor, did you really think you could get away?"

"This is impossible," Tremaine rasped, nearly mad with terror. "The poison…you should be dead!"

"Ah, yes, the poison. For shame, Doctor, trying to poison your patient. Primum non nocere? How fortuitous for me that I switched your 'serum'."

"You switched it? But why?" He asked, taking a step backward, looking for another escape.

"You see, Doctor, I'm not quite sure I'm ready to be, how did you put it…fully human again." She watched the doctor as he appeared a rabbit backed into a corner, the wolf near upon it.

"I…I don't understand…that is why you came to me, for a cure."

"What good is a cure to me without my Antonio?" she asked him.

"Surely he will come, you said as much yourself."

"Ah, yes, indeed he shall, but when? That is the question…when? The answer to that question I do not know. It may be years, decades, but what is time to one who does not age." She matched him step for step maintaining the same distance from him, not closing but not allowing him to recede. "But if I become human now, I will age…and he will not. No, when he comes to me, I will be waiting for him, just as he remembered me."

"But the cure…you need me to cure you both," Tremaine

said, stalling for time as he edged slowly along the wall.

"You think much too highly of your talents, Doctor. Now that you've discovered the key, I'm sure when the time is right, and when my Antonio has returned to me, we will be able to find another ambitious young doctor who wishes to enhance his reputation." Seeing Tremaine was moving toward the window, she said, "Go ahead, Doctor."

Tremaine tore open the heavy crepe curtain, hoping against hope that a last ray of sunlight might give him the chance he needed to escape.

"Ha ha ha ha ha..." came Abigail's laughter as the curtain fell, revealing only the faintest glow through the cracks in the shutter.

Tremaine put his hands to his ears to blot out the sound. "You...you planned to murder me all along..."

"Not true, Doctor. That thought only occurred to me after your lovely wife came to visit."

"Julia..."

"Yes, Doctor. Julia. Didn't you think her conversion came just a little too quickly and too completely?" Her cruel smile made him shiver. "She made such a willing victim."

Her mockery proved too much and Tremaine grabbed his walking stick from the table lunging toward Abigail, the tip aimed at her heart.

At the last possible second, Abigail deftly moved to one side grasping Tremaine's wrist with one hand and the stick with the other, snapping in two both the cane and the bones of Tremaine's lower arm, the broken cane skittering harmlessly across the floor. Now her hand grabbed the hair on the back of Tremaine's head, exposing his throat. "Soon your need for my bite will be so great you'll beg me to do this," she said as she lowered her head, then she hesitated as a thought occurred to her. "Perhaps I'll have you sacrifice your wife to me before I provide you the relief you will be begging me for…"

As Tremaine screamed, "No…" Abigail laughed once more, taking lurid pleasure in the doctor's terror.

"Abigail!" a familiar voice shouted.

Abigail snapped Tremaine's head back against the stone fireplace. He fell to the floor, unconscious.

"Sister," she said in a sarcastically sweet tone. "Whatever are you doing here? I've been meaning to speak to you about these impromptu visits. They are becoming quite noisome." She spoke as though they were discussing bric-a-brac over tea.

"You lied to me, Abigail. You've been lying to me all along."

"What? Do you mean him?" she asked, indicating Tremaine with a nod. "It might interest you to know that Dr. Tremaine was intent on murdering your sister this evening. Indeed, he would have had I not caught on to his plan."

"And what of Pierce?"

"We've gone over that; I told you that was a lie to trap you into a confession. Besides, sister, he was of no importance, a pathetic little creature.'"

"…and Inspector Andrews? Was he another pathetic creature?"

"Inspector Andrews?" She looked at her sister intently "So, I see you've been talking to that detective again, what was his name? Scrum? Or the other one, Holmes. Which one, dear sister, is turning you against me?"

"Strumm."

"Of course, Detective Strumm, I should have known he'd be

trouble when I heard the two of you together. Now, with what lies has he been filling that pretty little head of yours?"

"You are the one who's been lying, Abigail. Please, don't lie any more… don't." Emily put her hand to her mouth to stifle a sob as she steadied herself on a chair back.

"Poor Emily, so put upon," Abigail said, her manner suddenly changing. "You make me sick to my stomach," she said as she turned her back on her sister.

Shocked by the vitriol in her sister's voice, Emily stiffened, "What?"

"Poor, fragile little Emily," she said in a mocking tone as she walked casually about the room. "Always the one who needed to be coddled, always the favorite, the delicate, frail one. Remember when I was trapped in that mine and you 'rescued' me? I was the one who'd been trapped in that hole in the ground for hours on end, but it was you everyone fawned over."

"Abigail, that was only because I was ill."

"Yes, poor little Emily…always so ill. Always in poor health, too ill to make the trip to England when Mother and Father were killed. So, while you remained safe and warm with Aunt Lucie and Uncle Cedric it was I who was shipped off to Uncle Charles with his old world notions and ghastly demeanor. Too ill to make that trip? Ha. Oh, Emily, how you used that old line."

"Abigail…sister…" Emily didn't understand from where all this pent up vitriol came.

"And now, rather than take my part when I truly need you, knowing how horrid my affliction is, you take up for he who wished to destroy me. But I shouldn't be surprised. Perhaps that is what you want too. But you won't stop me, sister, not when I'm so close…"

Abigail grasped her sister's arms and dragged her toward the treatment table.

"What are you doing?"

"A change in plans, sister. Originally, I wasn't going to trade places with you until I was cured, but I'm afraid I shall have to hasten things a bit. Your Detective Strumm is expecting to find a vampire. I would hate to disappoint him." Abigail lifted her sister onto the table, strapping her to it.

A suddenly very frightened Emily sobbed, asking her sister, "What do you mean, Abigail? What are you going to do to me?"

Tremaine, dazed from the blow on the head, staggered to his knees. He could see Abigail across the spinning room, tying someone to a table. He didn't understand what was happening, but he knew what he must do. Picking up the shattered remains of his walking stick he stood up and ran the distance between himself and Abigail, hurling himself at her with a cry, "Aaaaggghhh…"

With lightning reflexes, Abigail turned on her attacker, taking the hypodermic syringe from her pocket as she turned. She plunged the syringe deep into Dr. Tremaine's jugular vein. But as her thumb depressed the plunger, Tremaine jammed the ragged tip of the broken walking stick up under Abigail's ribcage toward her heart. As they fell to the ground together, they tipped over the table on which Emily was strapped. The oil lamp fell to the floor, igniting the excelsior.

Chapter 30
...and the beginning of the end?

We raced the sun as Strumm drove the horse to its limit but still, before we went careening into the drive to Mauldin Place, it had set. The revelation from Murray that Barlucci could not be the murderer had caused Holmes to conclude that Abigail, not Barlucci, was behind the rash of homicides, including Inspector Andrews. He explained in shouted bits while we rode wildly through the streets of upper Manhattan, it had to have been Abigail, not Emily, Andrews met in the lobby of the Gilsey hotel. He'd undoubtedly given her the note to send her to Barlucci with him in hot pursuit. It revealed he knew too much, even though he wasn't completely correct in his surmisal, which prompted her to remove him before he could learn more. It was ludicrous to believe a woman of Emily Drake's breeding would be any match for an inspector from Scotland Yard. But a woman with the strength of ten...

It was the business about Pierce and his contact with the *Animus Lacuna* that tied up the loose ends. His story of creating an avalanche that buried Abigail Drake's fiancée must have so incensed her that she literally tore him limb from limb. Hell hath no fury, etcetera, etcetera.

As he stopped the growler, a violent explosion inside the

house showered the carriage with shards of broken glass from the windows. Holmes and Strumm leapt from the coach, Strumm pulling a long sliver of glass from his cheek just below his right eye. Holmes tore open the front door. Little other than flame could be seen inside the laboratory. They were about to abandon this entry and try the rear of the house when Holmes spotted Tremaine. Carefully avoiding flame and falling timber, he crossed the foyer to reach Tremaine just inside the door to the lab, but it was too late. His body was twisting and contorting in a grotesque fashion that Holmes recognized as the result of a strong poison. Holmes pulled the dying man out of the house and into the fresh air.

"What happened? Where is Miss Drake?"

"I killed her," Tremaine cried. "I killed the vampire."

"What about Emily? Where is Emily?" Holmes said, cradling Tremaine's head in his hands.

He coughed, spitting up blood, "No Emily...only Abigail." Tremaine's face grew suddenly slack. He stared into the darkness. "...Julia..." he said, before he slumped over dead.

Strumm darted back into the house. Using his overcoat, he beat at the flames making a path into the library. Once inside the room he saw Emily lying just inside the door, half of Tremaine's walking stick protruding from her chest. Despite the flames, he went to her, not willing to leave her to the fire. He placed his fingers on her throat, beneath her jaw bone. There was no heartbeat. He slipped his arm beneath her to carry her out of the room when he heard a cough. Turning, he saw a woman's feet beside an overturned table. She coughed once more.

Strumm made his way to her. The flames had not yet reached that corner of the room, which was near the door to the hallway that led to the cellar stairs and the kitchen.

"My God!" he called when he saw the woman's face. It was Emily. She was held fast to the table by a large leather strap around her waist. Quickly Strumm unfastened the strap. He heard a crack behind him. He turned in time to see the center section of the ceiling collapse over the place where he'd just been kneeling, onto the body of who he'd thought was Emily Drake.

Emily coughed again, then opened her eyes, "Detective Strumm?"

"Emily? Is that you, Emily?"

"Yes…is my sister…?"

"She's dead," he said without knowing if she'd heard him, her eyes closing once again.

With the path he'd entered now blocked with flame and debris, he picked Emily up in his arms and kicked open the door to the hallway. The smoke was thick, burning his eyes and throat, but he managed to carry her through the hall to the back of the house and out into the cold fresh air. He laid her on the ground and tried to revive her.

After a few minutes, she opened her eyes with a scream.

"Shh…" Strumm said. "It's okay, we're outside. You are okay."

"Is she…" cried Emily, "…is my sister dead?"

"Yes…" he said and pulled Emily close. She collapsed in sobs at his breast.

#

The house burned nearly to the ground by the time the first fire wagon arrived. It continued to smolder all the following day and it was early evening before Strumm and Dr. Rudalac, accompanied by

Holmes and I were able to search the ruins for proof the vampire was dead at last. Dr. Rudalac had his bone saw in a leather satchel at his side.

We searched the ruined house carefully, looking for Abigail's body. An unfortunate outgrowth of our search was the discovery of Detective Murray's body, drained of blood, in the upper loft of the livery stable. At first we feared Abigail Drake had somehow escaped. But we eventually found her pinned beneath a beam that had fallen through, probably just before Strumm had escaped with Emily. Her body was nearly consumed by the fire. The walking stick was charred and burned, up to where it entered her body, through the center of her chest.

Dr. Rudalac kneeled by the body. "Good," he said as he examined the wound, "The angle of entry is such that it certainly has penetrated her heart."

"Then she is truly dead?" Holmes said.

"Yes, but just to make sure, we need to remove her head."

"Is that absolutely necessary, Rudy?" Strumm said. It…it seems such a desecration."

Dr. Rudalac shook his head. "Mylo, you don't understand the power of the vampire. You see before you the remains of a woman."

"Yes, and what do you see?"

"I see the malignant form of a creature that could still be a danger to you, to me, but most especially, to Miss Emily Drake."

"Emily? Rudy, do you really think so?"

Holmes interjected, "In some of the old tales it is said that should the stake become dislodged from a vampire's heart before the head is removed, the vampire could once again rise from the dead. Is that not so, Dr. Rudalac?"

"You surprise me, Mr. Holmes. I was unaware you had such knowledge, a man of science and logic such as yourself. I cannot tell you if it's true, but…"

"Our knowledge of science is ever-expanding, Doctor. What is science today may seem superstition tomorrow and conversely, superstition, under the right circumstances, becomes science. I met a man on a voyage once who had some very interesting knowledge he shared with me."

"I see…and my knowledge tells me, at any rate, that we must sever the head to ensure the vampire does not cause any more mischief."

Strumm said, "Rudy…can you do it? She looks too much like…"

"Miss Drake? Oh, I'm sorry, it's 'Emily' now, isn't it?" he asked with a quick smile.

"Yes," Strumm said, matching Rudy's smile with his own. "As soon as she's up and around, I'm going to take her to the opera."

"Opera? Then it's serious," Dr. Rudalac said, still smiling. "I'm glad for you, my boy. It's about time some happiness found its way into your life."

"Thanks, Rudy. I'll wait in the carriage. Call me and I'll help you carry the remains out when you're done."

Holmes assisted Dr. Rudalac while I walked back to the carriage with Detective Strumm.

Strumm smoked a couple of cigarettes while Holmes and Dr. Rudalac carried out their grim mission. A few minutes later Dr. Rudalac and Holmes came carrying the body of Abigail in a sheet of canvas, with a separate bag in which we knew was Abigail's severed head.

"What does it mean, Mr. Holmes? Do you think Barlucci is still out there?"

"I would say that if what Mr. Pierce reported is true, we will probably not be bothered by Baron Barlucci again, at least as long as the frozen north remains frozen. What do you think, Dr. Rudalac?"

"I can't say, Mr. Holmes, but what I can say is that we were very lucky this turned out to be a much less experienced vampire. If it had been Barlucci, he would not have been defeated so easily."

Thinking of Murray, Strumm said, "I'd hardly call it easily, Rudy."

Two days later Strumm went by the Gilsey Hotel to see Holmes and Watson. They were having a last breakfast in the dining room when he came in. "Ah, Detective Strumm, please sit down. Join us."

"I'm not hungry, but I would like a cup of coffee," he said as he sat down across from Holmes. "I actually came by to apologize for not confiding in you more."

"Nonsense. I was encroaching on your grounds. What gamesman wouldn't have been leery. It is I who owe you an apology, Detective. I can see now why Murray held you in such high esteem." The mention of Murray's name caused visible pain in Strumm's face. He looked down at the floor in an apparent attempt to maintain his composure. "I'm sorry, Detective. Murray was a good man."

"And a better friend to me than I was to him, I'm afraid."

"I'm sure he might dispute that, old boy," said I in an attempt to salve his wound, which had the apparent good result.

Holmes spoke to break the awkward silence that had developed, "I went by to see Emily Drake and Mrs. Belmont

316

yesterday. They appear to be on the mend, so to speak."

"Yes, she told me you came by. I wanted to thank you for the kind words you left her with."

"She was still in bed. The entire affair was quite stressing for her, I'm sure. I hope I didn't disturb her too much."

"Not at all, they were very happy you came by before leaving."

"We also went to see Julia Tremaine," said I. "We wanted to give her our condolences for the loss of her husband, and to let her know he'd been instrumental in the destruction of the vampire."

"I'm afraid she didn't take it very well," Holmes said. "I've asked Dr. Rudalac to look in on her and see what he can do to help her. I'm afraid she's a living victim of Abigail Drake. Undoubtedly Dr. Tremaine discovered this and that is what caused him to attempt to destroy Abigail."

"Will she be all right?"

I said, "We have so little knowledge in this area that it's impossible to say. We hope she will, for her baby's sake."

"She's pregnant? How tragic," Strumm said.

"Quite," said I.

Chapter 31

Return to Baker Street...

Holmes and I had barely arrived back at our Baker Street flat when there was the sound of small feet flying up the stairs and series of quick knocks upon the door. I crossed the room and pulled it open. As I did, young Wittmore fell into the room, out of breath with his hat in his hand.

"Mr. 'Olmes," he said between pants.

"Yes, boy, to what do we owe this intrusion? We've just arrived home from America."

"Blimey, Mr. 'Olmes, I know that. Ain't I been on your doorstep these past weeks a-waitin' you to get back?" The young waif was obviously distressed, but for what reason I could not tell.

"'Ere, Mr. 'Olmes," he said holding out his closed fist. "Take it. The weight of it's made me nearly gibbous-backed the while you been gone. Take it and do wif me wot you will."

Holmes put his open palm beneath the boy's fist and into it was deposited a pocket watch, the very same watch he'd stolen some weeks ago.

"Ah, so you've decided to return my property, eh Wittmore?"

"Every time I looked at it, I felt guilty for what I done, Mr. Holmes. I wouldn't blame you if you called for the coppers and had me locked up in Newgate."

"It's the choices we make that determine who we are, Wittmore."

"I get it, Mr. Holmes, I'm nothin' but a thief of the lowest kind."

"No. Had you kept the watch you'd be a thief, a thief for which time would eventually run out. But you chose to return it. That shows you to be not only honest but courageous. Keep this, as both a gift and a reminder, it's never too late to do what's right."

"Wot? You givin' me this watch? What's the catch?"

"Only that you think more of yourself when you look at it than of your circumstances."

The boy took the watch in his hand and said, "Blimey, Mr. Holmes, I will…I promise."

"Now, run along, before I change my mind," said Holmes, a whimsical smile on his face.

After the boy had gone, I said to Holmes, "I suspect you've just done more for that boy's character than anyone in his life up to this point."

"I hope so, Watson. I've often thought a life, once it's taken the wrong turn, can only rarely be set straight again, but our little adventure in America is making me rethink more than one long-held conviction."

I must unfortunately end this tale on a sad note. While researching the facts of this case, I discovered that poor Julia never recovered from her illness. She did survive long enough to give birth to a healthy son whom she named Alan Cabot Tremaine. Upon Julia Tremaine's death, the newly married Mylo and Emily Strumm adopted the child with Julia's full blessing as she had come to know and become close to the couple in her final months. I am happy to report the lad has grown into a fine figure of a young man and has nearly completed his studies to become a doctor like his father.

Epilogue

"Three points to starboard," cried the lookout, "wreckage in the rocks."

"Lower the whaleboat; away the prize team."

Captain Thor Cutter was in his cabin when the prize team leader knocked on the door. "Enter," cried the captain.

Billy Bright stood before the captain, carrying a piece of what was at one time a life preserver. "It's her sir," he said. "Look."

Taking the piece of the preserver in his hand, the captain turned it over. On one side were the faded letters, 'M-U-S L-A-C-U-N-A'. "The *Animus Lacuna*," whispered Cutter.

Acknowledgements

As with any work of worth, and I hope this is, there are many people who've had a hand in seeing it come to fruition. I would like to express my gratitude to a few of those key people who in some way gave me inspiration, assistance, or encouragement in completing this novel. First, I would like to thank my wife, Nanette, for enduring countless nights when I would be in my Victorian cocoon responding to her attempts to converse only with grunts or silence. Her patience is boundless and her encouragement is without parallel, without which I would be lost. I would also like to thank those members of my family who read the early drafts of my book and gave me encouragement to continue, Theresa and Adrienne. A special thanks to Pete Rodill whose keen insights and recommendations took the book in a slightly different direction and, I think, made it the stronger for it. They say you should never judge a book by its cover, but it's the cover that first draws you to a book and I want to give a special thanks to Bob Gibson of Staunch Design for creating yet another stunning cover. I would also like to thank Officer Joseph Murray, with the Center City District of the Philadelphia Police Department. I met him only briefly while in Philadelphia on business. Officer Murray directed me to Independence Hall and then stopped traffic for me to cross the street. He left a lasting impression and was the inspiration for Detective Michael Murray in the book. In addition I would like to thank Jon Lellenberg of the Conan Doyle Estate for allowing the book to carry the estate's seal. Lastly, I would like to thank Steve Emecz, the publisher of MX Publishing, for having faith in the book and my ability to complete it. Oh yes, and a posthumous thanks to Arthur Conan Doyle, the beloved ACD, for creating a character of enduring popularity.

Also from MX Publishing

www.mxpublishing.com

MX Publishing is the world's largest specialist Sherlock Holmes publisher, with over a hundred titles and fifty authors creating the latest in Sherlock Holmes fiction and non-fiction.

From traditional short stories and novels to travel guides and quiz books, MX Publishing cater for all Holmes fans. The collection includes leading titles such as *Benedict Cumberbatch In Transition* and *The Norwood Author* which won the 2011 Howlett Award (Sherlock Holmes Book of the Year).

MX Publishing also has one of the largest communities of Holmes fans on Facebook with regular contributions from dozens of authors.

www.facebook.com/BooksSherlockHolmes

www.ingramcontent.com/pod-product-compliance
Lightning Source LLC
Chambersburg PA
CBHW072058020726
47501CB00003B/635